Finding a murderer requires 100% proof.

In Seneca Lake, New York, Norrie Ellington's Two Witches Winery has been selected by the local vintner community to host the annual Federweisser, a celebration of the season's first fermentation of white Chardonnay grapes. But the festivities are spoiled when Norrie learns that landowner Roy Wilkes has raised her neighbor Rosalee Marbleton's rent so high, she may have to close her vineyard.

Before the rent hike could go into effect, Wilkes is found dead on Roslaee's property—stabbed by a flowerpot stake—and she becomes the police's number one suspect. To clear her friend's name, Norrie conducts her own investigation. But as she gathers clues, Norrie finds herself targeted by a killer, and if she's not careful, her desire to see justice done may die on the vine . . .

Books by J.C. Eaton

The Sophie Kimball Mysteries
Booked 4 Murder
Ditched 4 Murder

And coming soon
Staged 4 Murder (July 2018)

And in E-Book

The Wine Trail Mysteries
A Riesling to Die
Chardonnayed to Rest

Published by Kensington Publishing Corporation

Chardonnayed to Rest

A Wine Trail Mystery

J.C. Eaton

LYRICAL UNDERGROUND
Kensington Publishing Corp.
www.kensingtonbooks.com

Lyrical Press books are published by
Kensington Publishing Corp. 119 West 40th Street New York, NY 10018

First Electronic Edition: September 2018
eISBN-13: 978-1-5161-0799-5
eISBN-10: 1-5161-0799-3

First Print Edition: September 2018
ISBN-13: 978-1-5161-0802-2
ISBN-10: 1-5161-0802-7

Printed in the United States of America

To Federweisser lovers everywhere, enjoy this mystery as much as you do the wine!

Acknowledgments

If ever a "ground crew" deserved thanks, it's ours. We are indeed indebted to Beth Cornell, Larry Finkelstein, Gale Leach, Ellen Lynes, Susan Morrow, Suzanne Scher and all the way across the continents to Australia, Susan Schwartz.

None of this would ever have been possible without our agent, Dawn Dowdle from Blue Ridge Literary Agency, and our editor, Tara Gavin, at Kensington. We thank our lucky stars you believed in us and took us on for this amazing ride. You're phenomenal!

Our production editors, Robin Cook and Renee Rocco, deserve a shout-out, too, for the incredible job they do.

It's definitely a team effort at Kensington and we are so appreciative.

Chapter 1

PENN YAN, NEW YORK

Catherine Trobert, owner of Lake View Winery, brushed the honey blond bangs away from her eyes with one hand and leaned across her chair to pat my wrist with the other. We were the first ones to take our seats at the semi-monthly Women of the Wineries meeting held at Madeline Martinez's establishment, Billsburrow Winery. It was the week before Labor Day and everyone was anxious for the fall winery events to begin.

Well, not everyone. I certainly wasn't. I was anxious to hear from my script analyst regarding the screenplay I had submitted for review. I was under contract with a Canadian film company that specialized in TV romances. Managing my sister's winery for a year while she and her husband, Jason, were off chasing after some elusive bug in Costa Rica was something I agreed to do in a weak moment. I had no intention of making it permanent. Besides, the study grant my entomologist brother-in-law got from Cornell's Experiment Station was supposed to be for a year. Even though I had heard a nasty rumor from Godfrey Klein, who worked with Jason, that the grant might be extended.

Bite your tongue, Godfrey.

For the past five years I had earned a decent living writing screenplays, and I intended to keep it that way. Overseeing Two Witches Winery was simply a favor. A favor that was due to expire in ten months, at which time I'd be back in Manhattan saying adios to the person who had sublet my apartment.

Catherine gave my wrist another pat and sighed. "I'm so sorry to break this to you, Norrie, but Steven won't be able to make it for Labor Day Weekend as planned. You wouldn't think his law firm would have such a big caseload, but it does. I suppose the state of Maine gets its fair share of crime, too."

"Huh?" All I'd heard were the words "Labor Day Weekend" and "Steven." I kind of pieced together the rest in my mind. Catherine Trobert had grand designs of fixing me up with her son, even though I'd hardly known him in high school. He was a few years older than me and hung out with the jocks and future leaders of America on the student council. I was too busy writing poetry for the literary magazine and articles for the school newspaper to take much notice of him.

"I know. I know," she said. "You haven't seen Steven since high school, but I'm certain the two of you would enjoy getting reunited."

Reunited? We were never united. Never ever. "Um, that's too bad. Send him my regards."

"I will, dear. I most certainly will. On a positive note, Gladys Pipp is back at work from her hip replacement. Moves around as if she was sixteen and not sixty."

"Um, is she one of your workers?"

"Oh, heavens no. Gladys is the secretary for the Yates County Department of Public Safety. Unlike those dour deputies over there who can barely utter a single syllable, Gladys is a wealth of information, if you need her. Shh! Don't tell anyone, but she gave me the heads-up about that nasty little speed trap just past Snell Road."

"I'll keep that in mind."

Just then, Stephanie Ipswich from Gable Hill Winery and Rosalee Marbleton from Terrace Wineries came into the room. I immediately greeted them. Anything to stop Catherine from lamenting about Steven or bringing up people I didn't know. Speed traps or not.

Madeline Martinez followed and placed a tray of scones, chocolate filled croissants, and butter cookies on the large coffee table. "Coffee and tea are on the credenza. Help yourselves, ladies. This should be a really short meeting. We've only got two things on the agenda—the Federweisser Festival and the inclusion of the Grey Egret Winery into our WOW association."

Rosalee moved her wire-rimmed glasses farther up her nose and sat up straight. For a small, stout woman in her early seventies, she looked as if she could command an army. "Let's be honest. If it wasn't for the Grey Egret, our West Side Women of the Wineries, which most of us simply refer to as WOW, abbreviated or not, wouldn't exist. And neither would the 'Sip and Savor' event or the Federweisser. It was Angela Martinelli who got the whole ball rolling."

"True, true," Catherine said, "but Angela no longer owns the Grey Egret. She sold it to Don and Theo a few years ago. They're the owners now. How can we have a winery women's group if two of the members are men?"

Stephanie selected the tiniest butter cookie from the tray—God forbid she eat something that would destroy that knockout figure of hers—and took the smallest bite. "Who says we have to be a women's group? Let's face it, the Grey Egret takes part in all our west side functions and that means endless phone calls when one of them could be at our meetings. I say we let them join the group."

"I second that!" I shouted.

"It's not a parliamentary procedure meeting, Norrie," Catherine whispered.

I shrugged. "I still think we should let them in. Don and Theo are great guys and amazingly supportive. When Elsbeth Waters' body was discovered in our Riesling vineyard this past June, it was Don and Theo who helped me get through that whole mess."

"That whole *murder*, you mean," Rosalee said. "I happen to agree with you." Then she turned to the others. "Invite them into our group, for heaven's sake, and let's get on with this meeting."

I'd never known Rosalee to appear so agitated, but I figured she had lots on her plate, so to speak, with the grape harvest starting and the fall tourist rush only days away.

Madeline nodded and gazed into her coffee cup. "Hmm, then what do we do about the name? WOW is so catchy."

I did at least three mental eye rolls and one silent scream. "Can't the initials represent something else? Drop the west side part of the title, since no one uses it anyway, except for my sister, and have the WOW stand for Winery Owners of the West. That would work, wouldn't it?"

"Norrie, you're a genius," Stephanie said. "So? Is it agreed, ladies? The Grey Egret joins our group?"

Everyone said "Yes" and Madeline announced she'd call Don and Theo to let them know the news.

"I hope the Federweisser portion doesn't take too long," Rosalee said. "I've got some pressing business to deal with."

"Everything okay?" Catherine asked.

"Not really, but I don't want to take up all of your time."

Madeline looked at each one of us. "It'll be fine. Go ahead."

Rosalee clasped her hands together and squeezed them tight. She sat up even straighter than before. "It's our water situation. At the winery, not the house. Fortunately the house is located close enough to the road in order to get its water from the village waterline. The winery wasn't that lucky, and the village has no intention of expanding its waterline. Anyway, we've been getting the water for our vineyards from the lake, and we truck in potable water for our own use at the winery. Lots of lakeshore wineries use a surface water source as well as a commercial one."

She paused for a moment and none of us said a word.

"We paid for a special waterline that went through the Baxters' property. For years we paid them for the land use. No different than someone owning a mobile home but renting the lot. It was a fair and reasonable price. Then, a few months ago, the Baxters sold their property and moved to Texas. The new owner jacked up the price to an astronomical level. He said if we don't pay, he'll cut off our water access."

"My God!" Madeline put her coffee cup down and covered her mouth.

"How can they do that?" Stephanie asked. "That's highway robbery."

Rosalee's voice sounded shaky. "I'm afraid they can and they will. Without water, our vineyards will be destroyed and our winery gone for good."

My heart began beating faster. "Isn't there anything you can do?"

"There are stopgap measures, like having non-potable water trucked in and placed in huge holding tanks. We've already started to do that, but it's an awfully expensive way to get water. That's why I'm headed into Geneva to see our attorney. Maybe we have legal rights. If not, we're doomed."

Catherine made a strange chortling sound. Something in between clearing her throat and gargling. "What kind of a selfish thug would do a thing like that? Terrace Wineries has been in the Finger Lakes since before I was even born. This isn't right. Clearly, there must be something we can do."

Rosalee gave a halfhearted smile. "Thanks, dear. I'm hoping my attorney will have an answer. Or even a decent idea. Anyway, I really must go. I'm sure you'll all get on fine with the rest of the meeting. Thank goodness the Federweisser event is at Two Witches this year and not my place. I'm sure Norrie will do a splendid job."

With that, Rosalee picked up her floral pocketbook, which looked as if it could double as a carpetbag, and headed out of the room. The rest of us sat there in silence for a few seconds before Madeline spoke.

"My husband's a county board representative. I'm going to see what he has to say about this. Rosalee was right, you know. About the wineries on the lake having to get their water from the lake. What if some of them are in the same predicament she is? Putting in pipelines and paying for land use because they don't own the property rights. A greedy landowner could really put the screws to them."

"I think we should call Henry Speltmore. He's in charge of the wine association. Maybe he has an idea or two floating around in his head," Stephanie said.

Madeline laughed. "If he does, that would be a first. But yeah, give him a call. He's a nice enough guy. It couldn't hurt. Well, I suppose we should get on with the last piece of business—the Federweisser."

I squirmed around in my seat, certain they were going to ask me what we had planned for the event. I knew I should've paid more attention to Cammy, our tasting room manager, when she went over the food menu for the Federweisser, but I didn't. I was too busy trying to get a dialogue straight in my mind for a scene that had to be worked out for my screenplay.

Same thing with Franz, our winemaker. He must've explained the process for making Federweisser to me at least three times, but I still wasn't a hundred percent sure I understood. Something about adding yeast to grapes so they fermented quickly. Oh, and the sugar. I remembered that part. The sugar in the grapes turned into alcohol and carbon dioxide and when it reached four percent, it became Federweisser, a really cool drink that tasted like a champagne soda. The thing was, the alcohol percent kept growing so the Federweisser had to be consumed within a few days. Otherwise, the stuff just became regular wine.

"Entertainment. Didn't you hear me, Norrie?"

"Huh?" I looked at Madeline and knew she had asked me a question, but I was too busy trying to recall the last two conversations I didn't pay attention to.

"Um, can you repeat that?"

Stephanie jumped in before Madeline could reply. "She asked if you were having any entertainment at the Federweisser. Last year, when it was held at Rosalee's, they hired a polka band."

I don't suppose watching Alvin, our Nigerian Dwarf Goat, spit at people constitutes entertainment. "Uh, yeah. We're working on that. But everything else is all set." *And if it's not, it will be.*

Madeline nodded and gave me a thumbs-up. "That sounds fine. Let us know if there's anything you need. We'll all make it a point to advertise for you and we'll be sure to drop by for the festivities. Goodness. That's only three weeks away. My, how time goes by."

Not fast enough, judging by the length of this meeting.

"Well, ladies," Madeline said. "That about concludes the meeting for me unless anyone else wants to bring up something."

My eyes widened and I held my breath.

Madeline clapped her hands together, startling us. "Okay then. We'll meet again right before the Federweisser. And if my husband has any bright ideas about how the county can help Rosalee, I'll let you know."

The next few minutes were spent commiserating about the mess Terrace Wineries was in before we all left Madeline's place. Stephanie motioned for me to chat with her once we got to the parking lot. I walked over to her car as she clicked the door open.

"You're a good sleuth, Norrie. Think you can dig up the dirt on that new landowner who's bilking Rosalee?"

"Me? I'm not an investigator."

"No. You're better. You get answers. They get red tape. Look, I'll be willing to do some checking, too, as long it's on the Internet. Between the winery and two first graders, I'm lucky I can get through the day with a coherent thought. Not to mention, we'll be closing on the Waters' property in a few weeks."

"That's right. I'm glad it worked out for you."

"Me, too. Elsbeth's niece, Yvonne, couldn't sell that B & B fast enough, but she knew it would be a tough sale with all that land. Fortunately, she was able to have it divided up so we could buy the property for vineyards and someone else could buy the B & B."

"Did she find a buyer for the business?"

"Uh-huh. I'm not sure who, but she said they were thrilled to run a bed and breakfast in the Finger Lakes."

"Did she say anything else? Like what she plans to do?"

"Not really. She was kind of tight-lipped about it. Can you blame her?"

"No, I suppose not."

"Anyway, let me know if you decide to poke around regarding that crummy water hog of Rosalee's."

"Sure thing."

"At least you don't have to find a murderer this time."

"Don't say that out loud!"

"You're not superstitious are you?"

"No, just careful."

I waved good-bye to the other ladies in the parking lot and drove home. Maybe I was just a tad superstitious, but at least I wasn't downright looney, like Glenda from our tasting room. I still couldn't believe I let her hold that ridiculous séance to contact Elsbeth's restless spirit. Stephanie was right. This time I'd be snooping around to dig up dirt, not a dead body.

Chapter 2

Theo Buchman was putting wine bottles into their rustic wooden bins when I stepped inside the Grey Egret's tasting room. The place was in full swing, with every seat taken, and I imagined it wasn't much different at my winery. At least Cammy would have things under control.

"Hey, stranger!" he shouted. "What brings you to our neck of the woods so early in the day? Aren't they keeping you busy enough up the hill?"

I walked closer to the wine bins. "Not if I can help it. I'm just the official overseer, or so I keep telling myself. Listen, I stopped by for two reasons, the good and the bad."

"Not the ugly?"

"Very funny. I'll start with the good, although you'll be getting a call from Madeline Martinez any time now."

"Sounds intriguing."

"Hmm, not a word I'd use. Here goes—the Women of the Wineries is now the Winery Owners of the West."

"Huh?"

"It was a WOW thing. We had to keep the WOW. Anyway, we changed the name because we want you and Don to be part of the group. You participate in most of the events and the Grey Egret started that little winery klatch to begin with. Besides, now I'll have someone to commiserate with after the meetings."

"That was the good news? We get to sit through gossipy meetings twice a month and listen to the rumor fests?"

"Sometimes we trade recipes."

"Wonderful. I'll send Don. But thanks for the heads-up. When Madeline calls, I'll act thrilled. So, what's the bad news?"

I proceeded to tell him about the predicament Rosalee Marbleton was in and watched as his expression got grimmer and grimmer.

"Geez, Norrie, that's awful."

"I know. I know. I was hoping you or Don might have some ideas about possible solutions for her."

"Not unless the new landowner's willing to sell her the property where the waterline goes. They *can* do that. Portion off a certain amount of acreage or, in this case, lakefront property and sell it while retaining the rest. The county figures out the tax adjustments and all that."

"I don't think the guy's willing to sell."

"Who is the new guy? I thought the Baxters still owned that land."

"Nope. They sold it and moved to Texas. I need to get the lowdown on the new owner."

"Unless you feel like purchasing a tax map from the county, ask Rosalee. Once you get the guy's name, we can do an unofficial background check on him. See what we can find out."

"Theo Buchman, are you telling me you're willing to snoop around with me?"

"Shh, as long as Don doesn't know. He's always afraid it'll get us into hot water."

"He may be right. Tell him hi. I'd better be going."

"Catch you later. And thanks for the updates. Especially the WOW."

I drove the rest of the way up the hill, aka our driveway, and raced into the house to see if there were any messages for me from the script analyst. I'd already checked my e-mails, but sometimes I got calls from the producer on the landline.

Nothing. The only greeting I got was from Charlie, the family Plott Hound, who got up from his dog bed and nudged his dog dish. I poured some kibble, booted up my laptop, and looked over my other projects. I had a deadline in November for a Valentine screenplay and was still roughing out the plot.

At a little past four, I walked down to the tasting room's bistro and grabbed a late lunch so I wouldn't have to monkey around with dinner. Lizzie was at her usual spot at the cash register and gave me a quick wave when I walked in. Cammy, our tasting room manager, and our employees, full-time and seasonal, were doing tastings. Like the Grey Egret, we were swamped, and it wasn't even Labor Day yet.

I was about to do a turnaround and head home when I realized something. I really had no idea if everything was going smoothly for the Federweisser. I seriously needed to pay more attention to Cammy and Franz.

"Psst! Cammy! Send your next customers to Glenda. I need to talk to you."

Cammy gave me a nod and mouthed, "Everything okay?"

I nodded and moseyed over to the T-shirt bins, where two girls were trying to decide whether to purchase the bright orange shirts or the screaming green ones. The logo and text were the same on all of them—Two Witches Winery, The Spell's on Us!

"We added a new color," I said. "Fuchsia. Those shirts are in the bins off to the right."

"Oh my God!" the tall brunette shrieked. "That's my favorite color."

She grabbed her friend by the arm, and I walked over to Cammy, who still had a concerned look on her face.

"Relax. I just need to know if we're all set for the Federweisser. It was the hot topic at the WOW meeting, along with some other stuff."

"We're all set to go on our end. We're serving pastry wrapped sausage bites, sausage cheese balls, and Kalamata olive bread. If those foods don't get people to drink and buy wine, nothing will."

"Sounds yummy. What about entertainment? The women went on and on about entertainment."

"We booked the Polka Meisters from Buffalo. Got a terrific price since they have to be in the area the next day for a wedding."

"Oh thank God! What about the publicity? Do we have any publicity?"

"Lots of it on our Facebook page, and we took out ads in all the local papers. Plus, the winery association always promotes it no matter which winery hosts it. And before you say another word, Catherine Trobert's husband dropped off the new banner earlier today. So, you see, there's nothing to worry about."

"Unless something goes wrong with the wine. Have you seen Franz today?"

"Uh-huh. He was in earlier to get a bite to eat and seemed perfectly fine. Trust me, Norrie, if Franz had a problem, you'd be the first to know."

"You're probably right, but it wouldn't hurt for me to double check. I'll give him a call at the winery lab when I get to the house. I don't want to walk in there and disturb him." *Or break something. Or contaminate something. Or give him a reason to look for employment elsewhere. We already lost our assistant vineyard manager. No need to lose the guy who knows what to do with the grapes.*

"Is that all that's bothering you? I feel as if you're holding back something. Spit it out. It can't be any worse than the murder we had right before the Fourth of July."

"It's bad, but not for us. For Rosalee at Terrace Wineries."

"Rosalee Marbleton? She's such a sweet lady. What's going on?"

For the second time that day, I spouted off about Rosalee's predicament. And while it wasn't exactly rumor mongering, it bordered on that very nasty line of gossiping, even though my intentions were good.

"Holy cow! That's highway robbery! Who's the jerk who owns the land?"

I shook my head. "I don't know, but I'm going to find out."

"Uh-oh. I see that look in your eye. Please don't tell me you're hatching a scheme to make that guy rethink his price tag."

"Whoa. I hadn't thought of that. But now that you mention it—"

"Don't! Remember what happened the last time you had one of those ideas? The tables got turned on you and you were nearly arrested."

"Aargh. I'm still trying to forget. Look, all I want to do now is find out more about this creep. Anyone who could do a thing like that must be a real loser."

"Agreed."

"I better let you get back to the tastings before Glenda goes nuts."

I meandered home and spent the rest of the day on my laptop, pausing for a ten-minute break, at which time I placed a call to Rosalee.

"Hi Rosalee. It's Norrie. I called because I was worried about you. We all are. I am hoping everything went well with your attorney."

Rosalee sighed and her voice was choppy. "We may have some legal rights since the waterline was installed decades ago and we had a lease agreement with the Baxters. I say 'We' because my sister, Marilyn Ansley, owns the land and my family owns the business and property. Our attorney is checking to see if that lease carried over, but frankly, I'm not too optimistic."

"Who's the new owner? That is, if you don't mind me asking."

"A miserable scourge by the name of Roy Wilkes. Real scruffy looking, too. I'm guessing he's in his late fifties, but it's hard to tell with that long beard of his. Reminds me of a mountain man."

"Yikes. By the way, why didn't you buy the property when the Baxters were selling it?"

"It's lakefront property. Outrageous taxes. The county and the school district rake it in. Now, in retrospect, I'm sorry we didn't. Never thought I'd find myself in this predicament."

"I'm really sorry, Rosalee. Please keep me posted. If I can think of anything to help you out, I'll let you know."

"I appreciate it, Norrie. It was nice seeing you today."

I felt lousy when I got off the phone. Rosalee sounded defeated. All the more reason for me to do some snooping around. At least I had a name and a description. It was a start. I made up my mind to do some background checking on Roy Wilkes the following day. As things turned out, I should've started the very minute I got off the phone with Rosalee.

Chapter 3

At first I couldn't place the sound. A sharp ringing. I was engulfed in darkness and a heavy weight bared down on my chest. Then the odor hit me. It was Charlie and he began to lick my face as the ringing continued.

"Geez, dog, it's the phone. Get down! Get down from the bed!"

I reached across the nightstand and grabbed the receiver. My eyes were gradually getting adjusted to the semidarkness, and I imagined that if I opened the curtains all the way, I'd see that the sun was about to come up. I seriously doubted it was a problem at our winery because the vineyard staff had made it a point to pound on my front door whenever something went wrong, no matter what obscene time it was.

"Hello?" I was hoping it was a wrong number.

"Norrie! It's Rosalee. Oh goodness! Oh my gosh! I'm standing over a dead body! Victoria found it. She took off this morning during our walk. I figured she was chasing after a rabbit. When I caught up to her, she was sniffing at the body. My poor dog. She must be traumatized."

Her voice stopped abruptly. Next thing I knew, she yelled at her dogs. All four Corgis, each named after British royalty. "No, Albert! You stop that! Philip! Elizabeth! Stay! Sit! Sit Stay!"

Then she was back on the phone with me. "You've got to help me. I'm literally a hair's breath away from a corpse. You're the expert, Norrie. What do I do? And speak fast. I only have one bar left on my phone."

"Me? I'm no authority."

"You're the only person I know who's had experience with these kinds of things. The only dead people I've come across in my seventy plus years were the ones who were gussied up in their coffins at the funeral parlor."

"Um, other than my vineyard workers finding Elsbeth Waters' body where our Riesling vines were growing, I've had no experience with this stuff. Zilch. Absolutely nada. Never mind. Where are you?"

"Near the pumping station, where our pipeline is. I'm standing on Roy Wilkes' land and if I'm not mistaken…"

And so much for the one bar Rosalee had left on her phone. I did the only thing I knew how. I hung up and called the Yates County Sheriff's emergency number. I gave them what little information I had, threw on some clothes, made sure I took a jacket because the mornings were chilly and raced downstairs. Moving at breakneck speed, I poured kibble into Charlie's bowl, refilled his water dish and charged toward my car.

When I got to the bottom of our driveway, I pulled up at Theo and Don's house and pounded on their door. No sense me being the only one to deal with Rosalee, her neurotic dogs, and a dead body.

"My God!" Don opened the door and ushered me inside. "What happened? You're usually not up until the break of noon."

"Rosalee Marbleton just called me. She found a dead body on the lakefront, next to her waterline."

"What? Who? Does she know? And why did she call *you*?"

"I think dead body discovery is now on my resume. Seriously, I have no idea. But it didn't sound as if she'd called the sheriff, so I did. I'm on my way over there now. I thought maybe you or Theo could go with me."

"I just heard that!" Theo yelled from another room. "Give me two seconds to throw on some jeans and I'll go with you. Unless, of course, Don wants to—"

"He doesn't!" Don shouted back. "I'll man the winery. You can go with Norrie."

Less than five minutes later, Theo jumped into my car and I drove across the road to Terrace Wineries.

"Which way is the pumping station?" Theo asked once I parked my car.

"Your guess is as good as mine. It can't be that far a walk if Rosalee does it every morning. How about you go left and I go right. First one to find her yells."

"How about the first one calls the other one on their cell. We'll never hear each other from a distance."

"Works for me. You and Don are on speed dial, you realize."

Theo laughed and I took off running. Well, maybe not running, but certainly walking briskly. The sun was now above the horizon, and I checked the time on my phone–6:37. I thought I saw some movement in the distance and figured it might be Rosalee's dogs, but as I approached, it turned out to be a couple of joggers. Both women.

"Have you seen an elderly woman with four fat little dogs?"

The taller one with frosted hair chuckled. "Sorry. We haven't. In fact, you're the first person we've seen on our jog, and we've be running for at least a half mile."

Just then my phone buzzed and it was Theo. "I'm with Rosalee. Turn around and head back. You can't miss us."

"Never mind," I said to the joggers. "My friend found her."

"Glad to hear that," the frosted-haired lady said, "because we've got to spin around and get back to our husbands. They've rented a motorboat for the day and are chomping at the bit to get on the lake. We figured this would be the only exercise we'd get, other than watching the men fish."

I nodded. "Hope you have a good time and don't forget to visit the wineries while you're here."

My God. I'm as bad as the women from WOW. Next thing you know I'll be doing an infomercial.

Years of walking all over Manhattan must've paid off because I was barely winded when I reached Theo and Rosalee. The Corgis were running all over the place, and Rosalee kept muttering, "Make it a heart attack. Make it a heart attack."

I pulled Theo aside and whispered, "What's going on with her?"

"The dead body…it's Roy Wilkes. She told me the second I got here."

"So, when she said she was standing over a dead body—"

"She meant it figuratively, not literally. She was about to tell you who it was when her cell phone went out."

"That explains it. No wonder she's going crazy. If the guy didn't drop dead from natural causes, those deputies will be pointing a finger at Rosalee. Geez, I sincerely hope Roy over there suffered a massive coronary."

Suddenly we heard sirens getting closer. Theo and I walked back to where Rosalee was standing. The dogs, thankfully, ignored the body and instead took turns rolling over what appeared to be a dead fish on the shore.

"Um, maybe we should get the dogs into your house, Rosalee," I said.

Theo immediately chimed in. "Good idea. What do you say we round them up, walk back to your house, and then come back to this spot? Norrie can hold down the fort."

"The dogs. Yes. The dogs. Did I call the sheriff? I don't remember doing that. Last thing I remember was talking to Norrie."

"Your phone must've gone dead," I said. "I called the sheriff's office."

Theo put an arm around Rosalee's shoulders and the two of them walked back to her house. Oddly enough, the Corgis didn't need to be called. They took one look at their owner leaving the area and were immediately on her heels. I figured if they were anything like Charlie, they were waiting to be fed.

Rosalee's house was close to the road, a good ways from the winery building and the lakeshore. It was just a matter of time before the cavalry came. If we were lucky, her vineyard workers might assume there was a drowning or maybe a missing tourist. Certainly not a dead body belonging to the guy whose land Rosalee rented in order to have a water supply. I knew the sheriff's car would come in guns-a-blazing, with their flashers on. And they'd have to use Rosalee's driveway and access road to reach the lakeshore. At least her winery building and her tasting room were a few hours away from opening.

I walked toward the pumping station and found myself staring at Roy Wilkes' lifeless body. Face-up. I wasn't as unnerved as I was the last time I found myself in this kind of situation. I figured it was because I only knew the guy from his wretched reputation.

The first thing I noticed was his work boots——well-worn brown leather boots that laced up to the ankles. The soles were still in pretty good shape, with plenty of tread left. Too bad he wouldn't be around to get his money's worth. I supposed I saw the boots right away because his feet were directly in front of me, given the direction I came from. He was wearing dark jeans and a dusty brown Carhartt jacket, with a few visible holes in the cloth. A large red stain seemed to be oozing closer to the emblem on the front pocket. Maybe Roy hadn't been dead that long. One arm was twisted above his head and the other rested across his stomach.

I tried not to look at his face, but it was near impossible. With that long brownish grey beard of his, the guy could've passed for thirty-eight or eighty-three. Hard to tell. His eyes, also dark, were wide open. Dead people in movies and on TV always had their eyes closed. Darn it! Why couldn't Roy's be closed? I was positive I'd be having nightmares for weeks.

My ears hurt from the siren sound, and I knew the sheriff's deputies had to be coming down Rosalee's driveway. What I didn't realize was there were two response vehicles, one with its flashers and siren in full force, and the other one not. That fact became clear to me when I heard a crunching sound a few feet from behind. I spun around and found myself face-to-face with Deputy Hickman. Deputy Gary (aka Grizzly Gary) Hickman.

"Miss Ellington. I should have known if there was a dead body anywhere in the county, you'd be within spitting range. Please don't tell me you were out for a morning stroll and just so happened to stumble across it."

"No. Rosalee Marbleton stumbled across it and called me. Well, actually one of her Corgis found the body. Then she called me."

"Unbelievable. The county has an excellent emergency response system in place, and who do people call? Their neighbor. So, I suppose you were the one who phoned it in. Am I right? I was out on another assignment when I got the word and drove over here. The other vehicle belongs to our forensics team."

Yep, couldn't miss 'em. They probably woke up everyone in a five-mile radius.

I looked behind the deputy. The forensics team was headed in our direction. Two men carried large black bags. I didn't see Rosalee or Theo, but I imagined the forensics guys told them to stay in the house and wait.

"Don't go anywhere, Miss Ellington. I still need to ask you a few questions. But that doesn't mean you need to be breathing over the investigators. You'll need to walk a few yards back."

Would the next county be too far?

I gave a quick nod, turned, and walked about ten steps when Deputy Hickman waved me over to him. "Forgot to ask, but, on the off chance, you wouldn't happen to know who our victim is, would you?"

"As a matter of fact, I do. Roy Wilkes, but that's all I know. Okay, not all." I figured he was going to get the information one way or the other, so I thought I'd save everyone some time. "Roy Wilkes owns the lakefront property where the Marbletons' waterline goes. Terrace Wineries rents that land from him. It used to belong to the Baxters, but they moved to Texas."

"You'll need to slow down. Roy Wilkes, you said?"

"Uh-huh."

The deputy took out a pad and pen and wrote the name down. Then he re-directed me to wait a good ten to twelve yards away.

I glanced over my shoulder. "Um, is that blood on his jacket? Looks like blood to me. Maybe he was shot. Or possibly stabbed."

"Miss Ellington, I would suggest you limit your observations to your writing and not crime scene investigations. That's why we have a forensics team. Now, please, wait a few yards back, or even better yet, why don't you go to Mrs. Marbleton's house? I can question you there as well as here."

I shrugged and took off for the house. Whoever shot or stabbed Roy Wilkes must've come from the north side of the lake. The joggers I'd seen said they'd been running for a half mile or so and hadn't come across anyone. Given the fact the blood was still oozing, I was pretty sure Roy had met his maker at the first sign of daybreak. In fact, had Rosalee arrived a bit sooner, it was likely she would've witnessed a murder. It had to be the first inkling of daybreak because no one went walking around the lake in the dark.

There were scuffle marks all over the sand and shoeprints everywhere. I doubted the forensics team would have much luck with the shoeprints. Probably every kid and tourist on summer break walked up and down that shore. Darn it. I should've looked around for a bullet shell.

Rosalee was on the phone and Theo let me into her house. White with black shutters. It was a typical upstate New York farmhouse, with a large foyer and doorways that led to separate rooms—dining, living and kitchen. No open concept whatsoever. He pointed to the kitchen, which was directly across from the front door, while we waited in the hallway. From my vantage point, I had a bird's-eye view of the room and immediately noticed the décor. Country kitchen for sure, with a round light oak table, not very different from my sister's, and chairs with blue and yellow cushions that matched the curtains. Small flowerpots with violets and asters lined the ledge over her sink, while an enormous spider plant hung directly above it.

"Shh! She's talking with her sister and the conversation's a doozy. Stay still and listen."

Rosalee's sister, Marilyn Ansley, owned the actual land, while Rosalee and her late husband owned the winery business.

Rosalee's voice was surprisingly loud. "I don't care if it is Pancake Day for your ladies' club. You need to get over here now. I mean it, Marilyn. For all I know, I could be a suspect. What?"

There was a slight pause and I held my breath. Then Rosalee resumed talking.

"No. I don't think he was out walking and dropped dead. I could've sworn I saw blood." Pause "What's that?"

Again, another pause.

"Of course I plan to do that, but his office doesn't open until nine. I told you before. The only number we have is for the office. No attorney in his right mind is going to give us his personal cell phone number. What's that again? Speak up."

Theo stifled a laugh, and I gave him a nudge.

"A bail bondsman? That's a little extreme, isn't it? No one's been arrested yet. Now get over here. You can eat pancakes some other time."

Rosalee slammed the receiver down, and Theo and I walked into the kitchen. Two of the Corgis were at their food bowls and I imagined the other two had finished eating and were sacked out somewhere.

"Is everything all right?" I asked. "I mean, with your phone call. Obviously everything's not all right with the dead body and all."

"Sit. Sit. I'll get us some coffee. I put on a fresh pot this morning. That was my sister, Marilyn, on the line. She's on her way over here. She lives right in town, a few blocks away from the Penn Yan diner. That's where she was headed before I called."

Just then there was a sharp rap at the door and Deputy Hickman swung it open. His voice was thunderous. "Mrs. Marbleton? Do you mind if I step in to ask you and Miss Ellington some questions?"

Rosalee called out from the kitchen. "We're in here. Come on in."

She took out four ceramic cups, each with a different dog on it, and lined them up by her coffeemaker. "We might as well have some coffee. There's sugar and creamer on the table."

"Thank you." The deputy took a seat at the table.

I skootched over to give him more room. He took out that same little pen and pad of his and cleared his throat. I expected the dogs to at least show up and bark, but they didn't.

"At this juncture in time, Mrs. Marbleton, I'm trying to establish a timeline and get a description of what you saw when you first discovered the body."

"What I saw? What I saw? I was horrified at what I saw. There was Victoria sniffing and prodding a body. I didn't know it belonged to Roy Wilkes until later. I called Norrie the minute I realized my poor dog had found a dead body."

I smiled and nodded, but Deputy Hickman ignored me. "Did you notice anything else at the scene?"

Rosalee furrowed her brow. "Like what? Isn't a dead body enough?"

The deputy sighed. One of those long sighs that usually signaled exasperation. "Were you acquainted with the deceased?"

"Unfortunately, yes. He owns, er...*owned* the land where our water pipeline runs."

The deputy glanced at me, as if to say, "Fine, you got the information right," and then he immediately focused on Rosalee. "What was your relationship with the victim like?"

"I paid him his rent, if that's what you mean. Listen, it's no secret. When Roy Wilkes bought the property from the Baxters, he jacked up the price for renting the land. In fact, I met with our attorney on Thursday to see if my sister and I had any legal recourse about the rent. My sister owns the land itself, and I own the winery."

I thought I heard a slight groan before Deputy Hickman continued, but I might've been mistaken. One of the Corgis was under the table and the noise might've been him or her.

"So, what you're telling me is you and your sister had an issue with the victim? Is that correct?"

"Don't say anything, Rosalee!" I blurted out. "Not until you speak with your lawyer."

Chapter 4

"Miss Ellington, no one has been Mirandized. Now, may we please continue?"

Theo kicked my ankle under the table and gave me a wink. I kept my mouth shut while Rosalee answered his question.

"Mr. Wilkes charged us an astronomical amount of money to rent that portion of the land. He threatened to cut off our water supply if we didn't pay him. Since the pipeline is on his property, he could've removed it and prohibited us from re-installing it. Either that or he could've shut down the pump house, which is also on his property. Either way, it would've meant curtains for Terrace Wineries."

Deputy Hickman rubbed his chin and leaned back "Do you own a gun, Mrs. Marbleton?"

"What a ridiculous question. Who in Yates County doesn't own a gun?"

I cringed as Rosalee dug herself deeper and deeper into the pit of "I could be the possible killer."

"I'm not asking for a county gun census. I'm asking you. Yes or no?"

"Of course I own a gun," she said. "In fact, I own at least five. All shotguns of one type or another. Twenty-twenties, a twenty-thirty, some sort of a pump action one…who the heck knows? They belonged to my late husband and are locked up in our gun case. Now, if you were to ask me if I knew how to shoot a gun, that would be a different story."

"Do you?" the deputy asked.

"No, but I imagine I could if I had to. I watch enough TV shows. All you do is aim the thing and pull the trigger."

Theo gasped and this time I was the one who kicked him under the table. At that moment, the deputy's phone rang and he stood up to take the call. None of us uttered a word while he left the room. A few seconds later he returned.

"The preliminary evidence from the forensic investigators points to a stab wound and not a gun. That's a good thing for you, Mrs. Marbleton."

Please Dear God, Rosalee, do not tell him you own any knives. Even kitchen knives.

The deputy went on. "We'll know more when the coroner completes the autopsy."

Gee, where have I heard that line before?

"I don't suppose anyone sitting around this table would know if our victim has any relatives around here?"

Theo and I shook our heads and Rosalee scowled. "Doubtful he's married." Then she turned to me, "Norrie, you probably took a good look at the body, was he wearing a wedding ring?"

"Um, I'm not sure. Maybe. Maybe not. I didn't really notice."

"Never mind," Deputy Hickman said. "Our team of investigators will be able to ascertain that information. In the meantime, I'd appreciate it if you didn't go all hog wild talking to everyone and spreading rumors. The crime scene will be cordoned off, and I imagine our investigators will be walking the lakefront in search of clues."

Rosalee reached across the table to pour more sugar into her coffee. She stared directly at the deputy. "If the man was stabbed, I truly doubt the perpetrator would leave the knife lying around for anyone to pick up."

"Murderers leave all sorts of clues, Mrs. Marbleton," he said. "And it's our job to find them, not yours. The last thing we need is for evidence to be tainted. And to make myself clear, let me remind all of you that this is an official investigation. Unless you've been hired by the Yates County Sheriff's Department, please do not take it upon yourself to go snooping around. There could very well be a dangerous killer out there. Leave it to the professionals."

When he said the last five words, his voice got noticeably louder, and he was looking directly at me. Then he excused himself and walked to the door. He opened it at the exact moment Marilyn Ansley arrived. She was taller than her sister and appeared to be at least half a decade younger. Short brown hair, not much makeup and sporting one of those homey sweatshirts with an embroidered design on the front. Hers featured a scene of two kittens playing with a ball of yarn.

Marilyn took one look at Deputy Hickman, clutched her large floral bag to her chest, and shrieked. "Dear Lord, Rosalee, have you been arrested?"

"No one's been arrested, ma'am," Deputy Hickman said.

Rosalee motioned for her sister to come in and introduced her to everyone. The deputy, who was on his way out, paused for a moment and eyeballed Marilyn.

"You're Mrs. Marbleton's sister? Is that correct?"

She jerked her head back, which exaggerated her double chin. "Yes. Yes, I am."

Suddenly, that familiar pad and pen came out of Deputy Hickman's pocket. "Were you acquainted with Roy Wilkes?"

Marilyn shook her head. "Not in the least. Wouldn't know him if I stepped over him."

"All right then," the deputy said. "I'll be on my way. And remember, keep your mouths closed about this case. And steer clear of the investigation."

With that, he was out the door.

Marilyn walked to the front window and stood there for a second. "It's okay. He got in his car. I want to know everything all of you know. I missed a good pancake breakfast for this."

"Eat a muffin, Marilyn," Rosalee said. "Try the honey raisin bran ones. Helps the digestion."

"The only thing I want to digest is what happened."

She helped herself to a cup of coffee, hung her bag from the chair and sat at the table. "Well? Isn't anyone going to say anything?"

Rosalee kept turning her head making eye contact with each one of us. "Roy Wilkes was a selfish and mean human being. Most likely he got what was coming, but I'm afraid that unless the sheriff's department finds evidence pointing to his killer, they'll be focusing their sights on me. Let's face it. Terrace Wineries had a darn good motive."

Theo tapped her arm and shook his head. "That may be true, but murders also require means and opportunity. Judging from his body, I'd say the guy was at least five foot nine and must've weighed over two hundred pounds. Rosalee, you can't be more than four foot nine and, while it would be in terrible taste to offer a gander at your weight, I'd say you were no match for him. Even if you were wielding a knife."

"I agree," I said. "Those sheriff's deputies must have some common sense."

Marilyn stopped stirring her coffee and put the teaspoon down. It made an annoying vibration as it hit the ceramic dish. "A knife? The man was killed with a knife? Nobody's told me anything. All I heard from my sister's hysterics was the man had blood on him. For all we know, he could've been shot. Seems like everyone's getting shot these days."

Theo told her about the earlier conversation we had with the deputy and the preliminary findings from the forensics team.

She looked at her sister and then at her coffee cup. "We're going to be in deep you-know-what if someone else doesn't appear on the horizon with a better motive and stronger biceps. What if the sheriff's department thinks you and I were in cahoots to stab that man? Dear God, Rosalee, this is a disaster. I hardly know what to suggest next."

Rosalee gave her a cold stare. "Then don't suggest anything. I'm going to call our attorney again. In the meantime, I'm sure Norrie will use all of her resources to find the real killer. You don't think I trust our sheriff's department, do you? Norrie happens to be an excellent sleuth."

A what? No way! I'm a screenwriter. Romances. Okay, fine. Maybe the occasional mystery, but I'm no detective. "I, um, er…I'm not an—"

Just then, there was another knock on the door. Actually three raps in quick succession. Before Rosalee said a word, a man's voice called out.

"Rosalee, it's me. Cal. What's going on? I saw one of the deputies leaving your house and the vineyard guys who were working down by the lake called my cell to tell me there's something going on below the winery. They spotted another sheriff's car and swore they saw a news crew van go down the long driveway. I got here as fast as I could. I was at the hardware store picking up a few replacement clippers. The old ones were really getting worn. Did someone drown?"

By now Cal had made his way to the kitchen and Rosalee motioned for him to grab a chair.

"Everyone, this is Cal Payne, our vineyard manager. Cal, you know my sister and these are our neighbors, Theo Buchman from the Grey Egret and Norrie Ellington from Two Witches."

Cal gave a quick nod but remained standing. I estimated him to be in his late thirties or maybe even early forties. Well-built with reddish hair and matching red stubble. "Nice to meet you. I won't be but a second."

"No one drowned," Rosalee said, "but I stumbled across Roy Wilkes' dead body first thing this morning on my walk with the dogs. He might've been stabbed to death. I called Norrie and she came over with Theo."

Marilyn grunted and cleared her throat. "Yes. And then she called me. I had to miss the monthly Pancake Day Breakfast at the diner."

Rosalee shot her a look, but Cal didn't appear to notice.

"Roy Wilkes? The guy who bought the Baxters' land? I only spoke with him once and it wasn't under the best circumstances. It was a week or two ago, and I noticed the water pressure had gone down. We weren't getting as much water in our vineyard aisles. I called him to let him know I'd be checking the pump house. He said even if the lake dried up, he still wanted his rent money. What a piece of work. Anyway, it turned out to be a small clog in one of the lines. We got it fixed right away."

"So, you never met him?" I asked.

"Nope. But some of my vineyard guys did. They saw him every now and then walking through the grapevine rows. Had to ask him not to. He wasn't exactly what you'd call compliant. Still, we never had any trouble, and I seriously doubt any of our people are responsible for what happened to the guy."

"If the sheriff's department runs their investigation the same way they did Elsbeth Waters' murder, they'll be questioning everyone at Terrace Wineries," I said.

Cal stretched his arms back, pinching his shoulder blades together. "No problem."

I might've imagined it, but I thought I detected some hesitancy in his voice.

Rosalee got up from the table and walked to the sink. "I suppose I'd better inform our winemaker and our tasting room manager. This is going to be a veritable nightmare until that killer is apprehended."

"Let's hope not," Cal said. "I'm on my way out. It's the harvest and none of us can afford any lost time. Rosalee, if you need anything, let me know. Okay?"

She walked him to the front door but unfortunately, I couldn't hear the rest of their conversation. Instead, Theo and I got to listen to Marilyn wailing once again because she had missed her morning with the ladies and the blueberry pancakes she had her heart set on.

When Rosalee got back to the kitchen, Theo and I excused ourselves and told her we'd be in touch.

Rosalee's parting words were, "Let me know what you uncover, Norrie," and I cringed.

"Hey, there's one good thing," Theo said as we got to my car. "Unlike your prior experience, Roy's body was found on the lakefront, not in her vineyard. That means she won't be besieged by crazy tourists. Cal said something about a news van. I imagine by five p.m., it'll be all over the Rochester and Syracuse TV stations."

"Yeah, nothing like a homicide to pick up viewers. Geez, up until this morning I thought the only thing you and I were going to do was conduct some background checks on the guy. Not tackle his murder."

"It all boils down to the same thing. We have to learn who he was, what he was into and all that good stuff before we can figure out who wanted to do him in."

"From what Cal and Rosalee told us, it sounds like anyone who's come in contact with him. Look, I've got to get some work done for my producer but in between breaks, I'll do some Google searches. What about you?"

"More of the same, only in between tastings, if I'm not too swamped today. How about we meet up after dinner and take a nice slow walk down that beach?"

"Theo Buchman, if I didn't know you better, I'd take that as a romantic gesture."

His face turned crimson, and I laughed. "Seriously, do you think we'll find any clues?"

He shrugged. "If not, we'll be sure to find lots of people out and about. Maybe one of them was an early riser who happened to see something."

It was a quick drive back to the Grey Egret. I couldn't believe it when I turned up the drive. Their parking lot was almost full.

"By God!" I said. "How long have we been gone?"

"Too long. Don's probably having a conniption. I'll catch you later. Hey, it wouldn't hurt if we told our employees about this. That way they can keep their eyes and ears open for any leads."

"Got it. Thanks, Theo. I know Rosalee appreciates it. I'm afraid she was right about being a prime suspect. And I can't sit back and let that happen. She's too nice a lady. Besides, it'll put a blemish on all of our wineries."

Chapter 5

I didn't want to bother John and his crew since every vineyard manager was stressed this time of year and John Grishner, our man-in-charge, was no exception. I figured I'd tell him about Rosalee's uninvited guest later in the day, or maybe I'd shoot off an e-mail. Much easier that way. I pulled the car over and made a quick stop into the winery building and informed our intern, Herbert, about "the situation across the road," as I began to call it.

"Maybe it was one of those random things," Herbert said. "Someone buzzed out on drugs looking for money."

I stared at his large brown eyes that matched the color of his skin. "That's more likely to happen in downtown Geneva, not the lakefront at dawn. Still, it's anyone's guess."

"Did you notice the type of stab wound? I once watched a program where they were able to tell the difference between a personal vengeance stab wound and a run-of-the-mill attack."

"I think that only happens on TV, but no, all I saw was blood."

"Not to sound callous, but at least it happened there and not here. Otherwise, we'd have to change our name to Two Murders Winery."

"Ha-ha. Let Franz and Alan know, okay?"

"Sure. Both of the winemakers have been going nonstop, preparing for the new harvest and monitoring what we have in the tanks. Not to mention making sure the Federweisser will be perfect. You do know what that entails. In fact—"

"I'm sure it's all good."

I got out of there as fast as I could before Herbert decided to give me another lesson on fermentation. It seemed whenever I got anywhere near those winemakers, that was the first thing they talked about. Sugar, yeast, bacteria, and a whole lot of other stuff that clogged up my mind and brought back awful memories of my eleventh grade chemistry class. Yeesh!

Our tasting room building was a few yards up the driveway and, like Theo and Don's, it, too, was packed. I parked alongside the building and looked around. A handful of tourists were out in front, reaching into Alvin's pen and petting him. Alvin, an enormous Nigerian Dwarf Goat, was my brother-in-law's idea to bring family friendliness to the winery. In my mind, that was akin to bringing the Marx Brothers to a coronation.

Alvin spit. Not often. But often enough, if he didn't like you. And, for some reason, I always seemed to wind up with his green slime somewhere on my clothing if I got too close.

Cammy waved to me the second I set foot in the door. Her auburn hair, although shorter than when I first met her two months ago, was pulled back from her face in a small, loose bun and tied with a bright orange ribbon that matched her Two Witches T-shirt. She had just finished a wine tasting with six or seven people and they headed to our wine racks and T-shirt bins.

"How's it going? As you can see, we haven't caught our breath yet."

"Um, speaking of breath, Roy Wilkes who owned the land that Rosalee Marbleton rented for her water supply, *that* Roy Wilkes, um…took his last breath a few hours ago."

Cammy wiped her hands on a dishtowel and set out more glasses for tastings. "Huh?"

"Dead. Rosalee found his body this morning while she was walking her dogs."

"On her property? Where?"

"Not exactly her property. On the lakefront. And get this, the guy was stabbed. I saw the blood on his jacket."

"What were you doing over there?"

I looked around the room and figured Glenda, Roger, and Sam could handle the customers. Same for our part-time employees. The closer we got to Labor Day, the more staff we needed.

"Come on. I'll tell you."

Cammy and I went into the kitchen and I helped myself to a large glass of orange juice from the fridge. I told her everything that happened across the road.

"Holy cow, Norrie! If ever there was a motive for murder, Rosalee's walking around with a capital M on her chest."

"No kidding. And you want to hear the worst thing? Okay, maybe not the worst, but still…Rosalee thinks *I* should be investigating. Me. Of all people. She doesn't trust the sheriff's department and, frankly, between her and her sister, Marilyn, I'm afraid the both of them are going to dig themselves into a hole. She already told the women in our winery group about how things took a turn for the worst when the Baxters sold the land to that wretched Roy Wilkes. Too bad Rosalee didn't snap it up. Guess she figured there was no reason to do so. Besides, lakefront land carries an outrageous price tag."

"Not as much as bail money and legal fees."

"Look, even if the motive does point to her, any deputy in his or her right mind would take one look at that little woman and realize she's no match for a strapping Brutus like Roy. I saw the body. Believe me, she would've been outgunned."

"True, but she could've hired someone."

"Rosalee? No way. Anyhow, keep your eyes and ears open and let the others know, too. People tend to talk a lot around here, especially when they've sipped some wine. If Roy's name comes up, try to get every last detail."

"No problem. I'll even let my aunts in Geneva know. They've taken over Rosinetti's and, believe me, no one can beat mouth flapping better than the patrons at a city bar. If there's something to be heard, they'll let me know."

"Thanks, Cammy. I've got to get going. I need to salvage at least part of the day for my writing."

"How's that going, by the way?"

"Not bad. I finished another round of revisions from my script analyst, and I'm waiting for the final review. Meantime, I'm working on another screenplay."

"Well, good luck with that."

* * * *

It was quarter to seven when I finished with my work. I got so engrossed with the tension between my two characters, I had completely forgotten about that Google search I was going to do on Roy Wilkes. Maybe Theo had had better luck. As planned, I walked down our driveway and we met in front of the Grey Egret. Don said he was too exhausted to go traipsing up and down the lake looking for nebulous clues, as he put it, and "engaging in banter with strangers on the beach."

"It's not banter," I told him. "It's calculated questioning. Maybe someone knows something."

He shook his head at Theo and me. "Maybe someone should let the sheriff's department deal with it. They already found Roy's motorcycle. It was parked in a wooded area a few yards from the pump house."

"How'd you find that out?" My voice was loud and squeaky at the same time.

"It was on the five o'clock news. Those reporters don't waste any time. Listen, whoever killed Roy is still out there. Did either of you think of that?"

"I, um, er, well…"

"Never mind. Keep your cell phones close and get out of there if something doesn't look right."

Theo and I bobbed our heads up and down in unison.

"I hope Don's not too mad at you," I said when I got into his car, an older Honda Civic in dire need of a wash.

"Nah. He worries. That's all."

Theo took the Terrace Wineries' driveway all the way down to the lakefront. No sense going the extra few miles to use the city access. The yellow crime scene tape surrounded the entire pump house and a good portion of the beach. It also beckoned every tourist and kid from here to Albuquerque.

"Holy cow! This is worse than when they cordoned off our vineyard. There must be at least fifteen people over there gawking. How long do you think the tape will stay up?"

"Anyone's guess. At least we won't have to walk far to get into the conversations. Let's go."

Theo was right. For the next hour, we watched the crowd intensify and dissipate, all the while trying to eke out information from anyone who might've been on the beach at dawn. It was frustrating as hell. First of all, I'd missed the evening news and so had Theo. It seemed everyone knew Roy Wilkes had been stabbed once in the chest with a long sharp object, but the investigators weren't able to find it. According to one of the rubberneckers, the word "knife" was never used. I made it a point to let Theo know my theory.

"It had to be some kind of pocket tool, like a screwdriver or one of those Swiss army knives. They've got all sorts of things like tweezers or files. You name it. And real easy for the killer to tuck away and keep walking."

"It's a strong possibility. After all, if the murder weapon was found, those reporters would've gotten that information. They're notorious for nagging the authorities to death. Look, we've got about another hour of daylight. What do you say we walk in the direction the killer used to make his or her exit? See if we can find anything of interest. Thanks to your encounter with those joggers this morning, we know our perpetrator left in the opposite direction. *And,* we know one more thing."

"What's that?"

"They didn't go up past the front of the winery because that's the route Rosalee took with her dogs."

I squinted my eyes and bit my lower lip. "Rosalee should've hired you. Are you sure you didn't study criminal justice at one point in your career?"

"Positive. But I read all the Hardy Boys novels, if that's a help."

"Remind me to introduce you to Lizzie in our tasting room. She's the Nancy Drew expert around these parts, but she'll drive you nuts."

Theo and I took a painstakingly slow walk up the lakefront toward Geneva, looking at all the lakefront houses and their driveways. Any one of them could've been the "getaway." Suddenly, I realized something.

"We're going about this all wrong. If our killer used one of those driveways to go from the lakefront back to his or her car, then the car would have to be parked by a house with a pull-off drive. You know. Where the road widens for a few yards so people can pull over. Only a few houses have those. The other homeowners have to pull directly into their own driveways. They can't park on the county road. And they'd be crazy to even consider it. Not much room. They'd be sideswiped."

"Now who's the genius? Okay, let's get back to my car, drive up the road, and jot down exactly which houses have pull-offs. Maybe we can come up with something and knock on some doors."

"If Grizzly Gary, oops! I mean, Deputy Hickman, finds out, he'll kill me. You heard him at Rosalee's. Those warnings were meant for me."

"How's he going to find out?"

"It doesn't matter. What's that saying? In for a dime, in for a dollar? I can't quit now."

"Good," he said. "Let's get a move on. Wouldn't want someone to steal my fabulous car while we're moseying around the lake."

"Ha! Ha!"

I was panting by the time I got into Theo's old Honda and put on my seatbelt. "It's a good thing I didn't bring Charlie. I was seriously considering bringing him, but I didn't want him to think he could leave our property, run across the road, and head for the lake. So far, that Plott Hound's been pretty content checking out the woods and sleeping in the kitchen or my bed."

"Yeah, he's a pretty mellow dog, all right. What do you say we take a quick run-through up the lake and count the pull-offs?"

"Do it!"

There were three pull-offs between Terrace Wineries and the sign that read, "Welcome to Geneva, New York, Lake Trout Capital of the World." Yep, the home of Hobart and William Smith Colleges, a world-renowned agricultural experiment station, an elegant opera house, wineries galore, and what did the city tout? Its fish. At least that was one step above Penn Yan, where we proudly showed off our buckwheat crop.

The house belonging to the first pull-off was a sprawling blue ranch in desperate need of a paint job. It had "rental property" written all over it. Its driveway and the pull-off had at least four parked cars. The next pull-off was a few yards down from an historic stone house with a carefully groomed garden in front. No visible cars. The house belonging to the last pull-off was a good ways back from the road. Thanks to the shrubs, bushes and trees, all that was visible was a white high-pitched roof with a red chimney.

"We've got time," Theo said. "Want to have a chat with the chipped paint blue ranch? I'll turn around at the next intersection and double back."

"Good. By that time, I might be able to think of something."

As it turned out, three women about my age were just getting into one of the cars when Theo pulled over. I jumped out and waved my arms. "Wait! Before you go, I need to—"

"If you're looking for directions," a petite blonde with short curly hair said, "we're not from around here. We're renting the place for the month and we keep getting lost every time we go out. In fact, maybe you know how to get to Uncle Joe's Restaurant in Geneva."

"Easy. Stay on Route 14 until you get to North Street. Then make a left and then a right on Genesee. It's up there."

"Left. Right. Thanks. Er, was there something you wanted?"

"If any of you were up real early this morning, did you happen to see if someone cut through your property to get to a car?"

"Sorry. None of us got up before nine. Of course, that's real early for us. Why? Is someone missing?"

"Not exactly. Hold on a second." I ran back to the car and asked if Theo had a pen and paper. He handed me an old gas receipt and a pencil from his console. I raced back to the blonde.

"Here's my name and phone number. I own Two Witches Winery in Penn Yan. If any of your friends remember seeing anyone, or even the car, please call me and let me know. It's really important. That's all I can tell you."

She raised her eyebrows and winked. "Someone's boyfriend cheating? Sure. I'll ask and if I hear anything, I'll let you know. We were at your winery a few days ago. Love that Cauldron Caper. I bought four bottles!"

"Wow. Thanks. And thanks about the other thing."

"On to the next house," I said. "The girls weren't even up, but the blonde will ask around and call me."

The occupant of the stone house wasn't as forthcoming. It was an elderly man who was hard of hearing and kept asking, "What?"

At the very moment when I decided it was a lost cause, a middle-aged woman, with her hair pulled back by two fashion clips, came rushing over to the door. "I'm so sorry," she said. "I was down in the cellar getting the laundry. My father's pretty much deaf. How can I help you?"

I figured she'd probably caught the evening news or, most likely, would catch the late night news, so I gave her the abbreviated version of the incident and asked if she was up early and if she saw anyone.

"I'm up with the roosters and enjoying my coffee with the sunrise. It's my only private time. Sorry, but I didn't see or hear anyone. Wish I could be more help."

I thanked her and trudged back to the car. The sun was setting, and I figured we had about fifteen, maybe twenty, more minutes of daylight.

"That figures," I said to Theo. "The last house on our list just so happens to be the dilapidated Victorian hidden away in the brambles. I'm not walking up to their front door alone."

"Don't worry. I had no intention of letting you. I'll park the car and we can both get snatched up and thrown into the oven by the witch."

"Very funny, Hansel."

"Make sure you've got your cell phone and let's move it. We've got less than a half hour before dark."

"Terrific. The creepy house on the lake at dusk. If I wrote horror screenplays, it would be my next title."

Chapter 6

At one time the house might've been a Victorian charmer, but it looked as if years of neglect had rendered it one step above an old shack. Well, a large old two-story shack. The windows were boarded up and there wasn't a spot where the paint wasn't chipping. Theo and I stood in front of it and shook our heads.

"No sense going to the front door," I said. "Besides, for all we know, the wood on that porch might be ready to give way. I wonder who owns this place. The lakefront alone must be worth beaucoup bucks."

Theo swatted at a few small flying insects. "It's probably tied up in probate. Forget the house, let's look around back and see if there's a path to the lake. And let's do it quickly. These bugs are going to get worse."

The right side of the house was impossible. Too many overgrown bushes and fallen tree limbs. It was highly doubtful anyone traipsed through there. Especially someone who had recently committed a murder. We skirted around the porch and saw what once was a gate to a small garden area. It was lying on its side against a rusty fence. It looked as if there might have been a path to the lake a few feet from where we stood.

It was as if we read each other's minds and walked to the back of the house. Old metal lawn furniture, with deteriorating cushions, was strewn everywhere—on the patio, off to the side of the building, and even next to some of the larger trees. A partially inflated beach ball, that might have been red when new, was perched against the remains of an old bike so old it was impossible to tell what kind it was.

"If I'm not mistaken," Theo said, "it looks as if we can get right down to the lakefront from here. It's a narrow path but, at one time, it had to be the access to the lake. You can still see the sand and gravel in between the weeds, unlike the rest of the property."

"We'll be eaten alive," I moaned, swatting the small insects like crazy. "You know, Jason could've had himself a field day with these bugs. They probably bite as much as the ones in Costa Rica."

Theo gave a quick laugh and headed toward the lake. I remained a good three or four feet behind him. At first it was a gentle slope but, about ten yards down, it reminded me of that scene in *Romancing the Stone*.

I shouted for him to slow down. "We're going to land on our butts. I just know we are."

"Then it'll be a soft landing. Come on."

My sneakers skidded against the gravel but somehow I managed to remain upright, even if Theo had beat me to the lakefront by more than a minute or two. At one point I thought his foot might have caught on something because he appeared to bend over. Stumbling maybe? Hah! Soft landing my you-know-what. We'd have gravel scrapes all over our arms and legs. At least he never fell.

As far as I was concerned, I was relieved when I reached level ground. "You *do* realize we have to make our way back up that steep path, don't you? No wonder that house is deserted. The prior owner probably had a coronary getting down here."

"Yeah, but it was worth it. Look what I found!"

He held up a small object and, at first, I couldn't make it out. "What've you got?" I asked.

Theo grinned. "If it wasn't for the soles of my sneakers being so worn, I never would've felt this bad boy. The metal all but cut through the ball of my foot. Tomorrow I'm buying a new pair of Nikes."

"Enough about your feet. Show me what you found. Better yet, hand it over."

I opened the palm of my hand and he let go of the object. It was a small silver hang-tab with the manufacturer logo. The kind that was on the front pockets of expensive windbreakers and jackets. This one had some blue threads dangling from it.

"Look carefully, Norrie. There's no dirt on that thing. None whatsoever. If it'd been here a while, you could bet your bottom dollar it would be caked with dirt. This is recent. Even the threads are clean."

"My gosh. You don't suppose—"

"I do. Whoever stabbed Roy Wilkes came down to the lake the same way we just did. He or she must've known Roy would be walking the shore. Maybe it was something our victim did all the time. Anyway, his killer didn't simply walk up to him and let loose with a sharp object. When we saw the body, it looked as if there was a struggle. I'll wager Roy grabbed ahold of that hang-tab and it got loosened in the melee. That tab was so loose it probably fell off by the time the killer made it back to the path by that house. That's why we found it here and not by the body."

I looked carefully at the design. "It's an Eddie Bauer. The name's etched right into the metal. They all do that. LL Bean, Denim and Company, Cabela's..."

"Man's or woman's jacket?"

"I can't tell that from a hang-tab, but I do know the metal ones are usually on the more costly jackets. And, in this case, one that *has* to belong to our killer. It makes absolute sense. Now what? We can't go to the sheriff's office. Grizzly Gary will have my head. Besides, we kind of contaminated the evidence by touching it."

Theo rubbed his ear and swatted at more insects. "If it *is* evidence, then our killer was wearing a blue windbreaker when he or she got into it with Roy. That's more than we knew a few hours ago."

"A zillion people own blue windbreakers. I think it's a law around these parts. So now what?"

"We can get the unofficial word out to the wineries to be on the lookout for someone wearing one that's missing the hang-tab on one of its front pockets. It should be pretty obvious. We'll go back to my house, stage the tab on a light background, and use our phones to send the photo to the wineries. By now, they're sure to know what happened by Rosalee's pump house."

"You can say that again. Between Rosalee calling the WOW women and the TV news making a big deal of it, Roy Wilkes' murder is bound to be a hot topic of conversation tonight."

"Don't forget Marilyn Ansley. She probably has her senior center on speed dial. God knows what she told those folks."

The uphill trek back to Theo's car took less time. We were somewhat familiar with the path, and it wasn't as slippery as when we were headed downhill. It was, however, getting darker and the insects were vicious. I swore I could feel blood trickling down my face and neck from all the bites. I had just gotten back into the car and buckled my seatbelt when a wave of doubt all but choked me. "What if the killer was a passenger on Roy's motorcycle? What if this hang-tab belongs to someone who took a shortcut up from the lake?"

Theo was silent while I went on and on. Finally, he groaned. "Slow down. Think about it. If the killer was the passenger, wouldn't those women joggers have seen him or her? The killer had to have come from the opposite direction. Besides, with Roy dead and his motorcycle parked, how was the murderer going to get out of there? I still think he or she used their own vehicle. I think we are on the right track."

"I suppose you're right. I tend to overthink things."

Don was sitting on their porch when Theo pulled up. The second we got out of the car, he ran toward us. "It's about time! While you two were playing 'Gumshoe Detective,' I did some real investigating. You can thank me later. Either that or split the fourteen ninety-five I paid to do a background check on our victim. Oh. And I still had time to heat up some calzones. Come on in. And do tell. What did the both of you discover? Or dare I say, 'uncover'?"

Theo gave Don a hearty slap to the shoulder and held out the hang-tab. "Evidence, my man. Evidence! Norrie can explain. I've got to snap a decent photo and get the word out to the west side wineries. Give me your phone, Norrie, I'll get a snapshot for you, too."

No sooner did I hand over my cell phone to him when he flung open the door to the house and ran inside.

"Okay. I'm game," Don said. "What was that thing Theo was holding?"

"One of those metal hang-tabs that you see on fancy windbreakers or jackets. They're usually on the front pockets."

I then proceeded to give him the long version of the story, including our theory about the pull-offs on the road and a getaway path for the killer. Finding the little hang-tab all but clinched it as far as Theo and I were concerned.

"You two might actually be on to something. Still, what do you plan to do if someone at one of the wineries sees a person wearing a windbreaker without both of its hang-tabs on the pockets?"

"Uh, um, we haven't gotten that far in our thinking, but I suppose we'll have to call the sheriff's office to tell them."

By now Don and I had gone inside and were sitting at the kitchen table, where Theo had just finished taking the photos. He handed me back my phone, told me he e-mailed the WOW women and planned to do the same with his winery managers. I immediately started messaging my own contacts.

"Let's hope the two of you don't get chewed out for interfering with an investigation." Don took the calzones from the oven. "I hate to use the oven when it's hot out, but microwaving Italian food makes it taste like plastic."

I tapped my foot and turned toward him. "It's not really interfering. For all anyone knows, we're simply trying to return a hang-tab to the owner of an expensive piece of clothing."

"Oh brother. Never mind. Listen, are you guys interested in hearing what I found out about Roy Wilkes or not?"

Theo and I all but drowned each other out with our Yeahs.

"Fine," Don said. "Here goes: First of all, I went to the public records online from a nifty little site I found. After that, I shelled out the money for more information."

"Go on already," Theo groaned.

"Roy Wilkes is, I mean *was,* fifty-five and—"

"Wow! Rosalee guessed the age right," I blurted out. "Sorry. Go on. Go on."

Don cleared his throat. "Believe it or not, he was born in Penn Yan but moved to Pennsylvania before completing high school there. He went to school for industrial technologies and worked for Beecher Rand, an industrial manufacturing company, in Athens, Pennsylvania, up until a year ago. Never married. No children. No criminal record."

"Did he retire from the company or was he let go?" I asked.

Don shook his head. "Don't know. But get this—there are no records for any mortgages for his properties. He must've paid cash. I don't know about anyone else, but I'm curious as hell. Why did the guy decide to move back here? It's not as if this town is the pinnacle of excitement."

Theo quickly grabbed some plates from one of the cabinets and silverware from the drawer nearest him. The napkins were already on the table. "The question I'd be asking is what did he do that got him killed. Let's face it, we don't need the deputies to tell us it wasn't a robbery. But yeah, what the hell was it?"

After putting the calzones on the table, Don opened the fridge and took out sodas, water, and a recently opened bottle of their Merlot blend.

I poured myself some wine. "The worst part about this is Rosalee. She's convinced herself I can find the killer. So far I have a hang-tab and a headache."

"Eat, you'll feel better," Don said. "Seriously, the sheriffs may have access to forensic clues, but good old-fashioned sleuthing often yields better results."

The calzone was enormous and when I cut into it, the aroma of tomatoes, sausage and cheeses almost made me drool. "I wish we had access to Roy's house. Imagine what we could learn about him."

Theo and Don didn't say a word. Not at first. But I could read the expressions on their faces. A combination of shock and fear.

Theo spoke first. "Don't even think it. We don't have enough bail money put aside for breaking and entering."

I wiped some of the warm sauce from the side of my lips. "Don't worry. I'll stick to..." What was it Don said? Oh yeah, "gumshoeing."

The three of us agreed to spread the word about the hang-tab on the off chance the killer decided to pay one of the wineries a visit. It was more likely he or she would attend the Federweisser since that was a major event that drew out tourists and locals. Of course, that meant waiting, since it was three weeks from now. Anything could happen between now and then.

It was after nine when I got home. Theo insisted on driving me up the hill. Charlie was waiting for me on the porch and all but knocked me over when I got out of the car.

"Oh my gosh! Did I forget to feed you?"

I remembered putting kibble in his bowl first thing in the morning, but the dog was used to eating another meal in the early evening. I raced inside and immediately fed him, making a mental note to buy one of those large self-serve pet dispensers just in case.

As I put the food away and stashed the hang-tab in a safe place, I noticed the red light blinking on the answering machine. I immediately pushed the button. It was Cammy.

"Hey, Norrie! Got your e-mail about that hang-tab. Call me if it's not too late. I'm up 'til ten thirty. I called my aunts about Roy Wilkes and you're not going to believe this. A few weeks ago, he was at Rosinetti's and got into a fight with another guy. It was the first time they'd seen him at the bar, but Roy used a credit card and my aunt Luisa remembered the name. Call me."

I looked at the microwave clock and it read 9:23. I was dying to chat with Cammy but whenever someone says, "I'm up until whatever time," what they really mean is, "Don't call me unless hell is freezing over." It was a no-brainer. I decided to shift my morning writing schedule around and be at the tasting room when she arrived for work tomorrow. At last we were getting somewhere.

Chapter 7

Saturdays are usually crazy at the wineries and this one didn't appear to be any different. Cars were pulling into our parking lot as if we were Costco. I didn't even want to think about next Saturday because that was Labor Day Weekend.

To add to the zaniness, an army of vineyard workers were fast at work with the first harvest—the Chardonnay. In addition to our regular crew, we had hired a number of migrant workers who operated under a cooperative in Dresden, a few miles from Two Witches.

The grinding and spitting sounds from our harvesters were unmistakable. I remembered Peter Groff, our former assistant vineyard manager, showing me the tow-behind harvester and the self-propelled one.

Chardonnay was always the first grape we harvested. Mainly because we used it to make champagne as well as wine. In less than three weeks, I'd be sampling a bubbly, frothy version of it at our Federweisser.

I had to walk past Alvin's pen in order to get to the tasting room's entrance. Sure, I could've skirted it, but the goat was busy eating from his bucket of grains, so I figured I was relatively safe. The minute he heard me approaching, he trotted over and leaned forward. I knew he liked to be petted but, for some reason, he got particularly ornery around me. Leaning as far back as I could, I managed to extend my hand and rub his nose as he pressed his face against the fence. So far so good.

"Don't you spit at me. Nice goat. Nice Alvin."

Suddenly, a few tourists approached and he trotted over to greet them. I watched as he nuzzled and rubbed against their hands.

"Hope you enjoy the winery," I said to them before making my way to the front door.

The tasting room and sales area were open a half hour before the actual tastings began. Cammy was busy setting up the stations when I pulled her aside. "I wasn't going to bother you last night. I got in really late."

"I figured as much when I got your e-mail. So you and Theo think that hang-tab belongs to the killer?"

"It's quite possible. Of course, I can't say a word to the sheriff's deputies so we'll have to be low-key about our sleuthing. Theo decided to join me. So, tell me more about the Roy Wilkes incident at your family's bar."

Cammy stepped behind one of the tasting room tables and moved one of the large pitchers we used for emptying wineglasses aside. "The incident happened on a Friday night. According to my aunt Luisa, he and another guy were really getting into it. It was the first time she'd seen Roy at the bar. Same for the other guy. That doesn't mean it was the first time he was in there, only that it was the first time she saw him. Anyway, she doesn't know what they were arguing about, but when they started to push and shove each other, that's when two of the bartenders got them out of there."

"Not your cousins, Marc and Enzo?"

Marc and Enzo had helped me out with a rather sticky situation two months ago and, even though I could've managed without their help, it was nice to know I had them on my side.

"No. They're back at college."

I nodded and she went on. "According to my aunt, the one guy paid cash, but Roy used a credit card. Whenever there's an incident at the bar, they try to find out who was involved and make a note of it. If that person returns and has another problem, that's when they tell him or her not to return. Everyone gets the first ride free, if you know what I'm saying."

"I do."

"My aunt wrote down Roy's name on their 'no-fly' list. Oh, and before you ask if she remembers what they were wearing, she doesn't. I called her this morning and told her about the hang-tab. Said she'd let the bartenders know and they'd be on the lookout."

"Cammy, you're the best!"

Just then, Lizzie motioned me over to the cash register. The tasting stations would be open in a few minutes, and I didn't want to hold anyone up.

"Norrie," she said, adjusting her wire-rimmed glasses and patting down her perfectly styled grey hair, "I want you to know you did a splendid job finding that first clue. Cammy shared the hang-tab photo with everyone. That Nancy Drew handbook I gave you must've paid off. What's your next move?"

Lizzie was a Nancy Drew aficionado and insistent that every good sleuth abided by Nancy's standards. Too bad this wasn't the 1930s. Fortunately for me, a customer approached the cash register and I told Lizzie I'd catch up with her another time.

I made a quick stop at the bistro and had our chef, Fred, make me a tuna salad sandwich to go. He said he'd be on the lookout for anyone wearing a blue windbreaker sans the hang-tab on one pocket. Word was getting out. I put the sandwich in the fridge when I got home and tackled the screenplay hanging over my head. At a little before noon I put the sandwich on a plate, grabbed a Coke, and plopped down on the couch. That was when the phone rang. Figuring it might be important, I returned both items to the fridge and picked up.

"It's me, Norrie. Stephanie Ipswich. Remember when I told you I'd be willing to do some sleuthing on the Internet for you? It was right after our WOW meeting on Thursday."

"Of course I remember. That was the day before yesterday."

"Geez, I'm so used to the other ladies forgetting everything. Oops. Don't tell them I said that."

"No worries. I won't. So, what's up?"

"When I got your e-mail with that hang-tab, I started thinking. That Federweisser is going to draw a huge crowd. Huge. Maybe we should put together a posse, for lack of a better word, to wander around the event for the sole purpose of checking out who might be wearing that windbreaker. I was going to suggest doing it Labor Day Weekend as well, but the crowd moves too quickly in and out of the wineries. It's a blur and our tasting room employees don't have time to scrutinize. At the Federweisser everyone stays in one place but none of us can afford to loan you our own employees for surveillance because we'll be swamped as well. But, what if we commandeer, let's say…another group of interested and concerned citizens?"

"Um, who exactly did you have in mind?"

"I have a few possibilities. Now, keep in mind, I haven't shared this with anyone."

Thank God!

"My husband's bowling team for starters, or the quilting group from my church. We can talk about this at the next WOW, but what if all of us chipped in and bought the bowlers or quilters a lunch coupon for the Federweisser? They'd get a free lunch and all they'd have to do is walk around and snoop. Listen, I'm friends with some of those quilters and they'd do that without being paid. What do you think?"

Disaster. Disaster. Disaster.

"I, um, er…"

"I know. I know. It's ingenious, isn't it?"

"It's, uh, certainly that. Listen, let me think about it and I'll call you back. Definitely before our next meeting."

"Okay, sure. How's Rosalee holding up? I really should call her, but I didn't want to bother her."

"She seemed all right yesterday. Her sister was over there."

"Poor Rosalee. It's been all over the news. They said it might have been a screwdriver or an ice pick. Who uses an ice pick? Now a turkey thermometer I can understand, but an ice pick?"

"Yeah, that is a bit much. Listen, I really need to—"

"Say no more. I've taken up enough of your time. Get back to me on that posse idea, will you?"

"Sure thing."

I walked back to the fridge and retrieved my lunch for the second time. Maybe Stephanie's hang-tab surveillance team wasn't such a bad idea after all. We'd have lots of eyes on those Federweisser tourists. That meant a good chance of finding our suspect. But only if he or she decided to wear the windbreaker and attend the winery event. Still…it was better than nothing.

I picked up where I left off on my screenplay, but it was a struggle. One minute I was writing dialogue and the next I was thinking about Stephanie's plan. What should have taken me two or three hours took closer to six. Of course, I didn't spend all that time on task. I stopped to make an omelet and then got trapped on Facebook for longer than I wanted to admit. And when I wasn't looking at someone's pet or staring at what they ate for dinner, my thoughts went right back to Stephanie.

Since Theo and Don were as deep in this case as I was, I decided to run the idea by them. It was late evening but still plenty light outside. Charlie and I moseyed down to the Grey Egret and caught the men sitting on their porch enjoying the sunset.

"Hey there!" I called out as the dog and I walked up to their porch. "Stephanie Ipswich had an idea about us finding the owner of the windbreaker. She called me earlier today. Didn't want to bother you on a Saturday."

"Good thing," Theo said. "It was like a sea of humanity in our tasting room. At this rate, I'll be a basket case at the end of Labor Day Weekend."

Don flashed him a look. "Don't be so dramatic. You love it. You know you do."

"I love it when I can talk with people, tell them about the wine and listen to their stories and reflections. But during the fall rush, it's 'fill my glass, fill my glass, fill my glass.'"

I laughed. "Now you know why I decided to leave and become a screenwriter."

Charlie sniffed around the porch and finally settled on a place to lie down—the small rug in front of the door.

"Don't worry about him blocking your door all night," I said. "I'm only going to be here a minute or so. I wanted to get your thoughts on Stephanie's idea."

I pulled up a chair, declined the offer for something to drink, and told them about Stephanie's brainchild using the bowlers and/or the quilters. I couldn't tell if Don and Theo were going to burst out laughing or what. They tried to look restrained, but it wasn't working.

"Tell me," I said. "Tell me what you're thinking."

Don finally gave a laugh and then laughed louder. "Sorry, love. All I can picture is that scene from the old *Andy Griffith* show. The one with Gomer Pyle making a citizen's arrest. I can picture it now—one of those quilter ladies screaming 'Citizen's arrest! Citizen's arrest!'"

"Really? You think it'll go that badly?"

Theo shook his head. "Probably not. But you'd really have to spell out the ground rules for surveillance. Not to mention keeping tight-lipped about everything."

Don sighed. "I suppose it would work. I mean, you'd get a lot of mileage in terms of scoping out the crowd. Look how fast word is spreading already."

"Okay. I'll let Stephanie know. She was going to bring it up at the next WOW. It's a week from Thursday. Which one of you will be there?"

Don and Theo shouted out each other's name in unison.

"Fine. The both of you. Well, I'd better head back up the hill before it gets really dark."

"We can give you a lift, you know," Theo said.

"Nah, the dog needs the exercise."

Just then, we heard a piercing scream. The kind that made every single hair on one's arms and the back of the neck stand up.

I was no exception. "Holy crap! Where's it coming from?"

Charlie got up from his resting spot and stared across the road.

"Somewhere on the lake," Don said. "On a quiet night, we can hear voices from across the lake. Whole conversations even. It's a stretch to believe, but it's true."

I nodded. "I know. I grew up here, remember?"

Then, as if on cue, the scream repeated.

Don, who was standing between Theo and me, grabbed both our wrists. "It sounds closer than across the lake. Yikes, you don't think it's coming from Terrace Wineries? From Rosalee's house?"

"Only one way to find out," Theo answered. "Come on. We can all pile into my car. Charlie, too. Don, turn around and make sure the door's locked. Don't need whatever it is coming over here."

I bit my lip for a moment, trying to remember if I had locked my house. It took me a second but I was sure I did.

The three of us raced to Theo's car, with Charlie at my heels. He probably figured it was some sort of game. The sky was quickly changing from soft pink and blue hues to heavier darker ones. It would be totally dark in ten minutes. Fifteen if we were lucky.

Theo all but flew across Route 14 and into the Terrace Wineries' driveway. Only the small nightlights were on in the winery building, but at Rosalee's house, which was closer to the road, I could see the kitchen light on.

"Don't go rushing in there." I shoved Charlie off my chest and onto the backseat next to me. "This is always the scene in the Stephen King movies where something jumps out at the innocent victims."

"Norrie's got a point," Don said. "Why don't you honk your horn? The worst thing that can happen is Rosalee's fine and annoyed with us."

Theo blared the horn, but nothing happened.

"Maybe we should call the sheriff's office." I was about to make the call when the porch light came on and Rosalee opened the door. We piled out of the small Honda as if it was a clown car, complete with its own dog.

Rosalee waved her arms in the air and yelled, "Did you catch him? Did you grab him?"

"Who?" we all seemed to ask at once.

"The killer. He was on my porch. Victoria and Albert growled and Philip barked once. I got up to see what was going on and that's when I saw someone in a hooded sweatshirt by the bottom of the steps. Next time, I'll look out a window and not open the front door. I screamed as loud as I could and whoever it was ran behind the house. It took me a minute or two to catch my breath, but I screamed again. This time, to scare him off."

Don elbowed me. "We really do need to call the sheriff's office."

As much as I would've preferred not to, Don was right. No way was I about to go after some maniac down by the lakefront in the dark.

"You make the call," I said to him. "I want to remain anonymous as long as I can."

"You mean until Deputy Hickman arrives, don't you? Forget it, Norrie, you've already made it to his PITA list."

"His what?"

Theo laughed. "Pain In The Ass."

Rosalee had stepped onto the porch and was scanning it. All I noticed was the small line-up of flowerpots that were here yesterday—geraniums, asters and some sort of daisies. Rosalee had used decorative stakes to hold the larger plants up. Each stake had a cartoon version of an insect on it. A few ladybugs, a praying mantis and a dragonfly. Right up my brother-in-law's alley. I glanced at the flowerpots again while Don called the sheriff's office.

"Uh-oh. Looks like one of your insect heads fell off," I said to Rosalee.

She leaned over and took a good look at the geranium, clearly visible under the porch light. "The head didn't fall off. The whole darn thing's missing. Drat! Why would someone snatch one of those things? Phooey. As if I didn't have enough to worry about. I don't think I'll be able to find another re-purposed metal stake. These are heavy duty and the tips can go through even the toughest soil, not bend and break off like the kind you get at a garden store. I bought mine years ago on a trip to Cape Cod. My late husband thought they were ridiculous, but I liked them."

Suddenly I had this awful feeling in the pit of my stomach. "Mind if I take a closer look at one of those?"

Before she could answer, I pulled up the ladybug and stared at the stake. A long round metal tube with one hell of a sharp prick at the end. Not exactly what one would find on Etsy. What was it Stephanie was saying about an ice pick?

"I don't want to get ahead of myself," I said, "but I think I know what killed Roy Wilkes."

Rosalee took the ladybug from me and ran her finger across the tip. Then she glanced at the other flowerpot stakes. "Dear God. He was stabbed with the butterfly. The lovely Monarch Butterfly. That cinches it. It *had* to be the killer on my porch. Attempting to put the evidence back where he took it in the first place."

Charlie began to paw and whine at the front door while Rosalee's dogs returned the favor by barking.

She opened the door and motioned us to follow her. "We might as well go inside and wait for a sheriff's deputy to arrive. That hound dog of yours will be fine with the Corgis."

The second she said that, all four of her dogs converged around Charlie and sniffed him all over. He stood there stoically and, when they were done, made himself comfortable on a small throw rug under her coffee table.

Theo, Don, and I sat at the kitchen table, and waited for the inevitable visit from Grizzly Gary.

Rosalee manned the front window, muttering to herself about murder weapons, butterflies, and dead bodies. I must've mentally rolled my eyes a dozen times.

"I see headlights," she shouted. "And those blue and red flashers. They're pulling into my driveway. Thank goodness they don't have that siren blaring."

Rosalee immediately opened her front door. "Don't just stand there lollygagging on the front lawn. There's a murderer loose behind my house. Go! Chase him! Gun him down!"

Theo got up and tapped her on the shoulder. "We don't know if it was the killer. It might've been a prowler or a burglar. Maybe even a homeless person looking to scrounge some food. Besides, he or she is long gone by now. Let the deputies inside to take a statement and they'll go from there."

Two young men, who appeared to be my age, stepped inside the foyer. Both of them were blond and clean shaven. If it wasn't for the difference in their heights, they might've passed as twins. Must be Deputy Hickman had the night off.

Charlie didn't bother to get up, but the Corgis raced over only to be admonished by Rosalee, who told them to sit-stay. Then she focused her attention on the deputies.

"Well, don't just stand there waiting for the next Ice Age, send for a S.W.A.T. team or something."

Chapter 8

"Who wants to tell her this isn't an invasion?" I whispered to Theo and Don.

Rosalee crossed her arms and refused to let the deputies go any farther than the hallway where we were all crammed in.

"We need a statement, ma'am," the taller deputy said. "We can't proceed without one."

"Fine. Fine. But don't come crying to me that your murderer escaped."

The next five laborious minutes were spent in the kitchen, where Rosalee described the noise she and her dogs heard and the person she had seen leaving her porch. When she finally stopped for air, I broke in with the information about the flowerpot stake.

"So you see," I said, "the murder weapon used to kill Roy Wilkes might very well have been Mrs. Marbleton's re-purposed metal butterfly stake. The killer probably grabbed it on his way to meet with the victim. Or, to surprise the victim. Either way, the killer snatched the stake and was off to commit murder."

Don and Theo looked at each other across the table from where they were seated. It was one of those looks where one person knew exactly what the other was thinking.

"Go on," I said. "Spit it out."

Meanwhile, the shorter deputy took copious notes on a similar pad that his counterpart, and my nemesis, Deputy Hickman, used.

Don't these people know we have iPads today?

Don swallowed and pushed himself back from the table. "The only way someone would've known about the flowerpot stakes is if they were familiar with Rosalee's porch. Or more specifically, her plants." Then he turned to Rosalee.

The color was all but gone from her face. "The only one who knew about those stakes was my sister, Marilyn, who helped me transplant some of my geraniums."

"That doesn't necessarily mean anything," the taller deputy said. "Anyone who walked across your porch at one time or another was bound to notice them. And not to sound dismissive, but we have no idea if one of those stakes was the murder weapon."

Then the shorter deputy spoke. "Listen, we don't want to disappoint you, but it's pitch black outside and chances are your intruder is no longer in the vicinity. My partner and I will walk around the perimeter of your house and your garage. We'll be back in a few minutes."

"Can you check the winery building while you're at it? It's a bit farther down the driveway. For all we know, the killer could be hiding out or trying to break in. These criminals are smart, you know. I read they can dismantle an alarm system like ours in a matter of seconds. And I also read they always return to the scene of the crime."

The taller deputy shook his head. "I seriously doubt we're dealing with Harry Houdini. Besides, it really would be a stretch for someone to return to a crime scene late at night, in the dark."

The other deputy nudged him. "Wasn't the crime scene by the pump house and not the house?"

Rosalee narrowed her eyes and glared at them. "Close enough. Check the winery building, will you? I'd hate to phone your dispatch a second time tonight."

The deputies assured her they'd check everything and keep her informed. With that, they exited the house and I clasped my hands together and leaned into the table.

I wasn't so sure Rosalee's nighttime visitor was returning to the scene of the crime. Or, to be more specific, the scene *before* the crime. "We don't know if the intruder's intent was to put the butterfly stake back in the flowerpot."

"What else could that person have been doing?" Rosalee's voice was sharp, but the look on her face spelled out fear, not anger.

"Can anyone stay with you for a few nights?" Don asked. "Not that you aren't perfectly safe with your dogs and all, but still…"

"He's right," I added. "What about Marilyn?"

Rosalee sighed, rubbing her hands together. "I suppose I could give her a call."

"If you'd like, we could drive to Penn Yan and get her. The village is only a few miles away."

"It's late and I'll be fine tonight. I doubt the perpetrator will be back. I'll call my sister first thing in the morning. God knows, I hope it doesn't interfere with her breakfast brunches."

The deputies returned a few minutes later to inform us that everything was clear. "We'll have someone from the forensics team stop by in the morning to look over those flowerpots. They'll want to take one of those stakes with them to see if the stab wound matches up to the metal rod. If so, at least we'll know what the weapon was, even if it's not in our possession."

When the deputies left, the three of us theorized about what possibly could've ensued in the events leading up to Roy Wilkes' murder. It seemed as if the more we talked, the more agitated Rosalee got.

"I think we should call it a night," Don said. "It's really late and we'll all be comatose tomorrow if we don't get some sleep. Rosalee, you've got our number and Norrie's. Call us if you need anything. And if it's an emergency, call nine-one-one first. Okay?"

Rosalee gave a nod and thanked us. I all but had to shake Charlie awake from his new sleeping spot. He ambled out to the car, followed by the four Corgis, who made their final pit stops for the night.

"Think she'll be all right?" Theo asked as he started the car.

Don hummed to himself for a few seconds before answering. "Yeah. I doubt whoever it was on her porch stuck around once they saw the sheriff's car. The question I have, the one we *all* have, other than who it was, was what they were doing and what did they want."

"That's two questions," I said. "Sorry. It's late and I'm getting persnickety. I think it was the murderer and he or she came back to plant evidence incriminating Rosalee. Her dogs scared him off. That scream of hers didn't help either."

"You mean to say you think the killer was putting the murder weapon back in the flowerpot when he heard her?"

"Yep, I do. The pot with the missing flower stake was pulled out farther from the wall against her house. I noticed it when we first got there, but I didn't think much about it. Now, in retrospect, I bet our murderer had pulled it from the wall and was about to stick the butterfly stake back in it when he heard Rosalee."

"Good news is," Theo said. "It's too late now. We're on to him. Or her. If the killer decides to make another try at it, the sheriff's deputies are already aware that the butterfly stake is missing. If it turns up, they'll know why."

Theo drove to the top of the hill and let Charlie and me off in front of the house. He and Don waited until I was safely inside and the lights were on. I blinked the porch light to let them know all was well and they drove off.

"Honestly, Charlie, I don't know what I'd do without those two. Francine and Jason were right about having good neighbors who are also good friends."

The dog yawned and ran up the stairs to my bed. I was about to follow when I noticed the red light flashing on my answering machine.

Now what?

The screen on the phone indicated the call had come in earlier in the evening. About the time I had originally walked to Theo and Don's. I pushed the button and replayed the message.

"Call me if it's not too late, Norrie. I'm up 'til all hours. It's me, Glenda. I have a horrible premonition that something awful is going to befall the winery. I knew we should've given the place a good smudging with sage sticks. In the meantime, I'll look into cleansing rituals. Bye."

Terrific. Of all the possible workers my sister and brother-in-law could have hired for the tasting room, we had to get our own personal psychic—Glenda. She was a sweet lady and meant well, but would drive all of us crazy if we let her. I deleted the message, made sure the door was locked and the downstairs windows were closed and then joined Charlie in my queen-size bed.

Apparently there was a light rain that night because everything was damp and muddy when I got up the next morning. It didn't matter. The ground would dry up by the time the tasting room opened for business and our tours began. In answer to the increasing crowds at the wineries, Two Witches decided to run hourly tours weekdays and weekends beginning in late August. Franz, who was terrified someone would get into the lab and winery, posted a giant "VERBOTEN" sign on the door. Of course, he was banking on the fact they understood German and didn't think it was a new variety of wine.

I breezed into the tasting room at a little past nine. Real early for me. I needed to touch base with Cammy when she arrived and Glenda as well. Instead, Roger was the first one to greet me.

"I'm on the early shift this morning," he said. "We were so exhausted yesterday we didn't get a chance to refill the wine racks. I offered to do it before we opened. Cammy should be here any minute, and Glenda's coming in early, too. What's with her, anyway? She seems a little spooked."

I walked over to where Roger was standing and made myself useful by opening a carton of Pinot Noir for the wine rack. "You mean more than usual?"

"She said she had a bad feeling that—"

"Something awful was going to happen?"

"How'd you know? Don't tell me you're psychic, too."

"Nope. Got her phone message last night. After responding to an intruder on Rosalee Marbleton's front porch."

"What?"

Roger listened intently while I spouted off my flowerpot stake theory. "Hmm, you may be on to something. From what you described, the tip of that plant stake sounds similar to the tip of the French Halberd, a cunning little piece of weaponry in the French and Indian War."

Oh no! I've fallen into the rabbit hole! Phooey. And I'd been warned, too.

Roger had a penchant for the French and Indian War. The slightest connection and he'd launch into a never-ending discourse on the subject. I started to say something, but I wasn't quick enough. Miraculously, he managed to keep it brief.

"Interesting thing about the Halberd. It was slender. Could slip under an infantryman's arm and not be readily noticed until it was too late. That little flowerpot stake of yours could easily have been hugged under the killer's armpit. Especially if that insect motif was flat."

I thought for a second. "It was. I mean, they are. Flat."

"You do realize something, don't you?"

He answered before I said a word.

"If that was the murder weapon, then the murder was premeditated. Whoever orchestrated it must've known about a weapon no one would suspect. They also had to have known that Roy Wilkes would be at the pumping station. Hmm..."

Roger rubbed his chin and clicked his tongue, making a strange clacking sound. "If you want my two cents, I'll bet the killer lured Roy to that very spot. You can't have a premeditated murder on the off chance someone will be strolling by."

"Good point."

I helped Roger fill the wine racks while I waited for Cammy and Glenda to walk in. I didn't have to wait long. No sooner did we finish when Cammy appeared. She was sporting one of the new fuchsia T-shirts. The color could probably be seen from the nearest solar system.

"Norrie might've come across the murder weapon used on Roy Wilkes," Roger announced as Cammy walked toward us.

"Long story," I said. "I'll fill you in while you get set up for the onslaught."

As Cammy hustled from table to table, making sure the wines were all in the small mini-fridges underneath for tastings, the glass racks easily accessible and the dump pitchers in place, I gave her the rundown in spurts.

Rosalee's shriek. The flowerpot theory. And, not to be missed, Stephanie's brilliant idea to ferret out the person with the blue windbreaker.

"Boy, you certainly don't let any grass grow under your feet, do you?" she laughed.

"The grass is the least of my worries. Glenda called last night and left me a message. She has a feeling something terrible is about to befall us. Her words, not mine."

"Oh brother. I don't suppose she was specific."

"Nope. Apparently premonitions don't present that way. Listen, I've got to get back to my own work. When she gets in, tell her I got her message and I'm taking it under advisement."

"Good deal. Catch you later."

While I knew Glenda was probably being overly dramatic, I didn't want to take any chances. I left messages on John and Franz's cell phones for them to call me. The last winery staff meeting I'd held was three weeks ago and everything had been topsy-turvy since then.

According to Cammy, Francine used to hold one or two meetings a month but during the fall rush, it was down to one meeting with lots of individual conferencing with the managers. Our next meeting wasn't for another two weeks, and I didn't want to wait that long. Especially with the Federweisser coming up. I had to know that everything was copasetic as far as our winemaker and our vineyard manager were concerned.

Knowing how the wineries are all interconnected on the Seneca Lake Wine Trail, I worried we'd feel the repercussions from the murder across the road as if it happened here. I knew it was silly, but until I got reassurances from John and Franz, I wasn't about to take chances with our establishment. Especially if a lunatic killer was making the rounds.

Chapter 9

I knew the only way I was going to get the reassurances I needed from our winemaker and our vineyard manager was to chat with them face to face. It was much easier talking with John because, even though he felt compelled to spell out every nuance involved with planting and harvesting, at least I didn't have to force my eyelids to stay open the way I did with Franz. Maybe it was the words Franz used. Like "malolactic process" and "botrytis." Words I didn't want to deal with early the next morning.

After feeding the dog and forcing myself to try one of Francine's homemade granola cereals, I threw a light sweater over my top and headed to the barn. I thought Charlie would chomp at the chance to tag along but instead, he went back to his dog bed and closed his eyes. Most likely he'd gone outside and run around while I was sleeping.

When I approached the barn, I heard heated voices and recognized John's immediately. I held my breath and listened. The second voice was familiar, too, even though I had only heard it once. It was Cal Payne, Rosalee's vineyard manager. What on earth were he and John arguing about? On a Monday morning, no less.

I backed up against the side of the barn and tilted my head so my ear rested close to the window. I doubted anyone could see me from the driveway and who would? It was way too early for the tasting room to open. From my vantage point, pressed against the barn, I didn't need to guess what they were saying. I had a front row seat.

"So why are you telling me this? Cripes. Go to the damn sheriff's office and come clean."

Come clean? It was John speaking. Had Cal done something that he needed to confess? Like murdering Roy Wilkes? I held my breath until I thought my chest would burst.

"That stupid oaf would have me behind bars in a second. Hell, what was I supposed to do? Sit back and wait for Roy Wilkes to put Terrace Wineries under the ground for good? He had it coming."

My God. He did kill Roy Wilkes.

My heart was thumping and my hands were shaking. I pressed myself even closer to the building until the scratchy wood grains butted up against my jeans. Cal was still speaking and I didn't want to miss a word.

"I told him he was killing us with those jacked-up land prices, but all he did was smirk. I felt like backhanding him to wipe that smugness from his face, but I didn't. And believe me, it took all the restraint I could muster. Instead, I called him an SOB, among other things, and told him he'd better watch his back."

"So you threatened him? Geez, Cal, how the hell do you know that nobody heard you? Like I've been telling you, you need to get this on record before someone pokes his or her head out of the woodwork and points a finger at you."

"I came to you, didn't I?"

"For what? To ignore my advice? Look, you said you got into it with Roy shortly before he turned up dead. I'm no detective, but what the hell? You're keeping company with the big three——motive, means and opportunity. Don't wait until you become a suspect."

"Hey, I just wanted you to know, that's all."

"So I can come to your defense later?"

"Something like that, yeah."

There was a pause in the conversation, or maybe it ended. I wasn't going to stand around and wait. Instead, I walked to the back of the barn, where I wouldn't be spotted. Peering out from the corner of the building, I saw Cal walking toward the lineup of parked trucks. A second or two later, I heard an engine start and that was when I walked into the barn.

John was standing in the middle of the room looking like a fish out of water. "Norrie. What's up? Is everything all right?"

I nodded. "Wasn't that Rosalee's vineyard manager I saw getting into his truck? He stopped by her house the day the body was discovered."

"Yeah, that was him. Winery stuff. That's all. So, what can I do for you?"

"With everything going on, I haven't paid a lot of attention to our fall harvest and thought I should touch base with you."

"You can relax. As long as the rains hold off, we'll be in good shape. A little rainfall won't hurt, but a deluge certainly will. Forecast looks good so far. Colder nights, warmer days. Especially important for the reds."

"What about the workers? Our guys and the seasonal staff. We're not going to be shorthanded, are we?"

"Got it covered. Robbie and Travis have really stepped up to the plate. I keep telling them they should get their degrees in viticulture from one of the local state colleges and work part-time. Like so many of the locals, they get a job at one of the wineries and never go beyond it. Heck, with all those online classes, they should be able to juggle both. I'll keep pestering them. In the long run, we're probably better off nurturing one of our own guys than recruiting."

"Hmm, got a point there. So, where are we exactly with the harvest?" I figured I really needed to show a genuine interest, even if I couldn't care less what grape got picked first and whether or not it was by hand or with the help of the harvester. In my mind, once the stuff got smushed, it would become juice and eventually turn into wine by the time we got done.

"We're going fast and furious handpicking the whites. Started with Chardonnay."

In a flash, my father's lessons came back to me. Harvesting follows the same pattern as tasting—white grapes first then reds.

"Wouldn't it be quicker with one of those harvesters?"

"Quicker, sure, but the end product would suffer. The harvesters snatch up all the clusters, but our pickers know enough to remove any grapes that show the slightest hint of mold. The more we can hand pick, the better off we are. Of course, when everything ripens at once, we don't have a choice but to use machinery. Aren't enough workers in all of Yates and Ontario counties to get the job done by hand. And none of us can afford to lose even a half hour on the job. Which reminds me, I was on my way over to check on Travis and Robbie when you walked in."

"Oh, don't let me hold you up. And thanks for the update. If you need anything, give a holler. By the way, what do you know about Cal Payne?"

"Know? Well, for one thing he's a capable vineyard manager, if that's what you're getting at. And extremely loyal to Rosalee Marbleton. Been with her for years."

"Loyal enough to commit murder?"

I couldn't believe those words came out of my mouth.

John clasped his hands together and took a breath. "Please don't tell me you overheard our conversation."

Now I was the one with hands clasped and my teeth tapping ever so slightly. "I may have caught some of it. I was right outside."

"I've known Cal for years, Norrie. He's no killer. But, I will admit, the circumstances don't look good. That's why I told him to be upfront about it. Look, not that I'm going to tell you what you should or should not be doing, but leave this to him, okay?"

"No worries there. I'm not about to go off and tell tales."

Well, not to the sheriff's deputy, anyway.

My next step was a jaunt to the winery lab. Technical vocabulary or not, I really needed to speak with Franz. If the tiniest thing went wrong due to my lack of oversight, I'd never forgive myself. Besides, I could almost see those WOW women shaking their heads and muttering things like, "Norrie was too self-absorbed in those screenplays of hers to manage that winery." Nope, I wasn't going to let that happen.

"It's only me," I called out when I opened the door to the winery building.

"Herbert and I are back here," was Franz's reply. "Alan is in the lab. Is everything all right?"

I imagined everyone was a bit jittery following the recent events. "Everything's fine." I walked into the little office. Franz and Herbert were both at their desks working on their computers. They immediately stopped and looked my way.

"I'm on my way back from the barn and thought I'd say hello. With the Federweisser coming up so soon, I figured I'd better make sure things are running smoothly on your end. I haven't been too attentive, I'm afraid. That murder at Terrace Wineries set me back a bit."

Franz pushed his chair back from the desk and ran a hand through his hair. "Leandre, their winemaker, told me he hasn't had a good night's sleep since the incident. He and I attended that winemakers luncheon a few days ago at Cornell. Poor man looked awful. Dark puffy circles under his eyes. I hardly knew what to say to him. To make matters worse, he's concerned that some of their old irrigation pipes might burst. They're in the process of replacing them, but you know how that goes. It's always the ones you don't replace that cause the problems."

Oh no. Something else to worry about.

Herbert, who saw the look on my face, quickly jumped in. "You can relax. Our vineyard crew replaced all of our old water lines last year."

My mind immediately jumped from water lines to wine barrels as I thought about Glenda's premonition. "Franz, where are the barrels for our Federweisser? Are they in the building or outside?"

"With the exception of one barrel of Chardonnay, which we use for the festival, the others are inside the winery building. If you're wondering what happens to the remaining wine in that barrel once the festival is over, it simply continues to ferment and will eventually be bottled."

"Is the barrel safe outside? I mean, can anyone tamper with it?"

Franz didn't answer at first and the silence was noticeable. "I suppose anyone can tamper with anything. I really never considered the possibility. Is there something you're not sharing with me?"

"No, nothing of the kind. But it's probably not such a bad idea to make sure we have a surveillance camera on that part of the building. I'll leave a message for John."

"Good idea. There's no such thing as being overly cautious."

I thanked Franz and Herbert and headed back up the hill. Long walks usually allowed me to clear my head but this one didn't. I couldn't help but relive the conversation I heard between John and Cal and, the more I thought about it, the more convinced I became that Cal Payne might not be the decent guy John thought he was.

True, I had told John I wouldn't say anything, but I was pretty certain he was referring to Deputy Hickman and not Theo and Don. Still, I kept my word for the next eight hours before I finally broke down and phoned the guys from the Grey Egret. Don picked up on the second ring.

"I better not be interrupting your dinner, but this is really important," I said.

"Juicy gossip or what?"

"Cal Payne lied to us when we met him at Rosalee's. He had an argument with Roy Wilkes, and it wasn't over the phone. Plus, it was shortly before Roy wound up dead."

"What do you mean by 'shortly'?"

"It was his word in a conversation with our vineyard manager, not mine. Cal wasn't specific."

"How do you know all this?"

"I overheard a schoolyard confession on my way to the barn to talk with John this morning. Cal was there and he told John that he and Roy got into a verbal altercation over the rate increase on the land rental. John wanted him to tell the sheriff but Cal refused. Why would anyone refuse if they were innocent?"

"Two reasons. Duh. Either they weren't innocent or they were hiding something else."

"Like?"

"Beats me. But I'm sure those little wheels of yours will keep spinning and find an answer."

"Very funny. Tell Theo I said hi. Talk to you later."

I tried to remember what Cal was wearing when he stopped by Rosalee's house. Somehow he didn't seem the Eddie Bauer blue windbreaker type. More the LL Bean canvas jacket or even a Carhartt, like the one Roy had on. Unfortunately, the only thing I recalled was his reddish hair and red stubble. If I was going to get anywhere with my so-called sleuthing, I'd have to be more observant.

Two pieces of buttered toast and an apple comprised my evening meal, while Charlie dove into his kibble as if I'd served him prime rib. I called it quits for the night and settled on the couch to channel surf, but it was useless. All I could think about was what Don had said about Cal. Either the guy was guilty or he was hiding something. I couldn't do much about the guilty verdict but, thanks to confidential background checks on the Internet, I could certainly find out if he was hiding a criminal background.

Nineteen ninety-five wasn't a whole lot of money for a year's subscription to Truth Seekers, Inc. I entered what little data I had and hoped it would be enough. It was. Within minutes, I learned that Calvin Payne was a registered felon. I all but bit my tongue when I read the screen. An additional premium fee of fourteen ninety-five promised salient details. Like someone hooked on a slot machine, I opted for that service as well.

It seemed that Cal had committed perjury regarding someone's divorce by lying under oath that the man had been unfaithful. It didn't make sense. New York had a no-fault divorce law. Then it dawned on me. That law was put into effect less than a decade ago. Up until then, divorces were granted under fault-based criteria or separation. Poor Cal. He was probably helping someone and paid a hefty price. The felony classification meant he would be "soiled goods" as far as getting another job. No wonder he was pissed at Roy Wilkes.

The caveat to the evening came with the seven o'clock news. The reporter mentioned the Seneca Lake Wine Trail and its popularity during Labor Day Weekend. Then she elaborated about the recent murders as if she was casually talking about food and wine pairings. "I'm sure visitors won't want to miss the action on Murderer's Corner, where two neighboring vineyards have something more in common than wine—dead bodies showing up on their property."

I bolted upright and reached for the phone.

"Rosalee," I said as soon as she picked up. "There's something you need to know."

Chapter 10

As if we didn't have enough tourists, tasters, and wine connoisseurs planning on spending their Labor Day Weekend on the wine trail, the commentator for that TV station virtually ensured we'd have every crackpot and curiosity seeker at our doorstep.

Rosalee took the news better than expected and told me she already had a crackpot who'd be staying at her place—her sister. When I got off the phone with her, I was too edgy to watch anything on TV but way too tired to write. Since I was on a roll with Internet searches, I decided to see who owned that abandoned house where we found the hang-tab. The Yates County Assessor's office had it all—property assessments and tax records.

Bold red letters immediately stood out for the past year and a half—DELINQUENT. Prior to that, the taxes had been paid in full. I scanned the top of the page to see who the owner was. Unlike the rest of the information, where the font was fairly large, the owner information appeared in a lower font. I squinted and took a closer look. Then I gasped.

Roy Wilkes. Roy Wilkes was the owner. It listed his home address in the village of Penn Yan but nothing else.

"Holy Crap, Charlie!" I shouted. "This is starting to get interesting."

The next thing I did was pull up the real estate information on Zillow. Roy Wilkes had purchased the property four years ago. But why? What the heck did he need an old dilapidated house for? Especially when he couldn't afford to fix it up. Heck, he couldn't even afford to pay the taxes. At least not recently.

Maybe, at one point, he'd thought about turning it into a bed and breakfast or maybe even flipping it to get a good return on his investment. Still, it sat there for a few years with nothing to show, except for more cobwebs, rotting wood, and overgrown weeds. I imagined Roy had gotten his fair share of notices from the county regarding the condition of his lawn.

It was too late to call Theo and Don, so I sent them an e-mail and called it quits for the night. My grand designs of sleuthing ended when Cammy phoned me first thing the next morning and asked if I planned to man the relief table over the weekend.

"I know how you feel about working in the tasting room, Norrie, but we're really going to be swamped. Inundated. Buried alive. We've got two tourist buses an hour lined up for all three days, and those are the ones that called in advance for reservations. We'll be suffocating if we get a ton of drop-ins."

"Uh, um..."

"The part-timers all plan to work full-time and overtime if needed. But it won't be enough."

"Fine. Fine. I'll do it."

"Great. We only use the relief table if our stations are so crowded we can't move things along. Maybe you'll be able to find some time during the day for your writing."

Yeah. Like that's going to happen. "Don't worry. I'll manage to meet my deadlines. I'd hate to have everyone all pissed at me for refusing to help during one of our busiest weekends. Besides, it gives me a chance to be on the lookout for that Eddie Bauer windbreaker."

"Speaking of that, are you going ahead with the covert spies for the Federweisser? You know, those quilters and bowlers?"

"Uh-huh. I gave Stephanie Ipswich the go-ahead a few days ago."

"Should be a real treat."

"Don't remind me."

With a holiday weekend only three days away, and every winery employee stretched to the limit with work, it was no wonder Theo, Don, and I couldn't find the time to meet. Heck, we couldn't even find the time to talk. I shot out an e-mail to Theo and got the following response:

"Let's sneak off and get a bite to eat after Thursday's WOW meeting. Madeline pushed it up a week and I drew the short straw."

I wrote back, "Lucky you. Madeline said the meeting would be brief."

His reply came in the form of a grimacing face. I returned the sentiment and got back to work.

At precisely noon, a frantic Marilyn Ansley phoned me. "Rosalee left your number on the refrigerator for me. I'd better be speaking to Norrie."

"Uh, yeah, you are."

"Less than three minutes ago, my sister was snatched out of our house and taken to jail for questioning. They think she's hiding the murder weapon. That moron of a deputy came storming over here after he read a forensic report."

"Deputy Hickman?"

"Yes, the one from the other day with the personality of a mule."

"All right. Slow down and tell me everything you know."

Rosalee had told me Marilyn was somewhat of a drama queen, but she seemed to have reached full empress status by the time she placed the call to my number.

"Those flowerpot stakes. The sharp tips. They match the wound. Exactly. The circumference. It was exact. I said that, didn't I? Not the weapon. The other ones they took. Ladybugs and beetles."

"Okay, okay. Stay calm. You are telling me there's a strong possibility the missing flowerpot stake was the one used to kill Roy Wilkes and the sheriff's department brought your sister in for further questioning. Is that correct?"

"Yes! That's what I've been saying."

"Marilyn, how do you know they think she's hiding the murder weapon?"

"Why else would they bring her in for questioning? Unless…Oh my God! They're going to arrest her. I'm on my way over there now. Right after I call our attorney."

"Hold on! Don't call anyone until we know what's going on. I'll head over there and meet you. And, by the way, it's the public safety building, not the jail. She hasn't been arrested and charged."

"Not yet."

Marilyn hung the phone up before I could say another word. So much for the lunch I was going to have at our bistro. I grabbed one of Francine's bland nutrition bars, tore off the wrapper, and chomped on it on my way out the door. Thankfully I had half a bottle of spring water in my car and gulped it down before I was even out of the driveway.

If there was good news to be had in all of this, it was the fact the weapon had been identified. Too bad it was missing. I was still ruminating about Rosalee's theory that the killer intended to return the bug stake to the flowerpot. If her dogs hadn't heard the noise and she hadn't let out that banshee shriek, no one would've been the wiser.

When I got to the public safety building, Marilyn had just slammed her car door and was thundering toward the entrance. I tried not to think about how many red lights she must've run in order to beat me to the door. Truth of the matter was, I ran a few myself.

"Hold on!" I yelled. "We'll walk in together."

The public safety building looked exactly the same as it did the last time I was there. Only the last time I didn't have to stop at the glass enclosed window to sign in and show identification. A hefty brunette with a bouffant hairdo and bedazzled glasses looked right at Marilyn and me. She squinted and leaned forward.

"They've got your sister in the back with Deputy Hickman and one of his underlings. Don't have a cow, Marilyn. She's not getting arrested."

Before the woman could continue, I put my driver's license in the tray and she slid it toward her.

"Norrie Ellington. Nice to meet you. I'm Gladys Pipp. Normally I'm at my desk in back, but Frieda's at lunch so I'm covering the front." She returned the license and kept talking. "Catherine Trobert told me all about you."

I can only imagine.

"Nice meeting you as—"

"Enough about Catherine," Marilyn broke in. "What's going on with my sister?"

"Gary Hickman's on a fishing expedition, that's all. Hang on a minute. I'll buzz his office and see if you can go in."

Her voice suddenly became very businesslike. "Mrs. Marbleton's sister and a friend are up front. Can I send them back to you?"

She put the phone down and looked up. "He's sending someone to escort you."

Good grief! It's not as if we're heavily armed and need to be frisked.

A second or two later a young deputy opened the door behind the reception window and motioned for us to follow him.

"Thanks, Gladys," Marilyn said. "I'll fill you in when we're done."

The row of cubicles looked familiar as we walked past them to Deputy Hickman's small office.

"I'd bring some chairs in," the deputy said to us as we took a step inside, "but you're not going to be here that long."

Marilyn rushed over to her sister as if Rosalee had spent the day at the Bastille and not the Yates County Public Safety Building. "Are you all right? I hope you didn't tell them anything without a lawyer. This is the United States. You're a citizen. You have rights."

I don't know whose eyes were rolling more, mine or Deputy Hickman's.

Finally, he spoke. "Mrs. Marbleton is not being charged with anything. Even though she does have a motive for murder."

"I knew it," Marilyn spouted. "I knew it. It's only a matter of time."

"Let me finish, will you?" he went on. "Motive, yes. And possibly means and opportunity. However, in this case, common sense has to prevail. Roy Wilkes was in excellent physical shape. I don't know how to say this politely, so I'll just spit it out. Your sister might've been able to stab Mr. Wilkes fifteen or twenty years ago, but at her age and in her physical condition, not only is it unlikely, it's preposterous."

I thought my jaw would drop and, from the look on Rosalee's face, I seriously wondered if she wasn't about to pick up the letter opener on Deputy Hickman's desk and prove him wrong. Before any of us could say anything, the guy kept talking.

"Our forensics team is quite certain the missing flowerpot stake, or whatever you call those things, is the murder weapon. What *I* need to know from Mrs. Marbleton is—who walked across her porch to the front door in the past month? Anyone and everyone. What about mail and package delivery? Anything delivered that couldn't be left in the box by the road? Who visited? When? What about the meter readers for gas and electricity? Did any of them come to the door? Mrs. Marbleton was putting together a list when the two of you came barging in."

I cleared my throat and spoke for the first time. "Actually, we were escorted by your deputy and—"

"Oh, for heaven's sake, Miss Ellington, you know what I'm getting at. And why does this not surprise me that you, of all people, would be here? I sincerely hope you're not going to pull a stunt like the last time and think you can conduct an investigation better than the professionals."

"Wouldn't dream of it."

Rosalee gave me a wink and I tried not to laugh. "I'm almost done with my list," she said, "and the deputy will have someone drive me home."

"I'll drive you home," Marilyn said. "We can stop at the diner for a bite to eat."

I shifted my weight from one foot to the other and sighed. "Um, I guess everything's okay here, so I might as well head back."

Just then, the deputy's phone rang and he picked up. "Are you serious? Her lawyer? Who sent for her lawyer? Sure, send him in. It's a regular circus in here."

I took a step closer to Marilyn and whispered, "You didn't tell your lawyer to come here, did you?"

"I might have," she whispered back.

Bradley Jamison wasn't exactly Rosalee's attorney. He was an attorney, all right, but not hers. Her attorney, Marvin Souza, was reading a will to a bereaving family and couldn't very well drop everything and drive to

Penn Yan from Geneva. So, the firm sent Bradley to find out whether or not a criminal attorney needed to be hired.

I was no stranger to good-looking guys, but the minute my eyes landed on Bradley Jamison, it was as if all the other men I'd ever seen were reduced to toads. That was how gorgeous this guy was. Sandy blond hair, cobalt blue eyes that matched his tie, and a physique that could put Chuck Norris to shame. He introduced himself to everyone, but I swore his gaze locked on mine for longer than usual. Then again, it was probably my imagination. I was wearing faded jeans with an equally old T-shirt with the word "Hodor" on it. Maybe the guy was into *Game of Thrones* and not me.

After an uncomfortable ten minutes or so, we all left Deputy Hickman's office. When we got to the front of the building, Gladys opened her glass window and called us over.

"I told you it was a fishing expedition, didn't I? If there's something you need to worry about, I'll let you know. Shh. I think someone's coming." Then, without warning, and with Bradley Jamison only a few feet from me, Gladys said, "I agree wholeheartedly with Catherine. You and Steven make a perfect couple."

If my mouth opened any wider, every insect in the county would've had a new home.

Chapter 11

"Can you believe it?" I kept repeating over and over again to Cammy. "Okay, fine. It's not as if I planned on dating anyone while I was stuck in Penn Yan babysitting the winery, but if I *was* to date someone, Bradley Jamison would certainly be top on the list. Oh hell. He would *be* the list! And now, thanks to big mouth Catherine, and even bigger mouth Gladys, Bradley thinks I'm seeing someone."

It was a little after three and I was spewing off in the tasting room's kitchen as Cammy hustled to put trays of glasses into the dishwasher. I had managed to grab a quick ham and cheese sandwich at the bistro before cornering Cammy.

She reached for an empty glass tray and looked up. "For all you know, he might be seeing someone. Or worse yet, he could be married."

"No wedding ring. That was the second thing I looked for."

Cammy let out a laugh. "I'm afraid to ask what the first was."

"Teeth. His teeth. A guy's got to have great teeth before I'll even consider going out."

"With dating criteria like that, I'm surprised you never sought out a career in dentistry. Hey, maybe you'll run into Mr. Good Teeth again."

"I wouldn't count on it. It's not as if Rosalee's going to be arrested and, with my luck, even if she was, her regular counsel, Marvin Souza, would show up. Bushy eyebrows and all."

Just then my cell phone vibrated.

"It's Franz," I said to Cammy. "I'd better take this. Catch you in a bit."

She carried a full tray of clean glasses back to the tasting room and I pushed the green button on the phone.

"Hi, Franz. Is everything all right?"

"Do you have a moment to stop over here? I need to show you something."

Franz never showed me anything so I became immediately concerned. "I'm on my way. I'm right next door in the tasting room."

"Meet me outside by the Chardonnay barrel."

I waved to the tasting room staff as I darted out the door. Franz was already outside standing by the Chardonnay barrel that housed our Federweisser wine.

"Look at this, would you?" He pointed to the side of the barrel. Someone had taken a magic marker and had written the words "Chardonnayed to Rest" in black ink. My hand flew over my mouth, and I stood there speechless. Franz paced back and forth in front of the barrel before speaking.

"This is not my idea of a joke. Alan, Herbert and I already checked the wine. It hasn't been tampered with, thank goodness, but this is quite disturbing. Quite disturbing! And to think only a short while ago I told you we had nothing to worry about. I rescind my earlier statement."

"It was probably one of the visitors. Some of them get tipsy from all the wine tasting on the trail and they do things they'd never consider on a normal day. Francine once told me we had a naked man run through the vineyards. They had to call the sheriff's department because Jason refused to chase after him."

"This isn't a naked man. If someone could stoop to writing graffiti, I fear they might do something even worse, like putting sugar in the barrel."

"I know we were going to see about having John put a camera back here. We talked about it yesterday. How's that going?"

"He'll have it installed by the end of the day, but I don't think a camera is going to be enough."

"We can't put an alarm system here. What about a makeshift fence around the barrel?"

"Already taken care of. It'll be temporary, but it'll be a deterrent. John got the materials and will have his crew put it up when they install the camera."

"Thanks, Franz. For being on top of things."

"I have to say, this has been a first. I pondered having you call the sheriff's office, but I'm afraid they'd dismiss it as a prank."

"I think you're right. Hey, I have another idea. We've got lots of those scarecrows all over the place to ward off critters and birds, what if we put one back here? In the dusk, it might look like a person."

"It can't hurt."

"Fine. I'll let John know. And please, call me if you see anything at all out of place."

"Shall do."

"Chardonnayed To Rest." It had to be someone's idea of a prank. The harvest season always seemed to bring out the kooks and nutcases. For years my parents moaned and groaned about it. My father in particular. He never liked the idea of college students hiring chartered buses so they could get inebriated and either pass out or throw-up. Winemaking was a skill. An art. And he wanted our customers to appreciate the nuances of our wines, not just the alcohol.

I took my time walking back to the house, pausing every now and then to look at our vineyards. The workers had already harvested one of the areas and had moved on to the next. I hoped I was right about the graffiti being someone's idea of a joke and not some sort of sick warning. The last thing we needed was another murder on our property. When I got inside, I poured myself a huge glass of juice and took out a piece of computer paper. It was time I put my thoughts about Roy Wilkes' murder in writing. Left alone in my head, they were way too scattered. And if there was some sort of connection between his dead body and those words on our Chardonnay barrel, I'd need to create a guide map to find it.

What I wound up with was actually more of a timeline with arrows that connected to stick figures. Above each figure I drew a bubble and filled it with pertinent information, or, in the case of the guy who had the altercation with Roy Wilkes at Rosinetti's Bar, a question mark. It was depressing. I had more questions than information. And the information I had was scant at best. Maybe my luck would change at the Federweisser and Stephanie's amateur spies would find someone wearing a blue windbreaker sans one of its hang-tabs.

I was about to call it quits and go back to my screenplay when the phone rang. Rosalee! As soon as she said hello, I held my breath, fearing the worst.

"Norrie, I thought you should know, I didn't give that deputy all the names of people who walked across my front porch."

"*Didn't* because you couldn't remember or something else?"

"Well, I might've forgotten a person or two but I deliberately left out Kelsey Payne, Cal's brother. He's a handyman and painter in Dresden, just down the road from here. This past spring he re-stained the porch deck for me. He had to move the plants as well as the doormat and my Adirondack chairs."

"Why keep that information from the sheriff's department?"

"Because Gary Hickman had Kelsey arrested for theft when Kelsey was in his teens. The matter was dismissed due to lack of evidence but, according to Cal, the Yates County Sheriff's Department has always had it in for his brother. I didn't need to pour salt into a wound. You get it, don't you? Besides, Kelsey would never commit murder. He's a nice guy."

So was Ted Bundy. I didn't say a word and waited for her to continue.

"I wanted you to have all the information so you wouldn't be blindsided on your investigation."

"Um, about that…I'm not an investigator. I'm more like an observer. An un-armed observer. Rosalee, we're dealing with a killer, here."

"All the more reason for you to have all the facts. What's your e-mail address? Not the winery one. Yours. I'm sending you the list of people I gave to Deputy Hickman. And try not to sound shocked. I know how to use e-mail."

"I, I, um…"

"Speak slowly and articulate. I want to be sure I get the right address."

Without wasting a second, I complied. Rosalee told me to expect her e-mail within the next five minutes and if it didn't arrive, to call her back. As I was about to hang up, I asked her if Terrace Wineries had experienced any graffiti on their property.

"Only once," she said. "Last summer our tasting room crew discovered a rather graphic rendering of the male anatomy on one of our restroom stalls. Other than that, no. Why?"

"Uh, same thing around here, that's all."

"It's those college students. They're worse than kindergarteners."

I told her I'd see her on Thursday for the WOW meeting and I'd check my e-mail for her message.

Sure enough, it arrived—a list of names and miscellaneous information. I printed out a copy and looked it over carefully. There were two sections, the first with her employees and the second for everyone else. I read the names over and over again. Along with Rosalee's commentary.

Leandre Moreau, winemaker.

Cal Payne, vineyard manager.

Letty Grebbins, tasting room manager.

Mickey Haldon, vineyard worker (only came by once to shovel my deck off in the winter).

Unknown UPS man with a package from L.L.Bean (wicked warm slippers I ordered for myself).

Census lady from the county (I told her I had better things to do and besides, I didn't want the government to get any more information than they already had).

My sister, Marilyn (on more than one occasion) and once with her obnoxious friend Erlene from the ladies' club.

Roy Wilkes (only once, but that was enough. Besides, it wasn't as if he stabbed himself with the darn flowerpot stake).

Howard the mailman with packages that didn't fit in my box.

Rosalee had also added a short note that read, "The deputy asked for everyone in the past month, but I figured I'd give them the whole shooting match. See what they do with it. If anything."

I laughed. Unfortunately, nothing whatsoever on that list stood out and, with the exception of Cal Payne, I'd be hard pressed to find anyone who might've had a connection with Roy Wilkes. However, two things gnawed at me. I e-mailed Rosalee about the first.

"What does Kelsey Payne look like?"

She replied, "Like his brother, only skinnier."

The second thought was more like an itch than a thought. Marilyn Ansley was a talker. She was also the person who helped replant those geraniums of Rosalee's. Surely she had to notice the heavy-duty repurposed insect-design flowerpot stakes. They were like miniature javelins. And what about her friend Erlene? What connections did that woman have?

I decided to forgo the e-mails and called Rosalee. "Rosalee, what do you know about Erlene? Marilyn's friend from the ladies' club?"

"Erlene Spencer. Bossy old bat. Always into something. Why? You don't think she's the killer? Besides, she wouldn't have to stab someone. All she'd need to do is talk and in a few minutes, the oxygen would be gone from the room."

"I wondered what connections she might have. That's all."

"Hmm, interesting point now that I think about it. Her husband used to be some big shot for a manufacturing company in Pennsylvania before they moved here. Heard he didn't part company on favorable terms, but that's scuttlebutt."

"Is he still alive?"

"Indeed he is. That's why she spends all her time with the ladies' club."

"You wouldn't happen to know his name, would you?"

"Bertie? Benny? Something with a B. Or maybe it was a D. Yes, I think it was a D."

"Never mind. Thanks, Rosalee. See you Thursday."

"Oh, before you hang up, tell your cleaning crew to try those magic erasers on the graffiti. It'll wipe stuff off a bathroom stall in no time."

"Will do." I didn't bother to mention our graffiti wasn't tucked away in the john.

* * * *

I didn't see or speak with Rosalee again until our WOW meeting two days later. All of the women and our new addition from the Grey Egret gathered as usual at Madeline Martinez's Billsburrow Winery. If Theo felt out of place, he didn't show it. I figured he was probably in shock.

Madeline, Stephanie and Catherine all shoved different trays of cookies at him as if the guy had never tasted food before.

"Thanks, but the coffee I'm drinking is fine as is," Theo said.

Then, to add insult to injury, Catherine asked if he was gluten or lactose intolerant or vegan.

"My cousin Arthur is gay and he's a vegetarian. Are you allowed to eat everything?"

Theo all but choked laughing. "I checked the manual and last I knew, they hadn't listed dietary restrictions for us."

Meanwhile, Rosalee got fidgety in her chair and let out a loud moan. "Can we please get on with the meeting and let the poor man eat whatever he wants or doesn't want?"

With that, Madeline began the proceedings. We talked briefly about Labor Day Weekend, which began the next day, assuming people took Friday off as well.

She reached for a folded newspaper on the end table by her chair. "According to the *Finger Lakes Times*, an even bigger crowd is expected this year. Word is out that it's going to be a banner year for our wines. Good vintage and all that. They interviewed a number of hotel and resort owners, and those places are completely booked up. Long waiting lists as well. And that doesn't include the locals or the college kids."

"Remember to remind your tasting room managers about the bus and limo warnings." Then, Stephanie turned to Theo. "If we get a bus or limousine with a number of inebriants who are out of control, we phone the next winery on the trail and give them the heads-up. It's up to them if they want to accept those patrons or send them on their way."

Catherine, who was seated next to Theo, elbowed him. "We only had to do that once or twice last year, if I remember correctly, but who wants to put up with shenanigans with so many people?"

"I think it's a great idea," Theo said. "Can we expand it to include any sightings of someone in a blue windbreaker that's missing its hang-tab on a front pocket? It may be a clue to the murder by Rosalee's pumping station. I know it will be zany with a million wine tasters, but you never know what your employees might manage to spot."

Stephanie all but jumped from her seat on the couch. "Did Norrie tell you about the brainstorm I had?"

Before he could open his mouth, Stephanie explained about the bowlers and quilters who were going to converge on Two Witches Winery during the Federweisser for the express purpose of "ferreting out" the killer. That was if the hang-tab came from his jacket.

"So you see," she said, "I thought of Labor Day Weekend, but it just wasn't feasible for such a covert operation. However, Theo's idea is fine. Let's tell everyone to be on the lookout. What do they call that? Putting out a BOLO? We'll have a BOLO of our own."

At that point, Madeline put her coffee cup on the end table and turned to Rosalee. "Any news so far?"

"That idiotic deputy in charge of the investigation thinks I might be involved. He hasn't said as much, but that steely look he gave me the other day at the Public Safety Building was enough."

"What were you doing at the Public Safety Building?" Catherine and Madeline asked at once.

It was a jumble of words—flowerpot, insect, repurposed metal…and then two words that really caught my attention—Bradley Jamison. Rosalee unraveled the entire scenario beginning with the night the intruder showed up on her porch and ended with the fact that "Marvin Souza sent over some pre-teen lawyer who hadn't reached puberty yet."

"The hot guy?" Theo mouthed to me when no one was looking.

"Yes," I mouthed back.

"Oh my gosh, Rosalee," Catherine said, "to think the murder weapon might've come from one of your own flowerpots."

Trying to get off the subject of Roy Wilkes' murder was like trying to take a lollipop away from a three-year-old. After a few attempts at shifting the conversation, I gave up and went along with the flow. Finally, we were able to move past the latest murder on the wine trail and get back to our regular business. By the time Theo and I left the WOW meeting, he had moved from shock to "dazed beyond belief."

"You can relax now," I said as we walked to our cars. "Don can attend the next meeting."

"What? Are you kidding? This is a hoot and a holler. I'm going to tell Don he's off the hook and I'll be attending these meetings from now on. I haven't laughed so much in I can't begin to remember when. Dietary restrictions. Can you believe it?"

Chapter 12

When I returned to the house, Godfrey Klein, the entomologist in Jason's office, had left a message on the answering machine. I wasn't sure if it was good news or bad. In fact, I wasn't sure what it meant.

"Jason is fairly certain the Aedes bahamensis may have crossed into Costa Rica. Thought you'd like to know. Spoke with him on the satphone last night."

I figured, if another stupid bug crossed into Costa Rica, let it stay there. I had enough to worry about. Like eating. Rather than traipsing over to the bistro for lunch, I scrambled up some eggs and shared them with Charlie. I picked up Rosalee's list for the umpteenth time and perused it again, in case I hadn't done a thorough enough job before. Still nothing. Her managers had been on staff for years and even that vineyard worker, Mickey Haldon, was a recent high school graduate from Penn Yan who had worked part-time summers for the winery since he was sixteen. Not a likely killer in my book.

As for Howard the mailman and the UPS guy, it was anyone's guess. Same for the census lady. Only, in her case, Rosalee would've been the victim, not Roy Wilkes. Unless Rosalee was keeping something from me, I had reached a dead end as far as her list was concerned. To make matters worse, I didn't think the Yates County Sheriff's Department was making any headway either.

True, Roy had only been dead for about a week, but I was getting impatient. Don's online search revealed the guy had worked for Beecher Rand in Athens, Pennsylvania. All I managed to pull up on my online searches from the *Chicago Tribune* and the *New York Times* was boring information about mergers, bids, divestments and stockholders. It finally dawned on me I needed small town papers that might focus on the human interest stuff.

Thanks to Google, I found three of them—*The Morning Call* out of Allentown, *The Morning Times* from Sayre and Scranton's *Times-Tribune*. If I was lucky, maybe Roy had won an award, participated on a local softball team or had been involved in some scandal that ultimately cost him his job and, if there was a link, maybe even his life.

By that time my brain had reached the point of muddling over and I traded my laptop search for a re-run on *Masterpiece Theatre*. The young Queen Victoria was being plagued by the palace to select a husband when my phone rang.

Cammy all but screeched into my ear. "Norrie! Get over to Rosinetti's Bar right now. Drop everything! My aunt just called. She recognized the guy who had the fight with Roy Wilkes. He's there but I don't know for how long. I'm on my way. Hurry up!"

The jeans I was wearing were okay, but I tore off the ratty T-shirt I had on and opted for a plain black one. I ran a comb through my hair and raced out of there, making sure the door was locked and Charlie was inside with his doggie door closed. No time to even grab a bag. I shoved my cell phone in my pocket, along with my wallet.

Rosinetti's Bar was located on the corner of Seneca and Exchange Streets, with its main entrance on Exchange Street. It was a large brick building that had been there since the Second World War. According to Cammy, the building and the bar had been in her family since that war as well. I'd never been in there since I was too young to drink when I was in high school and, by the time I went to college, my visits home were brief. No time for bar hopping. Besides, I never was much of a drinker. Funny, considering my family's livelihood.

The green, white and red flashing sign in front of the place read, "Rosinetti's Bar." It was shaped like the Italian flag and could be seen two blocks away. I parked across the street in a small lot, rather than torture myself with parallel parking in front. Cammy must've had the same idea because her car was also in the small lot.

I walked across the street and went directly inside. Like most bars, it was dimly lit but not so dark as to wonder about the goings on. The pungent aroma of beer permeated the room, but there was something else—the unmistakable whiff of pizza coming out of the oven. I remembered Cammy telling me they served pizza and hamburgers to their patrons, along with other bar foods.

To my right was a long bar with the usual stools, most of them occupied. Two bartenders, both male, were busy serving drinks. On my left were rectangular tables with red, white, and green tablecloths. Hard to miss the Italian theme. The walls featured an assortment of beer posters and a few mirrors. I spotted a waitress taking orders from one of the tables as I looked around for Cammy.

The crowd was a mix of college students and townies and the ambience was mellow. In the background, a Maroon 5 song was playing. I scanned the place, unsure of whether or not I should take a seat at the bar or stand there and wait for Cammy to appear. My eyes, now acclimated to the dark, darted all over the place. I prayed no one would approach me and ask if I wanted a drink. Then again, maybe I was overestimating my sex appeal.

In a flash, the door behind the bar swung open and Cammy stood there. She spied me immediately and motioned for me to join her in the kitchen. I skirted the end of the long counter and rushed inside.

A heavyset woman with dark curls, dangling earrings, and a red apron extended her hand to me. I guessed her to be in her early sixties. "Norrie, right?"

I nodded.

"I'm Luisa, Cammy's aunt. This is better than a spy novel. He's at the bar. The man who had the fight. Do you think he killed the other man?"

Cammy took a step toward her aunt and shushed her. "Our voices can carry. We need to be inconspicuous."

Her aunt moved away from the door and we followed her. Behind us, another woman was making a pizza. She was younger, but not by much. Also dark curls but no earrings. At least none I could see.

"You said he was the one at the far end of the bar," Cammy whispered. "Did he come in with the guy sitting next to him or did he come alone?"

Her aunt shrugged. "I don't know. I was making my calzones with Teresa. When I brought an order to the bar, he was there. That's when I called you. He's in the second to the last stool next to a man I don't recognize."

Cammy opened the door about an inch and looked out. "Our suspect's still there. Older guy. Ruddy completion. Looks kind of weathered."

I crept behind her. "What's the other guy look like?"

She stepped back. "See for yourself. Skinny. Younger. Reddish hair. At least I think it's red. Hard to tell in the dim light."

"Looks red to me," I said. "We've got to figure out a way to find out who he is and, before you say another word, I'm not going to go over there and flirt with him."

"Ew! That's the last thing I was going to suggest."

I stared through the narrow door opening and bit my lower lip. Why were these things always so easy in the movies? *Because dunderheads like me write the stupid screenplays.* Then it hit me. I reached into my pocket and pulled out my phone. I'd read about something like this on the Internet and figured it was worth a try. "Is your cell phone handy?" I asked Cammy.

"Handy? It's part of my anatomy, but it's too dark to get a decent photo of them."

"I have a plan. I'm going to take the empty seat between the two guys and those college students. You go to the bar and tell the bartender you're going to take a picture of me but need his help. He's got to shine your cell phone's flashlight above my head to give off enough light for the photo. Then, you take the picture. But not of me. Of those guys. Got it?"

"Sure enough. What have we got to lose?"

"A possible murderer if he leaves. Hurry up."

I walked out of the kitchen and as unobtrusively as I could, I plunked myself into the stool next to the suspect. Cammy grabbed the bartender by the elbow and whispered something to him.

"Anything for you, Camilla," he said.

"Thanks, Tony."

Then, Cammy handed me a bottle of Corona and shouted, "Smile and look like you're having fun. That should make Eduardo jealous."

Our plan went off like clockwork. The bartender used the flashlight beam to illuminate the area and Cammy snapped the photo using my phone. Not one, but three pictures, to be on the safe side.

"That should do it," she said, loud enough for everyone to hear. "Looks like you're partying with a group of good-looking college guys. That jerk of a boyfriend of yours is bound to get the message." Then she turned and walked back into the kitchen.

I got up from the stool, still holding the Corona, and followed her as if that had been our intent all along. She waved for me, phone in hand, to follow her into the storage room. Her aunt Luisa was also waving me over as well.

"Remind me to bring out another jar of the minced garlic. I meant to do that earlier," her aunt said. "Teresa's going to run out if I don't."

Cammy rolled her eyes. "Enough with the garlic. Let's see if this worked."

She handed me the phone, and I immediately clicked on the photo app. Sure enough, there was our guy and part of my shoulder. The skinny red-haired man was in the photo as well. I slid my finger across the screen and looked at the other two shots. They were perfect. Absolutely perfect.

"Now what?" Cammy asked. "Off to the sheriff's department first thing in the morning to share them?"

"With Deputy Hickman? Don't be nuts. He'll read me the riot act or, worse yet, find a way to lock me up for interfering with an official investigation. Nope. I plan to show these photos to our staff at the winery to see if anyone recognizes either of those men. I'm also going to e-mail it to all the other wineries on the west side. And Rosalee. She'll be the first one on my e-mail list."

"And if someone recognizes the guy, then what?"

"Then I'll consider two possible options—throwing myself on the mercy of the sheriff's department or becoming even more intimately acquainted with Google search."

"I wouldn't hold off too long on sharing that information if I were you. If that man really *is* a killer, let the authorities deal with him."

"Oh, believe me, I intend to. But only when I'm positive. When I have real evidence that can connect him with Roy Wilkes. Until then, all I've got is speculation and, at this point, I'm not even sure I have that."

Then Cammy's aunt broke in. "You girls need to be careful. Capisce?"

"Don't worry," Cammy said. "We will."

The three of us stepped out of the storage room just as Tony came into the kitchen. "Don't know what this is about, but I thought you'd want to know the two guys from the end of the bar just left. So, what's with that? What's going on?"

Before anyone could say anything, Cammy made a quick introduction. "Norrie, meet my brother, Tony. He's a firefighter in Geneva but has the night off. He's helping out."

Who in this establishment isn't related?

"Hi! Nice to meet you," I said.

Tony looked to be a few years younger than Cammy. Much taller and extremely well built with dark hair and brown eyes. When he reached to shake my hand, I saw the wedding ring. Not that I was looking.

"Likewise. Now, will someone please tell me what's going on?"

"You might've been serving beer to a murderer," Luisa said. "The girls aren't sure yet."

I took a deep breath and, as succinctly as possible, told Tony about Rosalee's discovery by her pumping station and everything else leading up to this moment.

"Holy cannoli. Can't you two leave the investigation to the sheriff's department?"

Cammy gave her brother a look. "Really, Tony? The sheriff's department?"

"Then at least promise me you won't do anything stupid. By the way, when you're ready to leave, I'm walking you to your cars."

I hung around long enough to finish my Corona and taste Luisa's pizza. It was, by far, the best pizza I'd had in I-don't-remember-how long and I told her as much.

"I've got to bring Don and Theo here," I said to Cammy when we got ready to leave. "They're not going to believe the pizza."

"Yeah, I keep forgetting you've never been here before."

"That'll change."

It was almost midnight when I got home, but I pulled up my laptop and shot out those e-mails with the mystery men photos attached. If I was lucky, maybe someone at one of the wineries knew something and I'd find out first thing in the morning.

Chapter 13

I got up earlier than usual, took a quick shower, and put in a good three hours of work on my screenplay before venturing down to the tasting room. As if solving a murder wasn't enough to deal with, the last thing I needed from the film production company was to wind up like Conrad Blyth.

Conrad wrote wonderful Amish romance screenplays but, for some reason, he had gotten kicked to the curb, so to speak. Something about audience interest according to Renee, my producer. In this business, any excuse was excuse enough to drop a series, and turning in a screenplay that was even a day late would most certainly put me on the "We Might Axe Her Next" list. I wasn't about to take any chances.

Charlie had inhaled his kibble and exited the house via his doggie door at daybreak. I opened the windows to let in some fresh air when he left and made sure to close them on my way to the tasting room. It was a little past ten and we were already inundated with customers. I had promised Cammy I'd help out at the relief table, but I hoped they wouldn't need me right away.

Lizzie was at the cash register ringing up a sale when I arrived. Cammy, Glenda, Sam and Roger were all manning their stations.

"It won't get really crazy 'til noon," Cammy said as eight or nine customers left her table to peruse the wine racks. "I got your e-mail with the photo and passed it around before we opened. Terrific background lighting by the way."

I laughed.

"You need to talk with Lizzie. She thinks she recognizes one of the men."

"What?" I raced to the cash register, all but bumping into our clientele.

"Lizzie! Quick! Before any customers get over here, tell me. Can you identify those men in that photo?"

Lizzie adjusted her wire-rimmed glasses and spoke softly, even though no one was near us. "I can't be a hundred percent sure, but the older man looks like David Whitaker."

"David Whitaker? Who's that?"

"He was on the school board a few years ago. Made a big stink about changing the mascot. You don't think he could be the killer, do you?"

"I'm not sure." *And I'm not sure if the man in the photo is really David Whitaker.*

"Are you following the guidelines I gave you from the *Nancy Drew Handbook*?"

"Absolutely." *Especially the ones that include wearing white gloves, training a carrier pigeon, and foiling a purse snatcher.*

Lizzie meant well, but I was no Nancy Drew.

"Listen," I told her, "don't say anything to anyone until I can be sure. Okay? Maybe someone else around here also recognized the man in the photo."

Unfortunately, no one else did. Sam thought he might've seen the younger guy around town but couldn't be sure. I wasn't banking on getting any calls from the other wineries right away because everyone would be drowning in tourists by early afternoon. And, as things turned out, so were we.

I manned the relief station from noon until five and thought I had seriously lost my mind. It was a blur of customers. Taste after taste. Wine after wine. By two, the line at the cash register had gotten so long we had to call Fred's wife, Emma, and ask her to step away from the bistro in order to handle all of the cash sales until things slowed down. Thankfully, we had hired a part-time college student to give Fred a hand with the food.

I tried unsuccessfully to do a Google search on David Whitaker while my customers were tasting wine, but it was futile. I gave up and stuck the iPhone back in my pocket. When the doors finally closed at five thirty, I all but collapsed. The tastings ended at five, but the winery remained open until five thirty for customers to purchase wine or gifts.

"I don't think I can think straight," Glenda announced after locking the front door. "I'll need to create a haven of repose the minute I get home."

Sam, who was busy stacking more wine bottles on the racks, paused for a second. "You mean burn incense and take a shower?"

Glenda gave her head a slight shake. "I mean, attending to my ablutions with essential oils and soft music."

"I'm going out for a hamburger and a brew," he said. "Enjoy your ablutions."

Cammy put her hands on her hips and rolled her neck. "If we think we're tired now, just wait until tomorrow and the next two days. This was only the precursor."

All of us left the building together, and I walked Cammy to her car. "Lizzie thinks she knows who that guy is. The one who had the fight with Roy Wilkes. He may or may not be David Whitaker, a former school board member. Sound familiar?"

She shook her head. "Sorry. It's hard enough keeping up with the Geneva City School Board where I live. I'm not at all familiar with Penn Yan's. If you find out anything, let me know."

"Sure thing. This may be the first break we've had, thanks to you. By the way, your aunt and brother are really sweet."

"The aunt, yes, but no one's described Tony as sweet. He'll get a good laugh out of it. See you tomorrow."

Charlie was waiting by his food dish when I walked into the house. Too tired to even crack an egg, I poured him some kibble and made myself a peanut butter and jelly sandwich. Then I plopped down on the couch and closed my eyes for what I thought was ten or fifteen minutes. When I reached for my iPhone to try that Google search again, I couldn't believe it. I had slept for over an hour.

"At this rate, your mistress will be like the living dead by Monday," I said to the dog. I knew Theo and Don would be equally whipped, but I was dying to find out if either of them recognized David Whitaker. No word from the other wineries, but I figured they might not have had a chance to check their e-mails. The fall rush consumed everything and Labor Day Weekend was a real eye-opener.

The Grey Egret and Theo and Don's landline were both on speed dial. I made one click and waited for someone to pick up at the house.

"Hey, Norrie," Theo said. "We were about to call you. Are you as wiped out as we are? Don's idea of dinner tonight is an English muffin with cheese and a tomato slice. That should tell you something."

"I'm putting oregano on it," Don yelled from the background.

I snickered. "Ugh, I know. I can barely move from the couch to the kitchen without feeling like I'm a hundred years old. That crowd today was relentless. It would've been impossible to be on the lookout for that blue windbreaker. Good thing we've got it covered during the Federweisser. Unless, of course, the sheriff's department solves Roy Wilkes' murder before then."

"I wouldn't count on it. If you think today was a bear, wait until tomorrow. Listen, we got your photo and the younger guy, the skinny one with the reddish hair, looks like Rosalee's vineyard manager, Cal Payne, only it's not. Cal's older and not as thin."

"He has a brother who was arrested for theft when he was a kid. Rosalee told me about it, but she's adamant he's not the killer. According to her, the brothers bear a resemblance."

"Did she give you a name?"

"Yeah. Kelsey. Kelsey Payne. And get this, the guy does handyman work for her. He even stained her porch."

"Hmm, that would give him *means,* if he snatched that flowerpot stake, and opportunity, if he knew when and where Roy would be, but what about motive?"

"I'll try to dig up any info I can on him, but frankly all I want to do is nap."

"Don't push yourself. Once the weekend's over, all of us will have more time for sleuthing. Hang in there, okay?"

"As always. Say hi to Don."

In spite of it being early evening, I could barely keep my eyelids open. I went back to the couch and dozed off again. This time it lasted for two hours. At nine thirty I awoke thirsty and ravenous. Charlie was fast asleep in his dog bed but immediately jumped to attention when he heard me rustling around in the fridge.

We shared some turkey salad I had brought back from the bistro, along with taco chips, some broken pretzel rods and string cheese. Not my finest culinary moment.

"Okay, dog," I said. "I'm going to rinse off in the shower and then get down to some serious Internet searching. I can't believe I showered this morning. Every bit of me reeks from sweat."

He followed me upstairs, jumped on the bed, and performed his own cleansing ritual, which was too graphic to discuss. I thought of Glenda and her essential oil bath and almost considered doing something similar. However, the only oils we had were olive and motor.

By ten fifteen I was wide awake and on the laptop. I started my search by Googling the Penn Yan Board of Education. Sure enough, David Whitaker's picture appeared in some archived photos. And while he looked like the man in Rosinetti's Bar, I really wasn't sure it was him. The face wasn't as angular and something about the jawline didn't look right. Still, the archived photo was a few years old and as people aged, they began to look different.

I was able to glean some information about David Whitaker, but nothing that grabbed me by the throat screaming, "He's the killer! He's the killer!" The guy was married with two grown children. Lived in Penn Yan for the past five years. Member of the Kiwanis Club and the Elks. Boring. I didn't press it any further.

Next, I turned my sights on Kelsey Payne and put my recently purchased subscription to Truth Seekers, Inc., to good use. Sure enough I located Kelsey G. Payne, age thirty-seven, one city of residence—Penn Yan. An old driver's license photo appeared next to Kelsey's name, and I was positive the guy at the bar was him.

What if Kelsey owed an outrageous amount of money to the other man and made a deal to get Roy Wilkes over to the pumping station in exchange for the loan to be dropped? I was singing my own praises until Cammy ruined everything the next day.

"What do you mean it's not him?" I whined when she insisted the guy wasn't Kelsey. "How can you be sure?"

"Because I sent that e-mail photo to everyone at Rosinetti's and asked them to keep an ear out if the guy comes in again. As it turned out, he was there last night with a woman. The bartender, no relation this time, said the woman kept calling him Richie."

"That doesn't mean anything. Richie could be a nickname."

"For Kelsey? That's a stretch. Anyway, you said that Kelsey Payne lived in Penn Yan. The bartender overheard the guy saying to the woman, 'Come on back to my place. It's only a few blocks from here. Great apartment overlooking the lake. I was lucky to nab it a few years ago.'"

"Oh crap."

While I crossed Kelsey Payne off my list, his brother popped back up like one of those Jack-in-the-box toys for kids. I knew Cal had a decent motive and he admitted to having it out with Roy Wilkes shortly before the guy turned up dead. *Shortly*. How on earth was I ever going to narrow that time frame down?

I put my potential murderers list to the back of my mind and set up the relief table in preparation for the blitzkrieg. Good thing I did. Customer after customer, taste after taste, it never stopped. If I wasn't serving samples, I was rushing into the kitchen with trays of dirty glasses for the dishwasher and returning with clean ones. I was going faster than that chocolate factory conveyer belt from *I Love Lucy*.

It would've been a real disaster if we didn't have the part-time college students working for us. A thin blonde with full lips and pinkish hair relieved me at a little past noon so I could get something to eat and hopefully regain my sanity.

I leaned back in one of our kitchen chairs and was about to chomp on a portabella mushroom sandwich when the winery phone rang. I got it on the second ring.

“Norrie? Is that you? It’s Stephanie. Listen, we just turned away a Diamond Johnny’s tour bus out of Ithaca. Those students are wild. We wouldn’t even let them into our winery. They must’ve been drinking from the moment they got on the bus. Catherine gave us the heads-up first. Apparently they all but trashed her tasting room and someone actually heaved into one of their potted plants.”

“Oh yuck! I’ll head outside right now and ward them off. Thanks for the warning.”

“Oh, by the way, got your e-mail. Sorry, but none of us can identify the men in that photo. One of our vineyard guys thought he’d seen the younger one around town but wasn’t sure. And no luck with the blue windbreaker either. All I saw yesterday were wineglasses being thrust at me. I couldn’t pour the stuff quick enough. I know I should be thankful my mother-in-law’s up here watching the boys, but you have no idea how that woman can talk. On and on. My God, I’m ready to throw myself off a cliff! Um, sorry to get rattling. You’d better hurry if you’re going to catch that bus.”

“Thanks, Stephanie.”

The busload of crazies was the least of my worries. The toilets backed up at a little past three and I all but had to offer Roto-Rooter a year’s supply of my blood to get them to come over. Sam had a friend at the Porta Potty company in Rochester, but it took them over two hours to arrive and get set up.

“We should’ve thought of this ahead of time,” he said as we watched the men unload those blue monstrosities from their truck. “And to think we’ve got to do it all over again for the Federweisser.”

The only place we could put the Porta Potties was next to Alvin’s pen, and he wasn’t too happy about it. Any time anyone went to relieve themselves, Alvin kicked up dust, dirt, and a fair share of hay. By late afternoon, I was ready to join Stephanie at that cliff. And by early evening, when we closed the doors for good that day, I felt as if I had already taken that jump.

“You look terrible,” Glenda said to me. “Here. Try this.” She handed me a small lavender pouch with crushed flower petals.

“Is that some kind of herbal poultice? Because, if it is, I’m not wounded.”

“No, it’s aromatherapy. Open it up, breathe deeply, and think calming thoughts. Go on, inhale and let your body relax.”

I undid the small ribbon on the pouch and took a whiff. It was a strange mix of roses, petunias, cloves and something with an odd cloying smell. I inhaled again.

"See?" she said. "You're starting to unwind already. The universe always rewards with its own natural scents."

Just then, Sam came tearing out of the kitchen and shouted, "Damn sink drain's backed-up. The stench is enough to gag a maggot."

I handed Glenda the pouch and smiled. "Guess the universe is rewarding us after all."

Chapter 14

Roto-Rooter returned and snaked out the kitchen sink. I sent everyone home and hung out in the office until they were finished. Most of the time was spent with my elbows on the desk and my head cradled in the palms of my hands. Occasionally I groaned. It was Saturday night and, according to everyone, the "worst two days were yet to come." I secretly prayed for a rainstorm, but the forecast called for bright sunshine and seasonable temperatures. I was beginning to despise the weather anchors every time I switched on the news.

I staggered up the hill and into the house, more exhausted than David Copperfield when he walked from London to Dover. At least I had had the foresight to have Fred make me two cold-cut sandwiches that I quickly scarfed down with a large Coke before turning my attention to the slew of unread e-mails I had received sometime between yesterday morning and now.

The script analyst Renee had assigned to the screenplay I submitted sent me a few of his thoughts. At least that was what his e-mail said—"a few thoughts." They turned out to be a four-page attachment that made my stomach roil. He gave me a three-week window to address them and resubmit. That would mean putting my current screenplay on hold and focusing on this one. Good thing I knew how to juggle.

Godfrey Klein sent me an image of the Aedes bahamensis because he didn't want me to confuse it with the albopictus. His words, not mine. I wouldn't confuse it. I'd swat it, step on it or fumigate it.

Catherine Trobert sent everyone in our WOW group a recipe for her apple tarts because, heaven knows, we didn't have enough to do.

Then there were the spam e-mails I couldn't delete fast enough. Bank offers. Clothing deals. Coupons for places in the city I wouldn't see for at least nine or ten months.

At the bottom of the list, there was an e-mail from Rosalee. Sent late last night. It read, "The skinny one looks an awful lot like Kelsey Payne, but it can't be him. He's in AA. The other one looks vaguely familiar. Which one had the fight with Roy Wilkes?"

I e-mailed back, "The vaguely familiar one," and called it quits for the night.

The next day, Sunday, turned out to be a repeat of yesterday, minus the stopped-up sink and toilets. Huge crowds and boisterous people, two things that meant booming sales. Who was I to complain? Everything in the tasting room was moving at breakneck speed, including me. All of that, however, came to an immediate halt the moment Lizzie waved me over to the cash register.

In addition to ringing up sales, she also answered the phone. Mainly because the winery's relic of a wall phone was right behind the counter where she worked.

"Norrie! It's urgent. Really urgent!" Her voice sounded even more shrill than usual. Fortunately, I had just finished a tasting for ten or eleven people and was on my way to the kitchen with a tray of dirty glasses.

"Be right there." I rushed into the kitchen and put the tray on the sink counter. No time to load it into the dishwasher.

Lizzie thrust the phone's receiver at me. "I think it's Rosalee Marbleton. Something about murdering a butterfly."

I faced the wall as I took the call. "Rosalee, what's up? What's going on?"

"I know he's in here. The murderer. She handed me the monarch butterfly."

"Who? Who's *she*? You said '*he*'s in here.' What are you talking about? Where are you?"

"A customer. In the tasting room. I'm here. She had the flowerpot stake in her hand. That means the murderer is here."

"Did you call the sheriff's office?"

"No. You need to get here first."

"Okay, fine. Stay calm. I'm on my way."

The second I hung up the phone, I told Lizzie to call the Yates County Sheriff's Office and tell them there's a problem at Terrace Wineries. Ask them to send someone.

"What if they want me to be specific?"

"Tell them we got an emergency call and if they want specifics, they need to send a deputy to Rosalee's tasting room."

Before Lizzie had a chance to say another word, I elbowed my way out of the building and ran up the hill. My hand tremored slightly as I reached into my pocket and pulled out my keychain. Minutes later I was in my car at the bottom of our driveway, waiting for the road traffic to slow down so I could get across Route 14 and pull into Terrace Wineries. The wait time was enough for me to clear my head.

If I decoded Rosalee's ramblings correctly, someone found the murder weapon in her tasting room. No wonder that woman was hysterical. Finally, the traffic started moving and I was able to get going with what I hoped was a break in this case.

Judging from Terrace Wineries' parking lot, they were having a banner day, too. I grabbed the first spot I could find, slammed the door, and raced into her tasting room. The building resembled a Swiss chalet, complete with a huge deck and white balcony that circled the entire structure. Winery barrels with potted geraniums, snapdragons, pansies, petunias, and coleus framed the entranceway.

I rushed inside, not knowing what to expect. Then, in a moment of clarity, I did something that ordinarily I wouldn't think of. That was because when I was dealing with someone else's catastrophe, I was levelheaded, unlike the scatterbrain I tend to be when faced with my own disasters.

Standing perfectly still at the inside entrance, I began to take photos of the tasting room with my iPhone. The large windows, with their curtains pulled to the sides, gave off enough lighting to ensure my pictures would be clear. I zoomed in on tables, counters and everything in between.

Suddenly, someone tapped my shoulder, and I spun around. It was Rosalee.

"Don't stand there like one of the tourists, do something!"

"I'm trying," I said, keeping my voice deliberately low. "I'm photographing evidence. One of these people might be the killer."

Rosalee took me by the arm and ushered me into a small foyer near the office. "The butterfly garden stake…the one that was missing…it turned up. A customer wanted to buy it. When she got to the cash register, Tiffany, our salesclerk, sent her to me since there was no price tag."

"And that's when you called me?"

"More or less. I think I scared the poor woman."

"What makes you say that?"

"Because I gasped and may have said something about a murder weapon."

I tried to stay focused. "Then what?"

"Then she dropped the thing on the counter and left without saying a word."

"Look around, is she still in the tasting room?"

Rosalee patted herself on the chest, took a breath and spun her head around. "Yes. Yes. That's her! Over by the souvenirs. Middle-aged woman with frosted hair. She's wearing a floral blouse."

I didn't know how Rosalee was able to spot the woman so quickly because I was struggling to find someone with frosted hair and a floral blouse.

Rosalee gave me a nudge. "Now she's moving to the wall with the jewelry."

"I see her. Look, you stay here and I'll have a word with her. Even better, wait out front. The sheriff's office will be sending a deputy. You might be better off talking to him or her while you're outside."

"I didn't call the sheriff. Didn't want to make a scene. You're the only one who knows about this."

"Not anymore. I called them." I didn't want to get into the fact it was actually Lizzie who placed the call because then Rosalee would want to know what Lizzie knew and I didn't have time for all that nonsense.

Before she could say a thing, I sprinted across the room and tapped the frosted-haired lady on the arm.

"Pardon me, I hate to bother you, but it's really important."

She stared at my Two Witches T-shirt but didn't say a word.

I went on, "It's about that flowerpot stake you wanted to buy."

"Not anymore. That woman in charge was really rude. She insinuated I was going to use it as a murder weapon. Can you imagine that?"

Oh yeah. At this point I can imagine anything.

"Um, yeah, well, about that…um, where did you find it? Was it with the other little souvenirs?"

"No. That's the funny thing. I found it on one of the windowsill ledges on the side of the building. The side that faces the lake. I had stepped outside to check out the view. I figured someone might've taken the cute little butterfly stake outside to look at it in the light and then changed their mind about buying it. So, they left it out there instead of bringing it back inside. Maybe they thought about shoplifting it, who knows? With all these crowds, it's easy to do. Some people have no morals these days."

"I'm really sorry about what happened. I'm a friend of the owner. I know she didn't mean to disrespect you. Anyway, if you decide to buy anything, tell the cashier you're entitled to a fifteen percent discount and if they have any questions, tell them to speak with the owner."

"Are you sure?"

"Positive."

I knew Rosalee wouldn't want to lose a customer, and if people think they're being treated badly at one establishment, they'll simply go to another. The Seneca Lake Wine Trail had a fabulous reputation, and I intended to keep it that way.

Rosalee was standing outside scanning the area when I approached. The sheriff's deputy hadn't arrived yet, and I prayed to the gods it wouldn't be Deputy Hickman.

So much for prayer.

I knew it was him the minute the car pulled into the lot. It all but skidded to a stop. At least I had time to let Rosalee know about the arrangement I had made with the frosted-haired lady.

No sooner had Deputy Hickman exited the official vehicle than I found myself standing directly in front of him. Rosalee trailed me by a few feet.

"Miss Ellington," the deputy said in a most condescending voice, "why, why, *why* am I not surprised to see you here? Do you intentionally look for trouble or are you drawn to it like a moth to a flame?"

"Um, more like a wrong place at the right time kind of thing, or right place and wrong time maybe?"

He brushed me aside and strode toward Rosalee. "Perhaps you can enlighten me. Our dispatch said there was a problem at your winery."

Rosalee cleared her throat, exaggerating each annoying sound. "The problem *is,* the murder weapon turned up in our tasting room. And if that turned up, then the murderer might be in there as well."

I waved my hands at both of them. "Um, if I could say something, um, the murder weapon wasn't exactly found in the tasting room, but it did wind up there. I spoke to the customer who wanted to buy it. She found it on one of the windowsill ledges that face the lake."

I paused and pointed in the general direction of the building. Deputy Hickman strode over there like a cowboy about to inspect cattle. "This the spot?" he asked.

"Uh-huh. That's what the customer said."

He continued to look around as Rosalee and I stood there. Finally, he spoke. "I see there's another set of stairs here leading off the balcony. It goes straight down to the lake. Quite possibly our killer darted up those stairs, stashed the murder weapon on that windowsill, where no one would see it right away, and took off. I'm calling my team to dust for prints."

I took a step closer to him and clicked my teeth. Not a terrific habit to have. "I thought the forensics team checked the area."

"The immediate area," he said. "I doubt they went as far as the tasting room balcony."

Yep, that's a real confidence builder.

Rosalee, who had been pretty quiet up until now, looked directly at the deputy and spoke. "Must you send that team this minute? It's going to disrupt business."

"Mrs. Marbleton, I must remind you, so does murder. I'll ask them to be discreet."

"It'll be all right," I said to Rosalee. "Most of the customers are up front." What I said next was meant for Deputy Hickman. "Maybe the forensics team could park around back. Much easier to get to the stairs."

He didn't say anything, but he certainly groaned loud enough before changing the subject. "The alleged murder weapon. Where, may I ask, is it?"

Rosalee put her hands over her heart as if she was about to swoon. "I left it at the cash register when I called Norrie. It's got to be there. My employees won't sell anything without a price tag. Unless someone stole it. Unless someone—"

"Let's check it out. I'll run in and you can follow." Leaving no time for either of them to object, I darted around the side of the building and walked directly to the counter, where I spied the garden stake laying next to the computer monitor, its red and black butterfly wings pointing up. I stood off to the side, keeping my eye on it until Rosalee and Deputy Hickman entered the building.

"It's right here," I said as they approached.

The deputy unfolded a substantial plastic evidence bag from his pocket and, using a tissue, picked up the garden stake and put it in the bag.

"The monarch butterfly was my favorite," Rosalee said. "But if it really turns out to be the murder weapon, I don't want it back."

"Understood," Deputy Hickman said.

Then she crossed her arms and tapped her foot. "How do you propose we isolate the killer? It could be anyone in this crowd."

"I seriously doubt our killer is in here sampling wine. My take is that he or she stashed the weapon on the day of the murder or maybe even the night someone was on your porch. Just stay alert for anything out of the ordinary." With that, he gave us a nod and proceeded out the door.

"Guess I should be going, too, Rosalee. My tasting room crew's probably going berserk with all the customers."

She thanked me and I charged out the door, making a beeline for the deputy's car. He had already opened the driver side door and was about to get in when I shouted to him.

"Wait! I need to ask you something."

"Make it quick, Miss Ellington."

"Did anyone come for Roy Wilkes' body? You know, family...friends, maybe? For funeral arrangements. That sort of thing."

"He left a trust and explicit directions for his burial. And that's all I'm at liberty to tell you. Humrph. I'm not even sure I should be telling you that much."

I shrugged. "The local papers will get that information eventually, but thanks."

"Let us do our job. All right?"

"Absolutely."

I made a mental note to call Gladys Pipp first thing Tuesday morning to find out what bank held Roy Wilkes' trust. I figured if I knew where he did his banking, I might be able to enlist Marilyn Ansley's coffee klatch crew for some help. One of those women was bound to work for the bank or know someone who did. All I really needed to see were Roy's bank statements for the past few years.

As I started the engine to my car, I wondered what the penalty was for unauthorized access to bank records. A misdemeanor maybe? It couldn't possibly be a felony. Then again, it might very well be a felony. I was way out of my league, but I wasn't without resources.

Chapter 15

"Are you sure, Theo?" I asked that night when I phoned him and Don. Theo was pre-law in undergraduate school and, even though he never made a career of it, his background was pretty solid. Or so I thought.

"Geez, Norrie. I'd have to look into it. Those things are pretty tricky. Why do you need to know?"

I told him about one of Rosalee's customers finding the alleged murder weapon and proceeded to fill him in on my ever-so-brief conversation with Deputy Hickman.

"So you see," I said, "no one's come forth to claim Roy Wilkes' body. It's been days since he was murdered. Shouldn't some family member or friend show some interest? And get this, Grizzly Gary told me Roy had a trust with the burial plans all lain out, so to speak. It was filed at his bank."

"I'm not sure where you're going with this."

"It's simple. No one can be that much of a loner. There's always some distant relative lurking in the woodwork or, at the very least, a friend. I figured if I could track down Roy's banking records, I might be able to see where his money was coming from and, in this case, more importantly, where it was going."

"If you do that, I'll tell you where you'll be going—to jail. I'm not one hundred percent sure, but it has felony written all over it."

"It's not like I'm going to take any of the money. I'm only going to have a little 'look-see.' Besides, I thought you said it was tricky."

"It is. There are zillions of felonies, but they all have something in common—a criminal record for the perpetrator. Listen, once this crazy weekend is over with, we can sit down and talk. Work our way around the sleuthing. Promise me you won't do anything rash before we get together."

"Don't worry. After today, I hardly have the energy. If I did, I'd backtrack our steps when we took that walk the other day behind the vacant house. Now more than ever I'm certain Roy's killer parked his vehicle on the Route 14 pullover. He didn't say it in so many words, but Deputy Hickman thought our suspect might've stashed the murder weapon on Terrace Wineries' deck as he or she was making a run for it back to the car. There's a path that goes directly to that winery building from the lakefront."

"If that's true, then even more reason for us to believe that hang-tab came from our guy. So, when do you want to break down and share that tidbit with the sheriff's department?"

"I don't, but if we're correct, I really could be withholding evidence. Terrific. Isn't that a felony, too? The hang-tab's in a safe spot, though. I put it in the kitchen drawer where we keep the potholders."

"Norrie, I really think—"

"Don't worry. I thought it, too, but I've got to give 'Operation Quilters and Bowlers' a chance to work the crowd at the Federweisser. If none of them can spot our suspect in the blue Eddie Bauer windbreaker, then I'll confess all to Grizzly Gary."

"I wasn't going to suggest that. All I was going to say is that you might want to put that hang-tab in a place where it's not likely to be removed by anyone."

"Trust me. The potholder drawer is the last place I go and the few visitors I do have don't cook."

Theo laughed. "Get some sleep. You'll need it tomorrow."

It turned out Theo was right. Labor Day was horrific. All morning long I kept asking myself, "Where do these people come from?" And when I wasn't doing that, I was muttering awful things about my sister and brother-in-law for talking me into this situation. Things that could not be said in polite company. Or any company, for that matter.

I knew it was bad when I couldn't even catch a break for a cup of coffee. Fred actually had to deliver the coffee to all of us at the tasting room stations. By quarter to two, my brain was fried. I was certain of it. Like a robot, all I did was pour wine samples, put the dirty glasses on the rack, take out clean ones, and repeat the process.

My right hand, aka my pouring arm, worked automatically. No matter what was thrust at me, I poured wine. That's why I did a double take when someone shoved a "Missing Persons" flyer at me. It was a middle-aged woman who somehow managed to elbow her way to my table.

"I'm going to all of the wineries," she said. "My friend's husband is missing. Please call the number listed if you see him. I thought maybe someone at a wine tasting station might've recognized him. Lots of people going through the wineries this weekend."

Yep, understatement of the year.

The picture was blurry but it did bear a resemblance to the man at Rosinetti's Bar. The one who Lizzie thought was David Whitaker when I showed her the snapshot I took on my phone. Then again, I was probably mistaken. I'd seen so many faces in the past thirty-six hours, I couldn't be counted on to identify my own mother.

I took a cursory look at the flyer and said "sure," not bothering to read the text. Then I told her to: "Give a copy to the lady at the cash register, too."

The woman disappeared into the crowd and I resumed the tastings. With the exception of one restroom break, and thank God we had a private restroom attached to the office, I was at that relief station all day. Cammy had had the foresight to hire a cleaning crew for afterhours during the busy holiday weekends. Normally it was something the regular tasting room crew did, but as she pointed out, it would cost the same, considering the overtime. Plus, I wouldn't wish that extra work on anyone. Especially our workers.

It was an eight-hour day that felt like eighty. When the last customer left the building and we locked the front door, I collapsed in the first bistro chair I could find. Lizzie was cashing out, but everyone else had the same idea I did.

"I'll be pouring wine in my sleep," Sam said.

Glenda glanced at him, leaned back, and stretched. "At least one part of your body will be moving. I don't think I can feel my legs. I'll need to surround myself with soft music and pleasant fragrances. I must get some sleep before I'll even consider a warm bath. I'd hate to drown in my own tub from sheer exhaustion. That's really my worst nightmare, you know, being found dead in my bathroom. If any of you find me dead in my bathroom, for the love of the universe, please move my body to the bed."

"At the rate we're going, we're more likely to be found keeled over in the vineyard," he replied. "But hey, good news! The next sideshow is two weeks away. We can all recuperate until then."

"No one's recuperating any time soon!" Lizzie shouted as she walked toward us. "Did you read the flyer? A former school board member is missing!"

Glenda's legs miraculously regained feeling. "I sense foul play in the air. We simply must smudge this tasting room with lavender and sage."

Sam burst out laughing. "Why not save the trouble and invite the Penn Yan Royal Order of the Moose to meet here? They all smoke cigars and pipes. That'll clean out any malevolent spirits."

"That's not funny," Cammy said. "It'll also clean out our customers."

I stood and walked to Lizzie. "Let me see that flyer for a minute. I must've left mine in the kitchen when I was cleaning up."

She handed me the paper and I took out my phone. "Okay, folks, these might not be the best photos, but they look like the same man. David Whitaker, right, Lizzie?"

She nodded. "That's him. But the flyer doesn't give a name. Only a hazy photo. The text says 'Have you seen this man? Missing since last night.' There's a phone number to call. A Penn Yan exchange. Look, I'm positive it's David Whitaker from the school board and I'm doubly convinced his family reported it to the sheriff's office. Unfortunately, the authorities have to wait forty-eight hours before they can do anything. Stupid, if you ask me. Heavens, the humane society begins to track down a dog immediately but as far as the rest of us are concerned, forget it."

She had a point. Unless it was a child or an incapacitated adult, the forty-eight-hour rule applied. I knew. I used it myself in some of my screenplays.

My eyes darted back and forth from the flyer to my phone. "If it *is* the same man from Rosinetti's Bar, then his disappearance might have something to do with Roy Wilkes' murder. The two of them had some sort of altercation at the bar. Pushing and shoving. They got tossed out before it could escalate."

"If you ask me," Sam said, "it makes this David Whitaker guy a prime suspect in the murder."

Yeah, a prime suspect that the sheriff's department knows nothing about because I never shared that information.

I was getting deeper and deeper into that hole of knowing enough stuff to get me in trouble but not enough to solve a murder. I wondered if that was how most amateur sleuths felt. At least none of them were at odds with the local law enforcement. Oh, what was I saying? None of them were real. I knew I was desperately sleep deprived and totally worn out because I couldn't even separate fictional detectives from the real ones.

"Norrie, are you all right? You look as if you spaced out for a moment."

I rubbed my eyes and stared at Roger. He'd been on the listening end of the conversation and I prayed it would stay that way. Last thing I needed was another discourse on the French and Indian War.

"I'm fine. Just tired, that's all. Well, I suppose we should lock up and get out of here while we're still mobile."

Like a defeated army, we exited the tasting room building. I watched the crew walk to their cars, turning once or twice to see what Alvin was up to. I imagined that obnoxious goat was exhausted as well, considering the ongoing attention he got all day from the customers. Glancing at his pen, I saw his grain bucket had been filled, his hay replaced, and the large water buckets filled to the rim. Nothing like room service for a goat. Too bad the vineyard guys didn't make house calls.

In spite of the fact it was Labor Day Weekend, the vineyard crew kept working and the winemakers never left their lab and winery unattended. I knew Franz, Alan, and Herbert had all taken turns monitoring the initial fermentation process for the Chardonnay. Once the grapes had been crushed—or was it pressed?—they had to check sugar and acidity levels. Not once, but lots of times. Then the mad scientist process of adding things like yeast and enzymes. Essentially, while all of us in the tasting room were busy getting customers to try the wine, those three men were working their tails off trying to make it. And holidays like Labor Day didn't translate into time off.

That was why it didn't surprise me to see Franz's and Alan's cars still parked on the side of the winery building when I started up the road. For a brief second I thought about turning around and checking in with them. Needless to say, I changed my mind. I figured they didn't need the interruption and I needed to throw myself onto the couch until the fog in my brain lifted.

I was so tired I literally went from the couch to my bed without even eating dinner or scanning my e-mails. I did remember, however, to feed Charlie. But that was only because he kept bumping my head as I tried to sleep. It was then that I realized the frightening truth about myself—I would make a terrible mother. Probably the kind that forgot to pick her kids up from soccer practice.

I awoke as the sun was coming up and made myself coffee, toast and a microwaved egg. A regular gourmet start to the day. The fog in my brain had lifted and oddly enough I felt energized. I put on my sneakers and went for a brisk walk around the vineyards, winding up at the winery lab. Franz and Alan were already there, and Herbert was pulling in. I stood on the gravel lot and waited for him to get out of his car.

"How's it going?" I asked.

"I should be the one to ask you that. The tasting room parking lot looked like Times Square on New Year's Eve."

"I think I poured wine in my sleep. Does that tell you something?"

He laughed and took a step toward me. "You'll be pleased to know I was able to take a steel wool pad and remove that graffiti from the wine barrel. Then I coated it with a bit of deck stain. It looks fine. Probably some foolish college prank."

"Is everything all right?"

"I'd be lying to you if I said yes. Franz is as nervous as hell and it's rubbing off on Alan. Leandre from Terrace Wineries called him yesterday. The sheriff's department has been questioning everyone over there about that murder. Not a one-time deal. They keep coming back with what they call 'follow-up' questions. Leandre told Franz they intend to broaden the search."

"Broaden the search?"

"According to him, those deputies think Roy Wilkes might've had some connections with area winemakers. That's what's gotten Franz in such a tizzy."

"Connections? Area winemakers? How? It doesn't make sense."

"It does if someone plans to start their own winery."

"Roy Wilkes? He was planning on starting his own winery?"

Herbert nodded. "Leandre overheard two deputies talking. Roy bought an old house with lakefront property less than a mile from Terrace Wineries. It's zoned commercial as well as residential, being lake property and all."

Drat! And I thought Theo and I were one step ahead of those deputies. "Go on."

"There's not much to say. The deputies think Roy was making offers to the local winemakers and maybe one of the owners got wind of it and did the guy in."

"That's the most ridiculous thing I ever heard. Even when that mega-winery tried to commandeer the local winemakers, the winery owners sought other means to deal with it. Besides, why should Franz be nervous?"

"Because Roy made Franz an offer."

"But he didn't accept." *Or he would have said something.*

"That's because Roy was found dead the next day."

"And he thinks *I* might have had something to do with it?"

"He saw your car pulling into Terrace Wineries just as the sun was coming up that morning."

"That's because Rosalee had already found the body!" *Dear God. And all this time Franz has been tiptoeing around me.* "And, for your information, I wasn't alone. Theo Buchman from the Grey Egret was with me. I wasn't about to check out a dead body on my own."

"Oh dear."

"You can say that again. I don't know how you're going to do this, Herbert, but, for heaven's sake, find a way to let your boss know I'm not the killer."

"Yes, indeed. Not the killer."

I shook my head and shuddered as Herbert turned and headed for the winery lab door. I don't know what bothered me more, the fact that one of my employees thought me capable of murder or the fact the sheriff's department seemed to be getting ahead of me when it came to tracking down who really murdered Roy Wilkes.

Chapter 16

Three days into the week and I was back to my normal schedule, if anything around here could be considered normal. With the huge Labor Day crowds gone, the regular tasting room staff would be able to handle the usual fall scene. I agreed to help out on the weekends but was adamant the weekdays were for my "real" job.

It took some convincing, but Cammy had finally accepted the fact that my screenwriting actually translated into a paycheck. That said, I secretly felt as if I dangled precariously over a cliff, wondering if, or God forbid *when,* the axe would fall.

Rosalee got a phone call from Deputy Hickman informing her that indeed, the butterfly flowerpot stake was the murder weapon. Whoever used it didn't bother to wipe it off completely before sticking it on that windowsill.

"What about fingerprints?" I asked when she called me on Wednesday. "Were they able to lift any prints?"

"You sound like one of those crime show people. No, the deputy said they couldn't find any viable ones. That was the word he used—viable. Now, the blood, that's a different story. It definitely came from Roy Wilkes. I'm never going to be able to enjoy looking at those cute flowerpot stakes again."

"Yeah, it is kind of creepy. Is Marilyn still staying with you?"

"God no! One night with my sister was enough. She's back at her own place. Erlene Spencer's husband took a powder and everyone's going hog-wild looking for him."

"Took a powder? Cocaine?"

"Don't you know English? It means he took off. Gone. Erlene has no idea where he could be and she thinks the sheriff's department is giving her the brush-off."

"Wow. That's the second missing person in Penn Yan this past week. Have you ever met Erlene's husband?"

"Nope, but being married to her, I can understand why the man got up and left. I did mention how bossy she is, didn't I?"

On at least two other occasions. "Um, yeah. I think so."

"Maybe he got fed up and left the state. Marilyn told me he walked out of his last job pretty well set for life. Hurrmph. Until Erlene tracks him down and takes her share of his money. Or clobbers him to death. Whichever comes first. Heck, she'd give a Visigoth warrior a run for his money."

I tried not to laugh. "I know it was a crazy weekend, but did someone come around with a flyer for that other missing person?"

"They must have because we found a few of those things in our tasting room. Posted one on the bulletin board near our front door. Posted it right next to the travel brochures. Why?"

"Uh, I can't really be sure, but *that* missing man looks like a man who was seen having a not-so-verbal altercation at Rosinetti's Bar with Roy Wilkes. Happened a few days before your Corgis found Roy's body. The only reason I know is because my tasting room manager is related to the owners of the bar."

"Wouldn't surprise me. The altercation, that is. Roy had a way of getting under people's skin better than a tick. Still, not a reason to kill him."

"Did Deputy Hickman give you any indication of how far along they were with the case?"

"His lips were sealed tighter than his ass. Pardon my French."

Rosalee certainly had a way of getting her point across. I told her I'd let her know if I heard anything, but I wasn't being a hundred percent truthful. I needed to guard what little information I had and only share it with my confidants. In this case, Don, Theo, and Cammy. And while I really felt Rosalee could be trusted, I wasn't so sure about her sister or her sister's bosom buddy, Erlene.

In an odd sort of a way, I felt badly for Erlene Spencer. Even if she was a bossy know-it-all who could wield a mean punch, according to Rosalee. No one deserved to have their life shattered by someone's disappearance. Especially a spouse. Maybe it was what Rosalee thought—the husband wanting to end the relationship. It wouldn't be the first time for something like that to happen. What surprised me the most was that there was no mention of her husband's disappearance on TV. Or that other guy, either. The one Lizzie thought might be David Whitaker after seeing the blurry photo on that flyer. Then again, the Rochester and Syracuse stations had enough crime to deal with in their own cities.

By Friday morning, nobody was any closer to solving the murder, or finding the missing persons, for that matter. My gut feeling told me I needed to get my hands on Roy Wilkes' bank statements if I was going to get anywhere with the case. In order to do that, I needed a plan. A plan that hopefully wouldn't land me in jail. Then again, there'd be a bright side—I'd hire Bradley Jamison as my attorney.

That night, over pizza and wings at Don and Theo's place, I told them what I had in mind.

"You want to WHAT? Impersonate a bank examiner? Are you insane?" Theo could hardly keep his voice down and Don wasn't much help either.

"Of the million and one things that could go wrong, let me begin with the most obvious—everyone in Penn Yan knows you. And the same could be said for Geneva."

Then Theo cut in. "You don't even know what a bank examiner does. What to look for. What to ask for. And I don't think they do it in person anymore. It's all computer records that get sent to one place or another. Heck, I don't even know."

"Are you two done? Because I really think I can pull this off."

The men looked at me and didn't say a word.

I clasped my hands together, propped my elbows on their kitchen table and grinned like the Cheshire Cat. "Roy Wilkes' savings and checking accounts are at Union Star Bank. That's where his trust is filed. Gladys Pipp told me. I really should send her a case of wine. Anyway, Union Star is a national bank, not a community bank, not a credit union. It's a big conglomerate national bank, like Chase, Bank of America, or Wells Fargo. That means if I were to walk into a branch, say, in Rochester or Syracuse, no one would know me from a hole in the wall."

Theo glared. "Until you opened your mouth. Norrie, this is dangerous. Worse than your little scheme two months ago to trick those developers from Vanna Enterprises."

It was a reckless scheme and I had put everyone in our winery at risk. Still, I got results. Pretending to be a bank examiner seemed mild compared to what I had already done.

"Like I said before, it's not as if I'm stealing the money, or even embezzling it. I'm simply—"

"Going to need a lawyer on retainer?"

"Theo's right," Don said. "And here's news for you—the minute Catherine Trobert gets wind of what you did, you can forget Bradley Jamison. She'll have her son, Steven, fly or drive here faster than any one of us can say 'Chardonnay.'"

I felt a sudden cramp in my stomach and knew it wasn't from the pizza. "So what do I do? There's got to be a way to find out what Roy Wilkes was up to that got him killed."

Theo wiped some sauce off his chin and reached for another slice. "Try the real estate angle. We already know the guy bought that vacant house. And, thanks to the conversation you had with Herbert, we now know he was planning on starting his own winery."

"Guys, this doesn't look good for Rosalee. I wonder what she's not telling us. What if he made her an offer for Terrace Wineries and the sheriff's department found out about it?"

Don turned to Theo and then back to me. "So?"

"They might put two and two together and come up with five. They might jump to the conclusion that Rosalee had him killed so he wouldn't force her to sell by cutting off their water access. And it really doesn't help that the murder weapon belonged to her."

"Hmm," Theo said. "When you looked into the tax records from the assessor's office, the taxes on that lakefront house were delinquent for a year and a half. Up until that point, everything was paid. Including the house. It was a cash sale. He didn't have a mortgage on it."

"How do you know?" I asked.

"I did a little sleuthing on my own."

Don let out a slow breath that sounded more like a moan. "Don't let him fool you into thinking he put a whole lot of effort into this. He made one phone call to the real estate agent who sold us the winery."

"It got results, didn't it? Up until a year and a half ago, Roy Wilkes had money. And prior to that, he was able to buy property outright, including the Baxters' land and that house. Something must've happened that made everything change. If we can figure out what it was, it might bring us a step closer to finding out what got him killed."

"I'll tell you what I'd like to figure out," Don said. "How come no one heard that motorcycle of Roy's on the morning of his murder. Those things make some serious road noise."

It was the first time anyone had mentioned the motorcycle, other than Deputy Hickman, who informed us it was found near the crime scene. I figured everyone already knew the answer.

"Oh my gosh. I can't believe I can actually answer this, but I can. CSX. The train. You know, Conrail. The trains run up and down Seneca Lake. Heck, the railway tracks are just a few yards from where the pumping station is, and I know for a fact, very long and loud trains run past there every morning. They would most definitely drown out a motorcycle."

Or a murder.

"Guess that would explain it," Theo said. "Too bad it wasn't a passenger train. No early morning witnesses. Only corrugated shipping containers from UPS to Walmart. Well, one mystery solved for the night. What do you say we move to the living room and make ourselves comfortable on the couch and recliners? If no one minds, I'll turn on the TV and see what we've missed today."

All of us cleared the table, grabbed our drinks, and moved to the other room. Isolde, their large, long-haired cat was sprawled out across the three-cushion couch and was indignant when Don picked her up and plunked her in a chair. "Hurry up if you want the couch, she'll circle right back if we don't move quickly. I'm grabbing the recliner."

I settled in and leaned my elbow on the armrest. Theo took the other side and turned on the remote. *Blue Bloods* had ended and the news was next.

"Shoot me if I have to watch another commercial for blood pressure," Theo said.

Don leaned back and sighed. "Just mute the damn thing."

We watched the endless stream of advertisements for cars, diarrhea, credit scores, and male performance-enhancing drugs before we heard the words, "This just in from our newsroom—no word yet on the disappearance of former Penn Yan School Board Member, David Whitaker."

"Lizzie was right! It *was* him!" I yelled. "The guy who had the fight with Roy Wilkes."

Theo gave my ankle a nudge. "Shh, let's hear what they're saying."

A photo of David Whitaker, that must've been taken when he was on the school board, flashed across the screen. It had the school district emblem on the wall in the background. The official orange and blue colors.

The news anchor indicated that he had been missing from his home in Penn Yan since Labor Day Weekend and if anyone had any information, they were to call the Penn Yan Sheriff's Department or Silent Witness. Two phone numbers appeared at the bottom of the screen.

Other than the dates when David Whitaker served on the school board, nothing else was mentioned. The news quickly switched to a traffic accident on Jefferson Road in Rochester and Theo lowered the sound on the TV.

"Coincidence or what?" he asked.

Don shook his head. "The 'or what' depends on whether or not the guy had a relationship with Roy Wilkes. I mean, for all we know, they could've been complete strangers who argued over something at the bar. A sports team. Politics. It doesn't take much for some people to get all worked up over that stuff."

Isolde left her spot on the chair, and made her way to my lap. I stroked her long fur and thought about what Theo and Don had said. "I Googled David Whitaker and came up with zilch. Family man, blah, blah. I suppose I could delve deeper."

"What about Roy? What did you unearth about him?" Theo looked straight at me and, for a second, I felt as if I was a little kid with my hand caught in the cookie jar. I remembered looking up the local newspapers for human interest stories that might include him, but I never got any further."

"Oh geez, I kind of got sidetracked."

Theo was relentless. "Where'd you leave off?"

"I tracked down the local newspapers, hoping his name might appear. Especially since they do stories about Beecher Rand employees. That's as far as I got."

"What papers?"

"Um, Scranton's *Time-Tribune*, *The Morning Call* out of Allentown and, uh, um… oh yeah, *The Morning Times* from Sayre."

Don chuckled. "No night owls in that part of Pennsylvania, huh?"

"I don't think they deliver evening papers anymore," I said. "This is awful. I really dropped the ball."

Theo reached over and patted me on the shoulder. "Relax. You're doing more than anyone. Three newspapers you said? Right? I've got an idea. We'll divvy them up. You can have the one in Scranton and Don and I will fight over who gets Sayre and who gets Allentown."

"I'm doing what?" Don asked.

"You're helping Norrie. Each of us will do an archival search from one of those papers. See what we come up with. If we're lucky, maybe we'll find something that links those two men. True, it's a longshot. We don't have forensics or access to bank accounts or any of the manpower the sheriff's department does, but we do have one thing."

I opened my eyes really wide. "What's that? Perseverance? Determination?"

"Boring social lives."

Chapter 17

I had just put my cereal bowl in the sink and was reaching in the cabinet below for a new bottle of dish soap when the phone rang. The call wasn't unusual for a Saturday morning, but the time was. It was only seven fifteen. I wiped my hands and picked up the receiver.

This better not be toilets overflowing, Alvin breaking loose and running down the driveway, or the return of the seventeen-year locusts.

"Hello?"

"Norrie! Thank God you're home." Rosalee sounded more stressed than ever. "Kelsey Payne's been arrested for murder. Those idiotic deputies think he killed Roy Wilkes. Poor Kelsey got hauled into the sheriff's office a few minutes ago. His brother, Cal, called me from there. He won't even be able to post bail until Monday. You've got to do something."

"Um, that's awful, but I'm not sure what I can do."

"Find the real killer, that's what! And do it before they hang my handyman."

I didn't bother to tell her hangings weren't an option in New York State. Instead, I asked her to calm down and tell me everything she knew.

Surprisingly, she managed to keep her voice steady. "They found incriminating evidence on Roy Wilkes' clothing that points to Kelsey. A fingerprint match, of all things. According to Cal, it was a really clear thumb print on one of the metal jacket buttons."

"But how did they—Oh never mind. You did tell me Kelsey was arrested when he was younger. Funny, but I always thought those records were sealed."

"Not to law enforcement, apparently. And knowing Deputy Hickman, he got a court order to release them."

"But why? Why suddenly decide to compare a thumb print from the crime scene with those on file for Kelsey Payne? It doesn't add up."

"It does if someone was trying to frame Kelsey. Cal said the sheriff's office got an anonymous tip."

"Oh geez. That really boils it down. What about a lawyer? Does Kelsey have one?"

"My next call is to Marvin Souza. About time he woke up. Of course, he'll probably send that Bradley whatshisname over to the jail."

It's Jamison and it's not the jail. It's the Public Safety Building.

"You think?" I tried not to sound too excited. Here I was practically salivating over an opportunity to see Bradley Jamison again while some poor guy got railroaded for murder.

"If I know Marvin," Rosalee said, "the last thing he's about to do is ruin a weekend. Of course he'll send that kid."

"Uh, it probably wouldn't hurt if I drove down there." *Who the heck am I kidding?*

I was positive they'd never let me see Kelsey, but nothing would stop them from me having a conversation with Gladys Pipp. I knew she worked on Saturdays from nine to noon because she mentioned it to me when I last spoke with her about Roy Wilkes' bank.

Rosalee cleared her throat for what seemed like forever. "Cal will still be there. I'd bet money on it. Tell him I'm getting a lawyer. This is the worst possible time of year for something like this."

The minute she said "worst time of year," it was as if someone had turned on a switch.

"Rosalee, are you going to be all right with the harvest? I mean, if Cal can't be around?"

"We've got two decent assistants and a lineup of migrant workers. All documented."

"Good. Good. Because if you need anything, I'm sure everyone in WOW will pitch in."

I would've offered my own workers, but I knew how stretched our resources were without an assistant vineyard manager and Federweisser looming.

"One more thing, Norrie. If you run into my sister while you're at the jail, tell her we could use some help in our tasting room. She hasn't bothered to return my calls since she left."

"Um, I don't know why I'd be running into Marilyn. Why would she be there?"

"Because she's glued to the hip to that Erlene Spencer. And last I heard, no one's found the missing husband."

"Oh."

"You can say that again. Erlene's been camped out over there, along with Marilyn. I suppose now they've arrested Kelsey, those deputies will start on their other cases."

"Yeah, I suppose."

"Idiots. Locking up the wrong man when the real killer's running loose."

"I know Kelsey's a friend and probably a great handyman, but can you really be sure he's innocent?"

"I'm sure. Hell, I've been on this earth for well over seventy years and in that time, I've learned a thing or two about human nature. Fingerprint or no fingerprint, Kelsey didn't kill anyone."

Granted, I was nowhere close to Rosalee's age, but I'd learned a thing or two about human nature as well. Number one being, "It doesn't hurt to sweeten the pot." The pot in this case being Gladys Pipp. I had to get her to talk. Since alcohol was forbidden in the public safety building, I had to rely on the next best thing—Francine's jams and jellies.

My sister had made an entire shelf-full of strawberry jam at the start of the season, and I knew Gladys would be a sucker for the stuff. I pulled out two jars, wrapped some pretty ribbon around them, and put them in a small bag.

Since it was so early in the day, I sent Theo and Don an e-mail about Kelsey's arrest, promising to call them later. I also promised to begin my archival search when I got back from the public safety building. What I failed to mention was Bradley Jamison and how I prayed my timing would work and that I'd run into him when I got there.

I selected a really cool turquoise tunic to go over my jeans and spent more than the usual two minutes on my hair. By twenty to nine, I was in my car and on my way to the village of Penn Yan. It was too early for the tourists, but our vineyard crew was on the job. The unmistakable vibrating sound of the harvester, as its rods shook the grapes from the vines, could be heard above my car's engine. It was a short drive and I got there in no time.

"Hi!" I said to the forty-something receptionist at the glass-enclosed window. "You must be Frieda. I need to speak with Gladys for a moment."

"We're not supposed to send anyone back there without clearance. Wait a second. How did you know my name? I didn't put my ID tag on yet. Did Gladys tell you anything about me? What did she say?"

"Uh, nothing. Just that she was working up here while you were at lunch one day last week."

The woman looked relieved. "Okay. What did you say your name is?"

"Norrie. Norrie Ellington from Two Witches Winery." I held out my license and she took a quick look.

"Hold on a second while I phone her."

As Frieda placed the call, I tried to sneak a glance at her upside down sign-in sheet to see if Bradley Jamison was anywhere in the building. No luck. I couldn't decipher a word.

"Gladys says it's all right for you to go back there. I'll sign you in." Then Frieda waved her hand toward her face and ushered me closer to the window. "She said to tell you Deputy Hickman is out on a call but she expects him back within the next thirty minutes. You need to make it quick."

I nodded and walked past her window, through the door that led to an endless lineup of cubicles and small offices. Gladys' workstation was adjacent to Deputy Hickman's office. No wonder she was concerned about my presence in the building.

"These are for you," I said handing her Francine's jellies.

"Strawberry! My favorite! Did you make them?"

"No. My sister's the one with the culinary touch. Enjoy. Listen, I don't have much time. I was hoping you could fill me in on Kelsey Payne's status."

Gladys made a tsk-tsk sound and leaned toward me. "Poor guy's in lockup on the other side of the building. I wasn't here when they brought him in, but I heard he was a wreck. Insisting they made a mistake."

"Rosalee Marbleton thinks they did. That's why I'm here. What can you tell me about the arrest?"

Since it was a Saturday, no one else was in the office except her. Still, she looked around the place at least twice. "I may have read the report when they were processing him. Mr. Payne's fingerprints were sent to our lab in Buffalo. It was a nine point match. Enough to book him, according to our jurisdiction."

"His prints could've been planted there, for all we know."

Gladys bobbed her head. "That's why we've got lawyers."

As soon as she said the word "lawyers," heat rose in my cheeks. I hoped she mistook it for concern over Kelsey.

"Yeah, uh, speaking of lawyers, did Kelsey's arrive?"

"Not yet. Unless he or she signed in with Frieda while you and I were talking. The only person who's been able to see Kelsey this morning is his brother, Cal Payne."

She paused for a minute to check the screen on her computer. "According to what it says here on the register list from the lockup, Cal signed out at a little past seven. I didn't get in until eight thirty."

"I don't suppose there's any chance I could have a word with Kelsey."

"Sorry, hon. Not unless you're family or legal counsel."

At that precise instant, something on screen caught her eye. "Looks like the lawyer just signed in. Maybe you can have a chat with him. He's out front getting a clearance card from Frieda."

Please do not let him be Marvin Souza. Please, please. Not Marvin Souza.

I thanked her and darted past the cubicles like a jackrabbit. My behavior was shameless. An innocent man, according to Rosalee, was in lockup and here I was hoping to have what? A rendezvous with his attorney? Francine would be appalled.

I caught Bradley Jamison's profile as I opened the door into the front reception area. *Yes! The gods are listening and Marvin Souza is probably still sleeping.*

Bradley turned and gave me a perplexed look. "Norrie, right? From one of the wineries."

"Two Witches. Across the road from Rosalee."

Bradley took a few steps toward me. "What brings you here so early on a Saturday?"

"Same thing that brought you. Rosalee. Unfortunately, since I'm not a relative and I'm not Kelsey's attorney, I can't speak with him."

"Hold on a second, I think I can fix that."

Bradley walked back to the window and told Frieda I was part of Kelsey's legal counsel. Not in so many words, but whatever he said worked because she issued me a clearance card for the lockup.

"Why did you do that?" I asked as the two of us exited the front of the building.

"Last thing I need is for your friend, Rosalee, to get my boss, Marvin, all riled up. Besides, from what I've heard, you're quite the sleuth."

"Grossly exaggerated, but if it gets me any closer to finding out what really happened and who really killed Roy Wilkes, I'll gladly take the honors. So now what?"

"Now we walk around the building to the back entrance where the county lockup is."

I followed Bradley and tried to stay focused. If I thought he was good looking the first time I saw him, he was even more spectacular today. With his short-sleeved ocean blue shirt and khakis, he looked as if he'd stepped out of a magazine. I could also detect a faint scent of citrus and clove, which made him even more appealing.

We walked into the lockup area, showed our identification, and held still while the deputy on duty used a metal detector to make sure we weren't about to bust anyone loose.

"I need to speak with my client, Kelsey Payne," Bradley said. "Joining me is Miss Ellington, who's also part of his defense team."

The deputy, who bore a strange resemblance to Beaver Cleaver, appeared to have little interest in us. He was more concerned about following protocol. "You'll need to empty your pockets and place your belongings in that tray. When you're done, everything will be returned to you. You are allowed to use a small recording device if you've brought one."

Bradley and I did as we were told. Next, we were ushered into a room that wasn't much bigger than a Porta Potty. There was one small metal rectangular table and four metal chairs that practically screamed "Uncomfortable as hell."

"Take a seat," the deputy said. "I'll have Mr. Payne brought in."

The table was small and my leg practically touched Bradley's. I crossed it over my ankle so there'd be no chance of contact. I was petrified he'd hear how fast my heart was beating.

"You look nervous," he said. "First time in an interrogation room?"

"Uh-huh."

"Don't feel bad. This is only my third time. Although, the first time probably doesn't count since I was only an intern."

"How long have you been working for Marvin Souza?"

"Not long. A little over a year. I completed my internship with Gabaldi, Fennick, and Wilson in Syracuse. When I got the offer to work with Marvin Souza in Geneva, I snapped it up. He's got one heck of a reputation."

"So you're from around these parts?"

"Baldwinsville. North of Syracuse. And you?"

"Born and raised in Penn Yan. Left for Manhattan when I graduated from college. Screenwriting to stay afloat. Guilted into returning for a year. Very complicated. Costa Rican bugs."

Bradley opened his mouth to say something but, in that instant, the deputy escorted Kelsey Payne into the room and directed him to sit opposite Bradley and me.

"You have thirty minutes, according to our regulations," the deputy said to us. "I'll be right outside that door if you need me. There's a buzzer on the wall."

Clearly, Kelsey Payne wasn't about to pose any threat. His hands were tied with one of those plastic things that always reminded me of garbage ties. At least his feet weren't bound together.

All I could think of was one of those classic lines from every cop movie I'd ever seen—"Are they treating you all right in here?" Fortunately, for everyone concerned, I didn't ask it.

Bradley introduced us and paused long enough for Kelsey to utter four words—"I didn't kill anyone."

Chapter 18

"Do you mind if our conversation is recorded?" Bradley asked as he pulled out a small device from his pocket.

Kelsey shook his head. "Fine."

Up close I could see the resemblance to his brother. Both of them had red hair, but not screaming red. More like a subdued version. And both of them were well-built but not exceedingly muscular. Kelsey was definitely younger and thinner. Probably in his thirties. When I met Cal for the first time at Rosalee's, he had a five-o'clock shadow. Looking at Kelsey's face, his was more like a five-day shadow.

Bradley slid the recorder closer to Kelsey. "Suppose you tell us what happened and why your fingerprints were found on the victim's clothing. How were you acquainted?"

"We weren't."

"Then how do you explain—"

"How my prints got on his jacket? It's a long story."

Bradley glanced at the analog clock that was on the wall behind Kelsey. "We've got time."

I didn't say a word, but I opened my eyes really wide to indicate I was interested in hearing what the guy had to say.

Kelsey leaned forward and stretched his bound arms across the table. "Mrs. Marbleton's been having a problem with rodents in her pumping station. Mice mostly, but a rat or two wouldn't surprise me. Anyway, she asked me to see what I could do to get rid of them. Damn things chew on the wiring in there and can do a hell of a lot of damage."

Bradley gave a nod. "Go on."

"That morning I had another job down the lake, and I couldn't be late. Since I set traps for those vermin the night before, I decided to check them before I left for my other job. I pulled my car way off the road and hoped it wouldn't get sideswiped. Then I took a shortcut through the woods to the pumping station. Used my penlight so I could see where I was going."

"Then what?" Bradley asked.

"I went inside to check the traps. Two of them were sprung, but no mice. I reset them. Had a jar of peanut butter in the building and used my fingers to spread the stuff. Wiped it off with a bandana I had in my pocket. The other traps were okay as is. I left the building and started back to the woods when I heard a commotion on the other side. The lake side. In the semidarkness I saw three people."

"Three?" I all but screeched.

"Yeah, three. It looked like a lot of pushing and shoving. Didn't know what the hell to think. I snuck around but hugged the building so no one would see me. Like I said, it was kind of dark. Next thing I knew, one of them was on the ground not moving and the other two were still fighting. I thought maybe they'd punched the guy who was on the ground."

Then Kelsey blew air out of his mouth. "One of the people took off running up the lakefront with the other guy on his tail. Looked like they skirted around a bit by the winery building, but not for long. I saw them moving farther up the lake. When I was sure they were a good distance away, I walked over to the person on the ground. I figured he was knocked out. Never heard a gunshot or anything. Holy geez! I bent down to shake the guy and my hand was on his chest. That's probably how my fingerprint got on one of his metal buttons. All that grease from the peanut butter made it real easy for a print."

At that moment, the deputy opened the door. "You have ten minutes left."

When he left, Kelsey went on with his description. "So, like I said, 'Holy geez.' The guy was dead. I felt something on my hand and it was blood. I didn't bother to stick around. I made a beeline for the woods and my car. Went straight to my other job and never breathed a word of it."

"But why?" Bradley asked, his voice slightly raised. "Why didn't you phone for help?"

"Can't help a dead man."

I bit my lower lip and looked Kelsey in the eyes. It was uncomfortable for me, and I imagined he felt the same. "You're not telling us something."

I held my gaze and waited. Then I asked again. "What was the real reason you didn't call nine-one-one?"

"Because I swore one of the guys running up the lakefront was my brother."

Bradley and I both gasped at once. The word "shortly" immediately sprung to mind, as in the verbal or maybe not-so-verbal altercation Cal had with Roy "shortly" before Roy was found dead.

"Cal?" My voice wavered. "You thought it was Cal?"

"I did at the time. Not anymore."

"What made you change your mind?"

"When I asked him this morning. Cal would never lie to me. I thought I was protecting him. Turned out I was wrong. And now what? I'm being framed for murder. This rots, you know. You have to do something."

Bradley turned off the recorder and pocketed it. "We will. We'll do everything in our power to defend you."

"It won't be enough," Kelsey said. "You have to find out who really killed that guy."

Bradley scratched his chin, never taking his eyes off of Kelsey. "Did you give a statement to the deputies when you were brought in?"

Kelsey nodded. "Same thing I told you. They asked if I wanted to call my lawyer, but I didn't know I had one. Besides, I have nothing to hide."

"One quick question. What made you think one of the perpetrators was your brother? Wasn't it way too dark to see anyone clearly?"

"When the train went by, I saw the hat. It was illuminated by the train's headlight. In the winter and on cold mornings, Cal wears one of those woolen hats with a reflective band. Really dorky looking. And there's another thing—Cal and Roy got into a big row about a week or so before. Cal told me about it. So, when I saw the hat, naturally I thought it was him."

Finally—"Shortly" was a week or so, not hours or minutes before.

The door opened again. "Ten minutes are up. You've got to go."

"I'll be back on Monday for your bail hearing," Bradley said. "Meanwhile, sit tight."

I felt as if I had been hit over the head with a sledgehammer. Of all things. Kelsey Payne witnessed a murder but kept quiet because he thought the killer was his brother. And for all any of us knew, it could be the brother. It gave new meaning to the term "Family Affairs."

Bradley took my elbow as we left the building and pulled me aside. "How did you know he wasn't telling us the truth about his reason for not phoning in the murder?"

"I didn't. It was a line I used in one of my screenplays. 'What was the real reason?' It's a popular line, you know. 'What was the real reason you broke up with him?' 'What was the real reason you left town?' That line could go on and on in infamy. It came to me all of a sudden and I blurted it out."

"Well, it worked. Not that it's going to help him much. They'll think he's grasping at anything to save his hide."

"Or his brother's."

"It doesn't matter. He's our client, not Cal, and I've got to prove him innocent. Listen, I don't know about you, but I'm starving. It was a choice this morning between shaving or eating. And believe me, I didn't want word to get back to Marvin I showed up to interview a client looking as if I stumbled out of bed. Even if that's true."

I laughed.

"So, do you know any good places to eat? I'm not that familiar with Penn Yan."

"The Penn Yan Diner's down the block and around the corner. Fantastic breakfasts and even better pies. You'll like it."

"Uh, guess it really is early for me. I wasn't too clear. Would you like to join me for breakfast?"

"I, er, um…"

"I really could use the company. Oh crap. That didn't come out right either. I would really enjoy your company, Norrie Ellington. So, how about it?"

"It's a date. I mean, a deal."

Bradley laughed and shook his head. "Mornings must not be your best time either."

The aroma of bacon permeated the air as soon as I stepped into the diner. I could've inhaled the entire grill, I was that hungry. I looked around and saw that Bradley was already seated at a corner booth.

"I ordered coffee for you as soon as I got here," he said. "I figured you'd want a cup."

"You figured right. Thanks."

The menu hadn't changed in decades, but I still looked it over. Bradley gave it a glance and groaned.

"What? Don't tell me there's nothing here you like?"

"Oh no. That's not it. Everything looks wonderful. It's just that I didn't have the heart to tell Kelsey that Marvin Souza's firm is only helping him out temporarily until we can secure a criminal lawyer. Our practice is family law—divorces, custody, real estate, wills and trusts…that sort of thing."

"I see."

"Yeah, no sense having the poor guy worry about it all weekend. Rosalee Marbleton was adamant that Marvin either take the case or, and I quote, 'Find me a damn good lawyer who will.'"

"Sounds like Rosalee."

"Marvin's got a number of contacts in Syracuse. He'll line up someone by the beginning of the week. Until then, we're the official counsel for Kelsey Payne."

At that moment, one of the waitresses appeared to take our order. She looked like a high schooler—lots of ear piercings, short black hair with blue and green streaks and red lipstick that could've come from Marilyn Monroe's private stash.

"Hi! I'm Cassidy. What can I get you?"

I ordered scrambled eggs, bacon, and sourdough toast while Bradley took another gander at the menu.

"I'll have the pancakes and eggs. No syrup but extra butter."

"Wow," I said. "That's how I like my pancakes, too. No syrup. Just butter." *Glenda would say this is a sign from the universe.*

"It's funny," I said, "but Kelsey Payne really does look like that guy our tasting room manager and I saw at Rosinetti's Bar a few nights ago."

"Rosinetti's? I've never been there but I heard the pizza is good. Is that someplace you go often?"

"Me? No. It was my first time."

I then proceeded to tell him the reason I was at Rosinetti's in the first place and how Cammy and I were trying to identify the man who fought with Roy Wilkes.

"Come to think of it," I said. "They all look similar—the Payne brothers and the man we're convinced is David Whitaker. Ruddy complexions, reddish hair but not too red. Aw, it's probably coincidence. Cal and Kelsey work outdoors, so that would explain their coloring. And David Whitaker? Maybe he's an outdoorsman, too, for all I know. *If* it's the same man."

"Hold on. Let me try to get all of this straight. You found out that Roy Wilkes had an altercation with a man in a bar who you think is a former school board member."

"Uh-huh."

"But you didn't report it to the sheriff's office."

"I know. Another long story. I wanted to wait until I was sure."

"So when you got a call that the mystery man was back at the bar, you and your tasting room manager went there."

"That's right. My tasting room manager is related to the owners."

Bradley listened intently while I told him about the photo we took and my unofficial sleuthing.

"I hate to say it, but David Whitaker is missing and, if it turns out that he's really the man from the bar, he may be the murderer. Norrie, you could actually be hindering an investigation."

"Only if someone rats me out."

Bradley groaned and took a gulp of his coffee. "Do you have any plans to share your intel with the Yates County Sheriff's Department?"

"My God. You sound just like Theo Buchman from the Grey Egret. He and his partner are friends of mine. And yes, I have a plan."

That led me to the next bit of information I held—the hang-tab.

"You really need to own up. The sooner the better. Look, I didn't want to say this, but here goes. I wouldn't put it past those sheriff's deputies to think Rosalee put Kelsey up to the murder so she could prevent her winery from going under. Everyone knows by now that, without a water supply, she'd be doomed. It won't only be Kelsey who's facing murder charges, it'll be Rosalee as well. My boss kept making a point of it, over and over again."

"It's that bad, huh? Last thing I want is for Rosalee to be unfairly accused of something. This stinks. The deputies are dragging their feet, even with the forensic evidence they have. That's why I have to go through with my plan. I really believe we can find the killer during our Federweisser event."

Bradley's mouth opened and I don't think he closed it until I was done explaining about the bowlers and the quilters. "You see, we might be able to pull together some real evidence—tangible evidence if someone with a blue Eddie Bauer windbreaker is missing a hang-tab. And, if the threads match. Did I tell you there were blue threads?"

"You—"

He never got to finish his thought because our food arrived and we literally dove into it. We made no mention about the murder, Kelsey's arrest, or David Whitaker's disappearance until after we had eaten.

Then Bradley spoke and what he said took me totally off guard. "I have to be back here on Monday to arrange for Kelsey's bail. That is, if they decide to grant him bail. Anyway, I'll have a chance to speak with him and I'll ask if it was him the night you and your tasting room manager were at the bar playing photo shoot. If it was, he's bound to explain who he was with and why."

"Cammy, that's my tasting room manager, really doesn't think it was him because one of their bartenders overheard someone calling the guy Richie when he showed up again. Still, I'm not too sure."

"All right. I'll see what I can do. When did you say this Federwhatever is taking place?"

"Federweisser. I can tell you're not all that familiar with fermentation. Don't worry. Neither am I. Federweisser is wine from the first fermentation.

The stuff tastes like Champagne but it's got a short shelf life. Very short. Anyway, the big shindig is Saturday, two weeks from today."

"Two weeks, huh? Are you really sure about those bowlers and quilters? Don't take this the wrong way, but your grand scheme kind of reminds me of a Woody Allen or Mel Brooks movie."

"Gee, not the Marx Brothers?"

"I wasn't about to go that far." He reached over and patted my hand. "You can relax. Your secret sleuthing is safe with me for now. But you can't hang on forever. If the Federweisser turns out to be a bust, as far as finding Roy's killer, then you seriously need to come forth with what you know. In fact, I'd wager that lead deputy would be genuinely appreciative."

"Grizzly Gary? Deputy Hickman? Appreciative? Not on your life. Or, in this case, mine."

"Please don't put me in a spot where I need to say something."

True, his words could've been taken as a threat, but I honestly didn't believe that was his intent.

"Okay fine. You've worn me down. Does this mean you'll be at the Federweisser?"

"I can't very well sit back and do nothing when I know what you've got planned. Oh yeah, I'll be there. So, guilt and bugs. Care to expound a little on that?"

The waitress refilled our coffees and I gave Bradley the long story. Holy cow, I don't know what got into me. I all but started with my elementary school years. I was clamoring to ask him if he was single but couldn't figure out a way to approach it without sounding desperate. Turned out I didn't have to wait too long. His phone, which he'd placed on the table, rang and I could see a photo of a woman named Pam. Real easy to read the name upside down. She looked downright gorgeous. Especially in a phone snapshot.

"Excuse me for a second. I really have to take this." He got up and stepped outside the diner, while I pretended to take another sip of my coffee.

"Everything all right?" I asked when he got back.

"Yeah, everything's fine. Well, I'm sure you've got a busy day ahead and I know I do, so we'd best get going. Oh, I paid the tab when I walked back in."

"How much do I—"

"It's on me. Thanks for introducing me to this place. Terrific food."

"Uh, yeah. Thanks for breakfast."

I figured if he was talking to a client, he would at least make mention of it, but since he didn't, I let my imagination do the work for me—girlfriend, fiancée, wife, ex-wife. Four very possible choices.

When we got to the door, he held it open. "Don't take any crazy chances with this investigation of yours. The Federweisser's bad enough. Truth is, Kelsey's explanation is credible right down to the details. Unless he's playing us, the killer could be anyone you know."

Chapter 19

"Does paying for someone's breakfast make it a date?" It was a little past five and I had moseyed down to the tasting room to catch Cammy before she left for the day.

She looked up from the wine bin, where she was rearranging bottles, and waited for me to continue.

"Because Bradley Jamison, that hunky attorney who works for the one Rosalee has on retainer, paid for mine this morning. So, was it a date?"

"Depends. Did he act as if it was a date?"

"No."

"Then it wasn't."

"Phooey. Not to sound all goo-goo eyed, and I know I said I wasn't interested in dating anyone since I'm not going to be here that long, but damn it all! This guy's a real hottie. He only has one flaw as far as I can tell."

"What flaw?" she asked.

"Pam."

"Pam. Who's that?"

"She could be anyone, but right now let's just say she's the significant other."

"And you know this how?" Cammy asked.

"He left the table to answer a phone call from her."

"That doesn't mean anything. He's a lawyer. She could be a client of his, for all you know."

"Then he would've said something."

"Not really. Haven't you heard of client confidentiality? And if she wasn't his client, she could've been his sister or a relative."

"I wouldn't bet on it. Never mind. I really don't have time to worry about my social life. I had breakfast with him because I was at the county lockup this morning trying to find out more about Kelsey Payne's arrest. Rosalee put me up to it. Those sheriff's deputies think Kelsey murdered Roy Wilkes."

"Whoa! Slow down! You're losing me. Kelsey Payne got arrested? I've heard you mention his name once or twice. He's Rosalee's handyman, right? The one who stained her deck and saw those flowerpot stakes. *That* Kelsey Payne?"

"Yes, yes. The very same Kelsey Payne whose brother is Rosalee's vineyard manager."

"It's beginning to sound like a soap opera."

"Worse. Bradley Jamison, the temporary legal counsel, was there to speak with Kelsey. I managed to wrangle my way into the interview, too."

"Impressive. I must say, I never knew you had such persuasive skills."

"I don't. He was scared of what Rosalee would do if I didn't get inside the lockup to hear what Kelsey had to say."

"Now this is beginning to make sense. That's how you wound up having breakfast with Mr. Hunk of the Day."

"Yep. That's about it."

I told Cammy what Kelsey told Bradley and me. About witnessing the altercation and Roy Wilkes' subsequent murder behind the pumping station that morning.

"No one's going to believe him," she said. "A solid fingerprint is like a full confession, and as for the motive…Oy vey. I don't even want to go there."

"You can say it. Bradley already did."

"That Rosalee put Kelsey up to it in order to save her winery?"

"Yep. That's it in a nutshell. Except for one thing. If it was a planned murder, how on earth would Kelsey have known Roy was going to be on the lakefront behind the pumping station at the break of dawn? Tell me that."

Cammy smacked her palm against her forehead. "Oh my God! You're right! How would he? No one goes walking around the lakefront at dawn hoping to run into someone so they can kill them. Even in the worst horror movies, they don't do that. Now what?"

"I'm not sure. Not until I finish with the boring stuff I've got to do. Theo, Don, and I are tracking down archival information on Roy Wilkes to see what we can find out. I intend to do my part as soon as I go back to the house. However, I did call Rosalee a few hours ago to tell her I spoke with Kelsey this morning. Apparently Bradley called her, too."

"How'd that go?" she asked.

"As well as could be expected I suppose. Her sister, Marilyn, was over there so I wasn't on the phone long. I could hear Marilyn in the background yelling about poor Erlene. Guess the husband never showed up."

"Speaking of not showing up, no word yet either on the other missing man, David Whitaker. Unlike Erlene's spouse, this Whitaker guy's been all over the news. They've practically canonized him for the work he did on the Penn Yan School Board."

"Before they nominate him for sainthood, I hope we can find out more about Roy and why the two of them were almost at fisticuffs at your family's bar. So, any other excitement around here?"

"Nope. Say, what did you mean by 'temporary legal counsel'?"

"Oh, that. Marvin Souza's firm is a family law firm, not a criminal law firm. They've got to find Kelsey a good defense lawyer."

"That shouldn't be too hard. There are lots of those firms in Rochester and Syracuse."

"Yeah, that's what I thought. Monday's the bail hearing and Bradley will be representing him."

"You going?"

"I'm tempted, but for the wrong reasons, so no. I'll be either buried in a screenplay or mired up to my elbows in research. Theo, Don, and I split up the workload."

"If you need me to do anything, give a holler."

"I will."

Alvin was chomping on a fresh pile of hay as I exited the building. I heard those guttural sounds of his before I actually laid eyes on him. It looked as if he had bitten off more than he could chew because a gigantic wad of the stuff was resting between the walkway to the tasting room and his pen. The goat must've leaned over his fence while he was eating.

Not wanting to have a mess the next day, I bent down to toss the stuff back in his pen and saw a cell phone in the hay. An Android. Someone was probably going nuts without it. I flipped the thing over and read the name scrawled on the cover—Travis O'Neil, one of our vineyard workers and apparently the lucky one who got to feed Alvin. That ornery goat probably spat at him and Travis dropped the phone in a hurry to get out of there.

Maybe I'd be in luck and Travis would still be working. I took off for the barn, sprinting as fast as I could. Only one truck was parked on the side of the building, and it belonged to the winery. Travis would have to make do without his phone until morning. Maybe his family had a landline and I could leave a message.

No sense walking any farther. I turned and started up the hill when I heard a rustling noise coming from the back of the barn. Maybe the guys hadn't left yet and had parked their cars out back. I skirted around the side of building and shouted. "Travis? Robbie?"

No answer.

Then, out of the corner of my eye, I spotted a kid who was lurking around our wine barrel. So much for a makeshift fence. "Hey! What are you doing?"

Before I could finish shouting, he got on one of those BMX street/dirt bikes and blew past me as if I wasn't there.

"Not on my watch, you don't." I screamed. "I know who you are and, boy, are you going to be in for it! I've got Deputy Hickman's personal phone number on speed dial."

Suddenly, the bike skidded a full one hundred eighty degrees and a skinny blond kid, who didn't look much older than ten or eleven, looked at me eye-to-eye. Without wasting a second, I took out Travis' phone and made like I was about to place a call.

"Wait!" he shouted. "Don't! I'll be grounded forever! I'm in enough sh—"

He let the bike drop to the ground and came running over. "My dad's gonna crucify me! He may act all nice to you guys at the wineries, but that's because he has to, being the head of the association."

The head of the association. My God! This has to be Henry Speltmore's kid.

"Talk fast and tell me what you were up to behind our barn. And you better not lie about it."

The kid shrugged and let out a sigh. "Tagging, that's all. Some of my buddies and me thought it would be funny to write stuff on the wine barrels."

"You? You're the one who wrote 'Chardonnayed To Rest'?"

He swallowed and nodded. "Yeah. I kind of play around with wine names and see what I can come up with. Sometimes I write other stuff, too."

"Don't! You can be arrested for that." *Damn. Pretty clever for a kid his age.*

He stood there for a minute and dug his hands in his pockets. "If you want, I can get a Brillo pad and scrub it off. I didn't write anything today. I hadn't even gotten to your barrels when I heard you."

"It's already been taken care of. Forget it. Just don't mess with our barrels again, okay?"

"Geez, you're sure a hell of a lot nicer than that crazy lunatic woman from across the road."

I figured he was referring to Rosalee. "What do you mean?"

"Remember when that dead body showed up? I ditched school that day so my buddy and I could catch some sunnies and rock bass in the lake. We kinda pulled a switcheroo on my folks and his. I told my parents I was staying at Todd's house and Todd told his parents he was staying at mine."

This kid was turning out to be a regular Tom Sawyer. My eyes widened and I kept listening.

"Anyway, we cut through the woods to get to this neat fishing spot. Both of us had flashlights, but we turned them off once we got out of the woods and near the shore. That's when that nutcase lady started yelling at us. Out of nowhere. What the hell, I mean, what the heck was she doing there? She started yelling we were trespassing and to go back where we came. I swear, that woman was louder than the train."

"Then what?" I asked.

"Todd got all weirded out and was afraid she'd call the sheriff, so we cut back through the woods and found another fishing spot about a half mile farther down."

"Did that lady have any dogs with her?"

"Hard to say. It was dark. She could've. No dogs barked, but that doesn't mean anything. Sometimes they don't bark and, all of a sudden, they take a piece out of your thigh. Maybe they killed that guy."

I laughed. "That lady was right. You shouldn't've been there in the first place."

"You're not going to call my dad, are you?"

"No. By the way, I'm Norrie Ellington. I'm one of the owners of Two Witches Winery."

The kid held out his hand. "I'm Eli. Eli Speltmore."

Boy are you going to keep your father on his toes!

"Nice to meet you, Eli. And if I were you, I'd write those puns in a notebook, not on our wine barrels."

He gave me a wink and dashed toward his bike. "Deal."

As I watched him take off down the driveway, I wondered why Rosalee never mentioned it. Then again, that encounter probably left her mind once Victoria spotted Roy Wilkes' body. Too bad Eli and his buddy didn't see anything.

* * * *

Once I got in the house, I made myself a ham sandwich, downed a Coke, and pulled up my laptop. As much as I wanted to get back to my screenplay, I had to get into Scranton's *Times-Tribune* if I was going to get anywhere with my search.

The entire process was worse than the first time when I centered on the *Chicago Tribune* and the *New York Times,* hoping to eyeball something earthshattering about Beecher Rand. I didn't. The only thing I found was an article about a patent infringement. The writer insinuated that someone working for the company provided another company with classified information about one of their inventions. However, Beecher Rand was unable to track down the culprit, and, worse yet, the other company wasn't located in the United States so the patent rights didn't apply. The end result appeared to be a financial loss for Roy's former employer.

I kept hoping I'd run into human interest stories about the company and its employees. No such luck. By ten after eight, I was ready to stick a fork in my eye. I opted instead for a giant bowl of ice cream and some microwaved popcorn. The kind with the artificial butter Francine would never allow in her house.

It was still early so I called Theo and Don to see if they were having any better luck.

"We're just getting started," Theo said. "It was an exhausting day. How long are you planning on staying up?"

"Ten, ten forty-five, maybe."

"Okay. If we run into anything worth noting, we'll call you before ten thirty. How's that?"

"Sounds good."

The popcorn had made me thirsty, so back to the fridge I went. Regrettably, I'd posted some personalized inspiration posters there and, instead of inspiring me, they made my stomach churn. Especially the one of Conrad Blyth getting kicked in the rump with the header, "Will Your Screenplay Get Rejected Next?"

After a fruitless hour and a half on my laptop, I reached the conclusion that Roy Wilkes was a ghost. Not a specter or spirit, but someone who simply made no mark on the industry he was in or the community he lived in. At least as far as the media was concerned.

I threw myself on the couch and stared at the ceiling. That was the moment the phone rang with Theo's exuberant voice at the other end. "We hit the motherlode!"

Don was shouting in the background. "What do you mean *we*? I hit the motherlode. You found bupkis."

"What? What did you find out about Roy Wilkes?" I asked.

Theo shushed Don. "Not Roy. David Whitaker. Were you aware he worked for Beecher Rand, too?"

I tried to think back, but I was tired and my mind wasn't cooperating. "Are you sure it's the same guy?"

"I'd bet money on it. There's a photo of him with the Kiwanis Club and it sure looks like the one floating around that says 'Missing Person.' He was getting some sort of an award and it mentioned he was a manager at Beecher Rand. Said he was married with two kids. Didn't you find that out as well?"

"Come to think of it, I did. On a Google search. But I can't tell you which site. I looked at so many. But yes, married with two grown children. I think it was part of a description about him when he served on the board of education in Penn Yan."

"You know what this means, don't you?"

"Other than the fact the guy has a predictable and boring life?"

"You must be tired. The guy worked at Beecher Rand the same time Roy Wilkes did. Duh! There's got to be a connection. That would explain the altercation at Rosinetti's Bar. Maybe this David Whitaker killed Roy Wilkes for whatever reason and took off before anyone got any the wiser."

"I'd better pull up Scranton's *Times-Tribune* again and start looking under a new archival search. This time with David Whitaker's name."

"Uh, you sound kind of tired and foggy. You know, it can wait until tomorrow."

"Actually, it can't. My mind would be bouncing all over the place and I'd never get any sleep. Might as well finish what I started. Do you want me to—"

"Call us? No offense, but even if you find out the guy was wanted for murder across the contiguous United States, wait until the morning. After seven."

"You got it. Oh my gosh, I can't believe what you found out. I wonder what other secrets are lurking around Beecher Rand."

Chapter 20

If ever there was a Horatio Alger story, it was David Whitaker's. From a low level entry position to the apex of the corporate ladder, this guy catapulted to the top like nobody's business. Why then, did he trade it all for early retirement in Penn Yan?

My eyes were glued shut the next morning, and Charlie's smelly tongue on my face didn't help matters. I got up, poured him his kibble, grabbed some juice, and staggered back to bed, where I remained until nine fifteen, an hour considered late by winery worker standards, but the crack of dawn as far as I was concerned. Besides, I told Cammy I'd help out in the afternoon if they really needed me.

"I don't get it," I said to Don, when I called him after getting up the second time. "David Whitaker seemed hell-bent to rise to the top of the food chain and then, poof! All of a sudden, early retirement in a village that pulls up the sidewalks at eight. It doesn't make sense."

"Maybe he got burnt out. It happens, you know. You said his children were grown. Maybe once he became an empty nester he no longer needed to prove anything."

"Maybe so, but there's something off. Darn it. I wish I knew the Roy Wilkes connection."

"Are you thinking maybe Roy had something to do with David's decision to retire?"

"I don't know what to think. Tomorrow I'll make a call to their human resources department. Prospective employers are allowed to ask for employment dates."

"So now you're their prospective employer? A missing guy and a dead man?"

"Beecher Rand won't know the difference. I can sound professional."

Don let out an annoying moan. "And to think the Academy Awards are wasted on actors."

"Very funny."

"Hey, how about joining us for dinner tomorrow night? Potluck."

"Great! I'll unearth one of Francine's vegetable casseroles for a side dish."

"Good idea. See you then."

Conrad's face on the refrigerator haunted me worse than the Ghost of Christmas Past. I made myself a cup of coffee, toasted a frozen bagel, and got to work on my screenplay revisions. The "few thoughts" my script analyst sent my way had meant some serious plot changes.

By quarter to one I was ready for a break and for something more substantial than a bagel. I rinsed off, put on clean clothes, and darted down the driveway to the tasting room and bistro. It was Sunday and Fred made amazing tomato and veggie frittatas on Sundays.

I managed to sneak in the tasting room without anyone noticing me. Something to be said for the crowd of post Labor Day tourists. The bistro wasn't too overwhelmed with orders but enough to keep Fred and his wife, Emma, busy.

"Hey, Norrie," Emma said. "I keep missing you. How's it going?"

Her long dark hair was pulled into a French knot that looked as if it was professionally styled.

Instinctively, I gathered my shoulder-length hair back behind my ears and gave it a pouf. "I'm doing okay. Better than the folks at Terrace Wineries, I suppose."

"I heard they made an arrest. I overheard some people talking about it this morning. By the way, what would you like?"

"The Sunday frittata, of course."

Emma gave a nod and walked over to her husband, who was at the grill. In a second, she returned. "I don't know the details or even if it's true, for that matter, but if they did arrest someone, that should make Mrs. Marbleton feel a whole lot better."

I didn't want to get the gossip train moving about Kelsey's arrest, so I simply nodded and grabbed a seat at one of the tables.

A few minutes later, Fred brought over my frittata. "I've got all the food orders set for the Federweisser. In addition to the canapes, we'll be selling sausage on rolls with sauerkraut or onions. The two college kids we have working for us on the weekends are really doing a decent job. We should be fine for that event."

"Make sure you've got enough of those sausage sandwiches. Remember, the WOW group is comping lunches for the bowlers and quilters."

"Don't worry. I already factored it in when I placed the order. Sure you're going to need that crew? I mean, if what Emma overheard is true, then the killer was arrested."

"Someone might've been arrested, but until we know for sure, the bowlers and quilters will be on the lookout for a blue windbreaker without a hang-tab in the front."

"You got it! Oh goodness. I turned my back for a minute and there's a lineup at the counter. I'd better get back to work."

"Thanks, Fred! Have a good day!"

The warm juices from the small cherry tomatoes gave a sweet taste to the egg and cheese mixture and I took my time savoring it. Then I glanced at the tasting room and got a knot in my stomach. I'd told Cammy I'd help out if they needed me, but I really wanted to get back to my screenplay. I walked into the tasting room as slowly as I possibly could without coming to a complete halt.

She spied me immediately. "You're off the hook! We're doing great. No need for the relief table today. Next weekend may be another story, but we're fine this afternoon."

"Yay! I've got a zillion changes to make on my screenplay and lots of back writing."

"Huh?"

"More changes, only earlier in the script."

"What about your other paperwork? The Roy Wilkes investigation? Were you able to find out anything else last night?"

"Not me, but Don did. It turns out Roy Wilkes and David Whitaker both worked for Beecher Rand. One guy turns up dead, the other disappears. It can't be a coincidence. Tomorrow morning I'm going to call the company and find out their dates of employment."

Cammy furrowed her brow. "Beecher Rand isn't about to give you that information."

"They will if I sort of stretch the truth and tell them I'm the owner of a winery and I'm conducting background checks for future employees."

"That's not stretching the truth. That's fabricating it!"

"Stretching. Fabricating. I really need to start somewhere."

"You better hope whoever you speak with hasn't read the papers lately. Especially the crime section and the obituaries."

"True, true, but for all they know, those guys could've applied for the job weeks ago and maybe we're just slow around here. If they say anything, I'd act shocked."

"Now you're beginning to sound like Lizzie."Cammy lowered her voice. "Are you aware she ran off little 'sightings' sheets for all of us in case we see anyone with that blue windbreaker? But Glenda's really topped the cake."

"Oh no. I'm almost afraid to ask. Not another séance?"

"Nope. That would be too easy. She believes we can channel the negative energy from the murderer if he or she sets foot in our winery."

"Please don't tell me it involves lighting anything on fire."

"It doesn't. She wants everyone to dose themselves in some sort of spiritual oil. Something about putting it behind our ears and on our wrists."

"That doesn't sound too bad."

"The stuff smells like rotten herring. She gave me a whiff from her little vial."

"If it smells that bad, then what's it supposed to do when confronted with negative energy?"

"It will turn black on the skin."

"Oh hell no. Absolutely hell no. We'll stick to the bowlers and quilters."

"That's what I thought."

Honestly, none of my friends back in Manhattan would believe any of this. What was I saying? I couldn't believe it either. I left the tasting room and went back home to finish what I had started this morning—addressing the "few thoughts" my script analyst sent. Thoughts that took me over three hours to rework into the script.

At least I felt productive, but it was short-lived. My cell phone rang and I picked up. I didn't think it was a winery problem because they usually called the house first or, in the case of the vineyard guys, pounded on the door and yelled.

"Hello?"

"Hi. Is this Nomie?"

"Nomie?"

"That's what my note says—Nomie. It's written in pencil on the back of a gas receipt and it says Two Witches."

The back of a gas receipt. My brain flipped back to the conversation Theo and I had had well over a week ago with the petite blonde who was renting the blue ranch house on the lake. I had jotted off my name and number in case she or her housemates remembered anything about the morning of Roy's murder or about the night before. Maybe one of them had seen something suspicious.

"It's me, only the m is really two r's. I'm Norrie Ellington from Two Witches Winery."

"Cool place. Love your Caldron Caper. I'm Bethany and we're renting the blue house on the lake. We were supposed to check out after Labor Day Weekend but got a two-week extension. It'll be cutting it close for us since college starts on September fourteenth, but what the heck. We're seniors so we can skip all that orientation stuff."

Sounds like a woman after my own heart.

"I meant to call you before now but I forgot," she said. "When I finally got around to throwing in wash, I found the crumpled note in my pocket. Mallory, one of my housemates, gave it to me. She said you wanted to know if any of us saw anyone cutting through our property around sunrise a couple of weeks ago. She even wrote the date down for me. It was the morning after one hell of a party night."

"I'll bet. So, did you see anything? Mallory said you were all sleeping."

"They were, but I wasn't. My head didn't hit a pillow until after six. I was out all night partying. I hooked up with a really hot older man and we made out all night. You might even know him."

An older man? Partying with coeds? That ruled out Don and Theo. And it damn well better not be John, Alan or Franz. And Roger wouldn't be partying, he'd be pontificating...

"Um, I kind of doubt it."

"Too bad. Like I said, Cal was one hot dude."

"Cal?"

My God, tell me this isn't happening. Ew!

"Did he tell you his last name?"

"He might've, but I forgot. Hey, there can't be that many older men with red hair, a fuzzy five-o'clock shadow and a physique to die for. Those biceps of his were like rocks."

My God. It really was Cal Payne. And ew! She's young enough to be his daughter. Of course, given what she just said, she's now his alibi. Or would be, if he was the one under arrest.

"Listen," Bethany went on. "I wasn't drunk or anything when I drove back to the house, but I kind of missed the pull-off in front and kept driving up the road. Missed the next one, too. I was really, really tired. I know, I know. I shouldn't've been on the road because tired people cause accidents, too, but I had to get back."

"Um, yeah. I understand." *I'm just trying to get the image of you and Cal out of my mind.* "So, then what? Did you see something?"

"Not at our house but at that creepy place a few houses up. The one that looks like something out of a Stephen King movie."

Bethany really had my interest at that point. "What? What did you see?"

"Two cars were parked there in the pull-off. Then, like out of nowhere, two people appeared and got into the cars."

"Out of nowhere, where? And what kind of cars? Did you get a good look?"

"Uh, yeah. Sort of. I pulled over to the side of the road because I was going to use the pull-off to swing around, but then they came out of the bushes and got in the cars real fast. I couldn't tell if they were men, women, or one of each. They were both large, though, if that's any help. Like I said, they were in one hell of a hurry."

Yep, two people. That's a help, I suppose.

"What about the cars?"

"Regular ones, I guess. Not sports cars or SUVs. Old folks' cars with four doors. Oh, and they were darker colors because I would've noticed if they were white."

"I don't suppose you saw any license plate numbers?"

"Sorry. I wasn't really paying that much attention. But, oh yeah, there was one more thing—that voice."

"Voice?"

"Uh-huh. I had my car windows rolled down to let in the breeze while I was driving. That's supposed to keep you awake. Anyway, I heard one of the people yelling, 'You stupid idiot!' only it sounded like 'id-jut.' It was a deep raspy voice, but it could've been a man's or a woman's. I was hoping they'd pull the heck out of there so I could turn around and head back. Why is this so important? Did someone burglarize a house or something?"

I wasn't sure if the summer rental girls paid a whole lot of attention to the local news, but I figured I had nothing to hide. "Someone was murdered on the lakefront a few houses down. The people you saw might've seen something."

"Oh yeah, *that.* It's been all over the news today. They caught the killer. Said it was the second murder in the county this past summer. The one before that was like decades ago. Can you imagine?"

More than you think. "I'm friends with the lady who lives right near there."

"Like I said, sorry it took me so long to call you. I kind of wasted your time since they found that guy. Guess it had nothing to do with what I saw. Oh, I almost forgot. Of course, it really doesn't matter anyway, but one of the drivers had a hard time pulling the door open. They stopped and had to use their other hand. Weird, huh?"

"Um, yeah. Weird. Thanks for calling me back, Bethany. If you visit Two Witches again, I'll give you a bottle of Caldron Caper for free. If I'm not in the tasting room, ask for Cammy."

"Wow. Thanks! Nice talking to you."

Bethany Whatever-Her-Name-Was didn't know it, but she'd eliminated one of my suspects and put real players into a timeline for me. That timeline matched the one Kelsey Payne gave Bradley and me. Real players and one of them was a killer. If not both. Something Deputy Hickman would dismiss as one of my theories because, number one, he didn't believe Kelsey, and number two, oh what the heck! It was the same as number one. Kelsey wasn't about to get a fair shake. Not with Grizzly Gary doing the happy dance thinking the case was over.

I looked at the time on the bottom of my laptop's screen—six twenty-three. I knew the Grey Egret would be closed so it wasn't as if I would be interrupting Theo and Don. I dialed their house phone but wound up leaving a message.

"Hey, it's me. Kelsey was telling the truth. There were two killers. Okay, maybe one killer and one accomplice, but still… Call me later and I'll explain. I don't want to wait until tomorrow night to tell you what I found out."

Then I walked over to the refrigerator and turned Conrad's photo around so I wouldn't have to look at his face, and put my screenplay away. Romance was the furthest thing from my mind.

Chapter 21

Kelsey Payne insisted he witnessed some sort of altercation that involved three people and Bethany said she saw two people appear out of nowhere behind the creepy house and get into two separate cars. Hardly coincidental, considering the timing. And what about the location? It would've been closer to park on the pull-off by the blue ranch, or even the pristine little place next to it, but no, they used the pull-off in front of an empty house. An empty house where no one would notice the comings and goings of drivers on the road. Or killers cutting through the yard to the lakefront.

This had to be a premeditated murder, except for one lousy detail. The one Cammy and I had batted around when we spoke about Kelsey. How on earth would anyone know that Roy Wilkes would be behind the pumping station at the crack of dawn? It wasn't as if he had to do any maintenance work there. The station belonged to Rosalee, and it was Kelsey and his brother who oversaw its operation.

There were giant chunks of this puzzle that I was missing, and, as much as I hated to admit it, I really should've shared what I knew with the sheriff's deputies. However, I was convinced they'd poo-poo it, especially with that ironclad evidence they had in the form of Kelsey's peanut butter-greased fingerprint on Roy's jacket button.

I had no other choice as far as I could tell. I had to rely on the surveillance at the Federweisser to catch the real murderer. Or one of them. That little hang-tab was evidence, too. All we needed was to find the windbreaker it belonged to.

Theo and Don called me back at a little past eight that evening. They'd stayed late in their winery to "put things back in order," according to

Don, and didn't check their answering machine until a few minutes before they called.

"Well?" I asked. "Is this the smoking bullet?"

"I think that's silver bullet, or smoking gun, but no, I don't think it's either," Theo said. "But that's only because we can't identify who those people were."

"It shouldn't matter. It validates everything Kelsey told us. Well, about there being two people anyway."

"Look, if you ask me, the one you should talk to about this is the lawyer, Bradley Jamison. You said Kelsey's bail hearing is tomorrow, right?"

"Uh-huh. Does that mean Bradley can present new evidence?"

"No. The judge will look at the scope of the crime, Kelsey's record, the possibility of a flight risk, that sort of thing."

"Aargh."

"You said those girls extended their stay for two more weeks?"

"Yeah. Why?"

"That girl Bethany may be called to testify for the defense."

"Oh my God! And I don't even know her last name or where she's from. Geez, I am so not cut out for this."

"You're doing fine. Give yourself some slack, and we'll see you tomorrow night. You going to be all right?"

"Sure, for a Nancy Drew screw-up."

The next morning I made it a point to get up early, get dressed, and call Marvin Souza's office so I could tell Bradley about my conversation with Bethany. Too bad he wasn't in.

"Mr. Jamison drove straight to the Yates County Courthouse this morning," the secretary said. "He has a bail hearing."

"I know. I know. That's why I'm calling. I have some new information and he's got to hear it."

"I can't give out his cell number, but I can try it and ask him to call you back. I'd put your call through to Mr. Souza, only he's not in yet."

"What time is the hearing?"

"Nine thirty."

I looked at the clock on the microwave. No time to wait if she fiddled around trying to reach Bradley. If I hurried, I could make it to the courthouse before the hearing. I thanked her, told her I'd drive there, hung up the phone and charged out the door. Route 14 wasn't too bad, but when I turned off on Route 54, the shortest way to the village, I ended up behind farm equipment. Slow moving, aggravating farm equipment that drivers were allowed to use on county roads in order to get from one parcel of their land to another.

It was impossible to pass any of those vehicles. They were so huge, I had zero visibility. I muttered all sorts of expletives under my breath and kept going. Finally, the last monstrosity left the road and I had a clear path into Penn Yan.

Miraculously, I got to the courthouse with seven minutes to spare. At least the parking lot was sparse, so I grabbed a spot and raced to the door. Another delay—identification check, a valid reason for my presence, and then the metal detectors. Penn Yan hadn't yet reached the point of x-ray machines for personal possessions, so a deputy did a quick search of my handbag.

"I need to speak with Bradley Jamison immediately," I told the deputy. "It's urgent. He's the legal counsel for Kelsey Payne, whose bail hearing is about to start."

The deputy must've seen the anguish on my face because he excused himself for a moment and made a quick call while I waited. "Hold on a moment, he'll be right out."

The double doors to the courtroom swung open and Bradley stepped forward. Brooks Brothers had nothing on him. From his tailored suit to the polish on his shoes, he looked every bit Wall Street.

"Norrie! What are you doing here?" he asked. "Kelsey's hearing is about to start."

"That's why I'm here. I have to tell you what I found out."

He ushered me into a small alcove near the double doors and I told him about my conversation with Bethany. "Kelsey was telling us the truth. The two people he witnessed with Roy Wilkes have to be the same ones Bethany saw. The timing adds up and so does everything else."

Bradley stood perfectly still and let out a sigh. "His defense lawyer, once Marvin secures one for him, will need that information, but I'm afraid it won't help with his bail hearing."

"That's what Theo Buchman from the Grey Egret said, but I was hoping he was wrong."

"Look, I'll do my best in there, but bail hearings deal with the arrest evidence, and that's pretty strong. I've got to hurry. It's an open hearing so you can come in."

He motioned me toward the doors and took off sprinting. I did a quick check to make sure my cell phone was on mute and then I followed him.

There were only four or five observers in the courtroom, and I recognized two of them—Cal Payne and Deputy Hickman. Both were seated in front.

A few of the others might've been Rosalee's vineyard workers, given how they were dressed, but I wasn't sure. All of them were male. I took a spot on the aisle in the back and pressed my lips together. I hadn't realized it, but my hands were clenched, too.

The hearing went the way in which Theo had described it would. Bradley stressed the fact that Kelsey had no arrest record as an adult and, because he had family in Penn Yan, he wasn't about to jump bail. It didn't matter. The judge, citing the magnitude of the crime, denied bail. I felt as if I had been kicked by a mule. A mule who went by the name of Grizzly Gary.

I left the courtroom and waited outside the building. A few minutes later, Bradley appeared. We walked away from the entrance and into the parking lot.

"Marvin will make sure Kelsey gets an outstanding criminal attorney," he said. "With that fingerprint, it was a slam dunk, I'm afraid."

"When will he go on trial? Did the judge say anything after I left the room?"

"The date hasn't been determined. Those things take time and the process itself is formidable, what with selecting a jury and all that."

"I suppose it's too late for me to go to the sheriff's department and tell them everything I've found out."

"Much as I hate to say this, you were right the first time. The scant evidence you do have, and the information you gleaned, isn't enough to get Kelsey off the hook or a new investigation started."

"What about Rosalee? She'll be devastated."

"In more ways than one. Once the trial gets started, the prosecutor will be pushing hard for motive and Rosalee Marbleton's bound to bear the brunt of that. She very well may be implicated, too."

"My God, what a nightmare."

"I've got a full client load this morning or I'd go over there myself. Best I can do is call her once I get into my car and tell her what took place. Unless, of course, her vineyard manager beat me to it. Did you see him in the first row?"

"Uh-huh. Hard to miss." *Especially when I pictured him mouth-to-mouth with Bethany. Ew!*

"I've got to run. I'll catch you later, Norrie. Thanks for driving over here."

Bradley took off before I could say another word. I walked back to my car and sat there for a good five minutes. Then I drove straight to Terrace Wineries. More specifically, to Rosalee's house.

It was almost eleven when I pulled into her driveway. Another car was already there. Some sort of nondescript old Buick. Beige. I figured

Rosalee's vehicle was in her garage. I took a breath, got out of the car, and walked to the house. The cutesy little flowerpot stakes were still in their original pots, minus the murder weapon and the one Deputy Hickman took for comparison.

A quick rap on the door and she stepped outside onto the porch, closing the door behind her. "I've just had horrible news and, of all things, my sister showed up with that dreadful Erlene Spencer. The two of them are like hyenas, laughing one minute and shrieking the next. I don't know how much longer I can stand it. I wanted to warn you first before you came inside."

"I imagine Erlene's a basket case by now, considering her husband is missing."

"Erlene's a pain in the patoot. Missing husband or not. She thought he might've gone back to his home town, but none of the relatives have seen him."

"What about her children? Doesn't she have children?"

"Yep. Two grown sons. One in Colorado and one in Geneva. They haven't seen him either. She's thinking foul play, but the sheriff's deputies aren't buying it. They think he scuttled off with some younger woman."

"Why on earth would they think that?"

"Let's just say the man had a reputation for philandering. 'Course, if you ask me, a cockroach would scuttle off, too, if it had to live with her."

"Yeesh."

"Anyway, you might as well come on in, I got some bad news from that lawyer Marvin stuck me with. The kid's as green as a cow pasture in July."

"Um, actually—"

"Bail's been denied for Kelsey Payne. Now everyone's scrambling to find him a good criminal lawyer. Seems I should be worried, too, according to what that lawyer had to say."

At this point we had entered the house, walked past the foyer, and into the kitchen. I re-introduced myself to Marilyn, because I wasn't sure if she remembered me from that day when Roy Wilkes was discovered dead and Deputy Hickman showed up at Rosalee's door.

Marilyn mumbled hello and introduced Erlene. Rosalee wasn't exaggerating. Erlene was a large woman, but not what I'd consider overweight, simply built large. Her hairdo was anything but natural, and I wagered she'd been through more cans of hairspray in a week than most women used in a decade. It gave new meaning to the term "voluminous hold." She was wearing a bulky grey sweatshirt that made her appear even bigger. But it was her voice that gave the impression I was in the room with "a force to be reckoned with."

"They can't arrest you for conspiring to commit murder," Marilyn said to her sister, "because they can't prove it. You need to quit worrying."

"You're not off the hook either, you know," Rosalee chirped back. "The land's in your name."

Just then, Erlene pounded her fist on the table. "I say 'Let the accused hang.' Face it, Rosalee, your handyman's guilty. Guilty as charged. I heard those news anchors over the weekend. The sheriff's department found a matching fingerprint on the dead man's clothing. His button or something. It wouldn't be there had it not been for your guy. If you ask me, Kelsey Payne was probably high on drugs. Happens all the time."

Rosalee's face turned beet red and, for a moment, I was certain she was about to get physical with Erlene. "That's preposterous. I've known those Payne brothers for years and drugs would be the last thing either one of them would do."

I pulled out a chair, slid into the seat, and made one of those calming gestures with my hands. "Shh. No one knows about this, so don't breathe a word. I happen to have a witness who saw the real murderers. That's right. Murderers. Two of them. My witness can corroborate Kelsey Payne's story. I'm working on getting everything in order for the sheriff's department. Once they take a closer look, I believe things will change for Kelsey."

Erlene opened her eyes and glared at me. "Murderers, you said? Two of them? Who's your witness?"

"I can't go running off at the mouth about this but, trust me, the fingerprint is circumstantial evidence. A witness is—"

"Leave her be," Rosalee said. "If Norrie says she's got witnesses, then she's got witnesses."

I had mentioned all of that to quell Rosalee's fears about Kelsey going on trial with a motive for murder that would've pointed the finger right at her. In retrospect, I should've kept my mouth shut. True, Bethany witnessed two people getting into two separate cars around the time of Roy Wilkes' murder, and true, she did see them coming up from the lakefront behind the dilapidated house, but whether or not they were the ones who killed Roy wasn't something Bethany had seen firsthand. Now I had everyone believing something that was more speculation than observation.

I was about to clarify what I'd said when all of a sudden Erlene stood up, yanked Marilyn by the arm, and announced, "I can't sit here all morning. Not with a missing husband and a diabetic cat who needs his insulin injection. For all I know, the cat could be comatose and my husband might be in worse shape. I need to have another chat with those deputies and get a fire lit under them. My husband and I happen to be upstanding community members. Not idle riff-raff. Come on, Marilyn, you need to drive me home."

Rosalee stepped out of their way and I mumbled, "Have a nice day. I don't think my car's blocking you, but if it is, let me know and I'll move it over."

Neither of the women paid any attention. They were out the door and gone within minutes.

"Don't say I didn't warn you about her," Rosalee said. "For the life of me, I can't imagine why my sister pals around with that woman."

"Um, Erlene must have some redeeming qualities."

"Unearthing them would require a major excavation. Would you like a cup of coffee while you're here?"

"My gosh, that would be heavenly. I barely had time for a sip of coffee when I left for the courthouse this morning."

"You were at the courthouse? You didn't mention it."

How could I? I was bulldozed the moment I arrived here. "Sorry. Our conversation kept moving in all sorts of directions. That's the reason I stopped over. To tell you I was at the courthouse."

Rosalee handed me a hot cup of coffee and placed some small cinnamon rolls on the table. "Help yourself. Made them this morning. Had to hide most of them from my sister and Erlene. Offered them some old Lorna Doone cookies I had in the cupboard."

Both of us burst out laughing.

Then, all of a sudden, Marilyn thundered into the house. "Don't mind me. Erlene thinks she left her sunscreen/bug spray in the bathroom. I told her I'd check."

Rosalee quickly threw a paper towel over the cinnamon rolls.

"I told Bradley Jamison about the witness who could substantiate Kelsey's story," I said when Marilyn was out of earshot. "It stinks, but they don't take that stuff into account at a bail hearing."

"Someone's got to take it into account. And it'll be too late when it comes time for his trial. They'll railroad him."

"Not if we can find the real killers first. I can't go into detail," *because they're so darn sketchy,* "but I've been working with Theo and Don to catch the true perpetrators."

"Honey, as much as I need your help, and heaven help us, so does Kelsey, you can't put yourself in a dangerous position where you could be killed."

"Don't worry, I won't."

The thud from Marilyn closing the bathroom door jolted Rosalee and me. "I'm back. There's no sunscreen in the bathroom. Did she leave it on the table?"

"I don't see anything," I said.

Marilyn grunted and left the kitchen. "It's probably in that bag of hers. Poor woman can't even think straight. I'll talk to you later, Rosalee."

Another thud, this time the front door. Gingerly, I removed the paper towel and picked up one of the cinnamon rolls. It made it to my mouth in a nanosecond. The sweetness and texture were amazing. No wonder Rosalee hid most of them from Marilyn and Erlene.

"Here," Rosalee said. "I'll put a few of these in a bag for you. You can munch on them later."

I thanked her and tried to reassure her that I was on the right track as far as the killers were concerned. And while that might've been true, I seriously wondered if any trains were running.

Chapter 22

I thought about what I had just said as soon as I closed the door behind me and walked to my car. That entire business about me putting together new evidence for Deputy Hickman was more for Rosalee's sake than Marilyn's and Erlene's. I'd have to do a lot better than going to the Yates County Public Safety Building and retelling the phone conversation I had with Bethany. Theo was right. I needed that girl's contact information, a really detailed timeline, and an honest-to-goodness written accounting of everything she witnessed.

It was a little past noon and fat chance those girls were sitting around the house. I figured I'd have better luck in the evening. Maybe after my dinner with Theo and Don. Meanwhile, I had enough to do at home. Screenplays didn't write themselves.

My car had only been parked in Rosalee's drive for an hour or so, and yet it still managed to accumulate a smattering of leaves and some miscellaneous debris from the trees. In another few weeks, there'd be more leaves falling and crunching under the windshield wipers. I caught a whiff of something on the sweet side as I opened my car door but couldn't quite place it.

The engine started up immediately, and I pulled out of her driveway to the road. The car seemed to tug a bit when I came to a full stop, but I didn't think much of it. Maybe I'd driven over some piece of trash or ugh, worse yet, roadkill. I waited for a clear shot then crossed Route 14 to the driveway we shared with the Grey Egret.

With my foot pressing on the gas pedal, the battle-worn Toyota made it up the hill like a champ, but when I hit the brake, it swerved and skidded all over the place, loosening gravel and sending small rocks everywhere. *Crap! When was the last time I had the darn thing serviced?*

Unlike Charlie, who constantly reminded me when he needed food, the car was somewhat of a silent trooper. I paid attention to the gas tank but, as far as everything else went, it was hit or miss. Francine told me to use their Subaru, especially in the winter, but if I was going to do damage to a car, I figured it might as well be mine.

The Walden family on Pre-Emption Road had been servicing my family's cars as far back as I could remember. Francine had left their number for me on her large list of emergency contacts in the kitchen. I picked up the phone, and dialed the minute I got inside the house. Hank Walden answered and I told him who I was.

"Hmm, we serviced the Subaru not too long ago. What's going on?"

"It's not the Subaru. It's my car. An older model Toyota Corolla."

"How old?"

"Two thousand seven."

"Okay, what's wrong?"

"When I step hard on the brake, it goes weird."

"Uh, can you be more specific?"

"It wobbles. And kind of swerves as it tries to come to a stop."

"Could be the brake pads, could be a loose caliper bolt…"

"Whatever it is, I need to bring it in so you guys can fix it."

"Got a tight schedule today, but I'll try to fit it in if you can get it right over to me."

"Do you know how long it's going to take?"

"Depends on what we find. We've got a loaner you can use. It's an older car, but it's newer than yours. Oops. Not trying to be funny."

"Don't worry. Everyone's cars are newer than mine and a loaner's fine."

"Listen, drive slowly and gently tap on the brake if needed. You should be all right. Probably needs pads."

"Thanks, see you soon."

"Well, Charlie," I said as the Plott Hound plopped himself at my feet, "that should wipe out my bank account until the start of next month. I forgot to ask if they take credit cards."

My car emergency didn't constitute as a winery or house emergency, so I was on my own as far as expenses went. I figured if it was going to cost me a fortune, I'd beg the Waldens to put me on a payment plan. Then again, I was probably worrying for no reason. Who didn't take credit cards these days?

* * * *

That evening, I hoofed it down the driveway to Theo and Don's for tacos and refried beans. We ate on their deck and watched as the sun sank slowly into the horizon. Our conversation didn't stray from the events earlier in the day. None of us were particularly optimistic about Kelsey's predicament but, as Theo pointed out, "We're still going gung ho with the Federweisser plan."

"Plus," I said, "I still think we might be able to convince the sheriff's department to take another look at the situation once we get a written statement from Bethany. Which, uh, was the next thing I was going to ask. Can one of you drive me over there? I'm hoping she'll be in. I'd take my car, but it's in the shop for wonky brakes and I don't want to use the loaner. Last thing I need is to dent that car or worse."

"You go with Norrie," Don said to Theo. "There's nothing to clean up. We used paper plates. When you get back, we can have dessert—homemade strawberry shortcake with whipped cream. It'll give me time to get it ready."

I stood up and gave Don a hug. "I'm salivating already. We'll be quick. Promise."

Once we were in Theo's car, I told him how weird my brakes had gotten all of a sudden, but he didn't seem too concerned.

"That kind of stuff happens all the time and we never notice it until whatever's wrong finally falls apart. At least you called the mechanic before anything awful happened."

"Look! The lights are on at the blue ranch. With any luck, the girls will be home."

Theo pulled off the road and parked next to one of their cars. We could hear music playing from inside the house and, for a moment, I felt funny interrupting the girls. Then I thought about poor Kelsey and hightailed it to their front door.

Mallory, the petite blonde, answered when I knocked. "Hi there! Bethany told me she spoke with you. Took her long enough to call. Come on in. She's in the living room. Everyone else went bar hopping tonight, but we were too tired. It's not like we're eighteen anymore. The twenties creep up on you."

Geez, tell me about it.

I introduced Theo to Mallory and Bethany and explained about needing a written statement.

"You mean they locked up the wrong guy?" Bethany tossed her hair and gave her head a shake.

"That's what we think," Theo said. "Do you mind helping us out?"

"No problem. I brought my laptop, but I don't have a printer. Wait! I can e-mail it to you, right?"

"Absolutely," I said. "Make sure it's got all of your contact information. And go to the toolbar under options so you can do an e-mail signature. If the sheriff's office needs another one, they'll contact you. We really, really appreciate it."

Bethany left the room and returned with her laptop. She sat at their small bistro table and started writing. "What is it exactly that you need?"

I spoke slowly. "Everything you witnessed. Oh, and the time. Even if it's approximate. Also, your name, home address, this address, e-mail and phone number."

"Sure thing."

"You might as well take a seat on the couch," Mallory said. "This could take a while. We've got beer and wine in the fridge if you want something."

I smiled and gave her a nod. "Thanks, but we're fine."

"You know," she said, "for a bunch of small towns on a lake, you've got a lot a crazy stuff going on. Some lunatic woman went all postal at the sheriff's office in Penn Yan because they couldn't find her missing husband. It was on the evening news. She was screaming that they had to find her damn husband before she did, or they'd be sorry. Bethany and I were cracking up."

I turned to Theo and opened my mouth but no words came out.

Mallory went on to say that the news anchors speculated about the husband walking out on the marriage or something like that because his car was missing, too. "And he took all his credit cards and stuff with him," she said. "It didn't sound like a kidnapping to them. Duh! No ransom. That would be my first clue."

"Did they give a name?" I asked.

Mallory shook her head. "If they did, I wasn't paying attention to that part. You know, if someone murdered him, wouldn't a body turn up?"

"Usually," Theo said.

Just then, Bethany got up from the table. "All done and e-mailed. Glad this place has Wi-Fi!"

We thanked her again and I reiterated that we'd give her a bottle or two of complimentary wine if she and her housemates visited Two Witches again.

"I've got to watch the evening news more often," I said to Theo, once we were in the car. "I seem to be missing everything. That crazy woman at the sheriff's office had to be Erlene Spencer. I ran into her and Marilyn Ansley at Rosalee's today. She didn't seem all that broken up over her husband when I walked in, but then, it was as if she finally remembered she *had* a husband and told us she needed to light a fire under those deputies. She was headed right over there."

"Sounds like a strange bird to me. So what do you think happened to her other half?"

"I think he ran off with another love interest. Middle-aged men are prone to do that, you know. Midlife crises and all. Although, he wasn't as much middle-aged as he was a senior. Maybe they're prone to doing that, too."

He gave me a poke with his elbow. "Only in your screenplays, I'm afraid."

When we got back to Theo and Don's, dessert was already on the table.

"Sorry it took us longer than expected," I said, "but Bethany's a slow typist."

Don motioned for us to sit down. "Hey, at least you got what you needed, didn't you?"

"That and a refresher on the local gossip. This time it was the Erlene Spencer show at the sheriff's office and we missed it. According to Mallory, who caught the news, Erlene was screaming, 'Find my damn husband before I do or you'll be sorry.'"

"What's that supposed to mean?" Don asked.

"Not to sound overly dramatic, but it sounds as if she might kill the guy herself!"

"Let's hope she does it at Terrace Wineries and not across the road at one of ours," he chuckled. "Come on. Enjoy the strawberry shortcake. You'll have to add your own whipped cream because I didn't want it to get runny."

I reached across the table for the can of whipped cream when I suddenly remembered something. "Oh crap. With all that hubbub about the bail hearing this morning and then the other goings on, I completely forgot to call the human resources department at Beecher Rand to see if the dates coincided for Roy Wilkes and David Whitaker. Although I'm pretty sure they do, since both men are about the same age."

"There's always tomorrow morning," Theo said in between bites of shortcake.

"I'll have to be really clever about how I go about it, too. I really need to find out if they worked in the same department."

"That information's on the up and up for prospective employers. You should be fine."

"I can't believe I forgot to do that. I was never absentminded before. That's only happened since I moved back here. Some days I can't even remember if I fed the dog, and the way he begs I always feed him again. Honestly, I was never like this."

"You never had to deal with murders before, either," Don said. "That stuff can really mess up someone's mind."

"I suppose. Anyway, at nine tomorrow morning, I intend to be on the phone with Beecher Rand."

Theo squirted more whipped cream on his shortbread and looked up. "If you find out anything consequential, call us in the tasting room."

Consequential wasn't the word for it. Cataclysmic seemed more apropos. And I found that out at daybreak the next morning, when Hank Walden from the garage called. So much for nine o'clock and Beecher Rand.

Chapter 23

"I don't mean to upset you, Norrie," Hank said, "but it appears as if someone tampered with the front driver's side brake. I had some time last night to check your car out and well, that's what I discovered."

I was still in bed and nearly tumbled out of it trying to get untangled from the sheets. "Tampered? What do you mean 'tampered'? Like sabotaged? Like in the movies where they cut your brakes? My God! Is that what happened? Someone cut my brakes?"

"Take it easy. Calm down. No one cut your brakes. This seemed like something a juvenile delinquent would do, like putting sugar in the gas tank or slashing tires."

"What did they do? What did they do?" I was beginning to sound like one of my parents' vinyl records when it got stuck.

"They put something sticky on the brake cylinder. Real easy to do. They could've wiped it on, sprayed it, pressed it on if the gook came from a tube… Not rocket science. Heck, they didn't even have to lift the hood or get under the car."

I took deep breaths in and out as I tried to focus on who could've done such a thing. Then my thoughts moved from *who* to *why*.

"Norrie, are you all right? You're not saying anything."

"Um, uh, yeah, I'm fine. Really I am. Fine."

When I got over the initial shock, I asked Hank a pivotal question. "When could this have happened? I mean, like when could they have put the gunk on the brake before I noticed it?"

"Hmm, hard to say. Depends on what they used and that, I really couldn't tell you. But if you want my best guess, I'd say maybe a two or three hour range. Makes a difference if you were driving it or not. Listen, the good news is the car didn't need any parts and nothing was really broken. I took the brakes apart, used solvent to clean everything up, and put it all back together. Oh, and I used a decent lubricant for the calipers in case you were worried—Permatex Ultra Disk. You can pick up your car any time today."

I thanked him and told him I'd be there before one. Then, trying to remain as calm as possible, I fed Charlie, took a shower, and made myself a cup of coffee. When I sat down to drink it, I realized my hands were shaking. I thought back to the only times when the car wasn't parked in front of the house and that left two places—the courthouse and Rosalee's.

I seriously doubted Marilyn and Erlene had time to pull off a little stunt like that, and, besides, why on earth would they? That left the courthouse. I took slow breaths and tried to think back to the moment when I pulled into the parking lot. There were lots of parking spaces and I chose one that was off to the side under a large tree. Living in Manhattan, I'd learned to park as far away from other cars as possible, even if it meant longer walks to wherever I was headed.

There were no other cars coming or going when I walked into the courthouse. But there was one thing—Cal Payne and the four or five other people who were at the bail hearing all left before Bradley and I did. That meant it could've been any one of them. Hank Walden told me it only took a minute or two to do the nasty deed to my brakes. The thought of Cal Payne or one of his vineyard workers trying to sabotage me was ludicrous, but then again, was he trying to give me a not-so-subtle message to stay the hell away from the case? I had no clue.

What I did have was a growing sense of dread. I couldn't hang on to the information I had much longer. It was time to come clean, as far as Deputy Hickman was concerned. I pulled up the e-mail and printed out Bethany's detailed description of the morning in question. Then I put it in an envelope and headed over to Walden's Garage to pick up my car.

"It's only a labor charge," Hank said. "Forty-nine dollars. Goes by the hourly rate, but I gave you a break."

"Whew. I was really worried this was going to cost me a fortune. Do you take checks, debit cards, credit, what?"

"All of the above."

I handed him my debit card and eyeballed my car. "I can't believe someone would do something like that."

"Sad to say, but this kind of stuff isn't all that uncommon. I've seen worse, though. Mainly from ex-boyfriends, girlfriends, or spouses trying to get even. Look, it was probably a prank. You said you parked by the courthouse, right? The high school and the middle school are only a block or two away. Maybe some kid ditched a class and decided to mess around."

"Maybe, but the worst part is thinking it could be personal."

"You might want to report it to the sheriff's office. Not that they can do anything, but they might consider putting some surveillance in that parking lot. Like a camera or something. Honestly, the place looks the same as it did when they built it."

"Yeah, I suppose that's the charm of these quaint little towns."

"I'm sure it was a one-time thing, but if you notice anything strange about the way your car's acting, park it and call me right away. No sense taking a chance. Okay?"

"Absolutely."

I thanked him and plunked myself down in my comfortable old Toyota. As I tossed my bag on the passenger seat, I could see the tip of the envelope containing Bethany's written statement. This whole mess had gone way too far, and I didn't want to wind up as another statistic. *Young screenwriter's car veers off highway and plunges into lake.* Hank Walden might've thought the damage to my brakes was vandalism, but I was convinced it was deliberate and personal. And, I had a gut feeling whoever did it wasn't about to stop.

Gladys Pipp was at the reception window when I walked into the public safety building.

"Frieda must be at lunch again," I said as I approached her.

"Like clockwork. Nice to see you again, Norrie. Are you here for a visitor's pass to see Kelsey Payne? Because, if you are, they're only allowing relatives and his legal counsel."

"Um, no. Actually, I'd like to speak with Deputy Hickman if he's in."

"You're in luck. He got back a few minutes ago from the diner. Early lunch. You didn't hear this from me, but if you have to speak with him, make sure it's after he's eaten. Hold on, I'll phone his office."

I waited while she let the deputy know I was here.

"All set," Gladys announced. "Right through those doors and—that's right, you know where he is."

"Sure do. Thanks."

I walked past the lineup of cubicles, trying not to make eye contact with anyone. The door to Deputy Hickman's office was open and he leaned against the doorframe studying my every move.

"Good afternoon, Miss Ellington. If you're here about the Kelsey Payne case, you might as well turn around and go back."

"I'm here because someone tried to kill me." *If that doesn't get me into his damn office, nothing will.*

"In that case, you'd better come in and take a seat."

I sat in the same uncomfortable chair as the last time I was in his office, only this time Marilyn Ansley wasn't in the room and Deputy Hickman remained standing.

"So, what's this about someone trying to murder you?"

I told the deputy what Hank Walden discovered about the brakes on my car and then backtracked to the courthouse, where I parked it for Kelsey's bail hearing. Then, pulling what best could be described as a "bait and switch," I got to the real reason for my visit.

Deputy Hickman rubbed his chin and glowered. "I should've known nothing would be simple as far as you're concerned. Suffice it to say you're not really here to fill out a vandalism report."

"Not really. I needed to show you this." Without wasting a second, I thrust Bethany's statement at his chest and didn't say a word.

He walked around to the other side of his desk and sat down, his eyes not budging from the paper.

Finally, he spoke. "Let me get this straight. Despite my directive for you to leave the investigation to the professionals, you decided to go off on your own little escapade to track down a killer. Is there anything I might have missed?"

"Uh, no. Not really."

"Good, because I want to be perfectly clear. We have the suspect in custody. With indisputable evidence. Indisputable. You're a writer. You know what that word means."

"I'm not disputing the fact that Kelsey Payne's fingerprint was on the button to Roy Wilkes' jacket. Kelsey admitted that. He explained why. It was after the fact. After he witnessed a murder, although he didn't realize it was a murder at the time. He saw the real killers. And this note proves he wasn't the only one."

"Miss Ellington, all this statement proves is that someone by the name of Bethany Montgomery saw two people come up from the lakefront and get into two cars that were parked on the pull-off near the house she was renting."

"But the timing—"

"Doesn't mean a thing. And even if it did, it's not enough to erase the incriminating evidence we have. In fact, it was so convincing, a grand jury wasn't needed for this case. Mr. Payne's trial date will be set shortly and any new evidence that comes to light, I'm sure, will be presented by his defense attorney and shared with the prosecution. Now, for the umpteenth time, please go back to your writing or your winemaking, or whatever it is you do on Two Witches Hill, and leave the police work to those of us who have a degree and experience in criminal justice."

"Wait! I do have tangible evidence."

I handed him a Ziploc bag containing the Eddie Bauer hang-tab, complete with its blue threads. I had removed it from the potholder drawer in the kitchen and stuffed it into my oversized purse. "Theo Buchman and I found this behind the house where Bethany said she saw those two people. We found it the night of Roy Wilkes' murder, when we kind of went snooping around the lakefront. Take a close look. It's a new hang-tab. It isn't coated in dirt or anything. That means it got there recently. And given the threads, it probably fell off one of the murderers during the scuffle."

"Miss Ellington, if I seriously thought this had any validity whatsoever, I'd have you arrested for withholding evidence. However, all you found was another piece of lake litter. That's right, lake litter! Anyone walking up and down the lakefront is bound to find stuff like this—old buttons, shoelaces, keys. Good heavens, the list never ends and that doesn't include the kinds of things I won't mention in mixed company."

"But, but—"

"I'll hold on to the statement from Miss Montgomery, but you can keep your little trinket. Trust me, it would never stand up in a court of law. It wasn't found at the scene of the crime or anywhere remotely close to it. A quarter mile down the lake hardly suffices. Now, getting back to the other matter at hand, your car brakes. I seriously suggest you *do* file a report in our office. This could be a pattern, you know. Disgruntled teenagers taking it out on private property."

"Yeah, all right. I'll do that."

I started for the door. No amount of persuasion was going to get Grizzly Gary to change his mind about Kelsey Payne, still I couldn't help but get in one final dig as I walked out. I spun my head around. "You've arrested the wrong man." True, it was cliché, but I couldn't come up with anything else at the moment.

"How'd it go?" Gladys asked when I reached the outer office.

"It didn't. Or I should say, *he* didn't. Believe me, that is. He wouldn't even consider another possibility regarding Roy Wilkes' murder."

Gladys motioned me closer to her window. "That's how Deputy Hickman is. Once he believes a case is ready to go to court, he never waivers. He's also compartmentalized, but not in a good sense. He has to finish one thing first before he tackles the next. At this juncture in time, my money is on David Whitaker's disappearance."

At that moment her phone rang. "Sorry, hon. Got to take this. Try to have a nice day."

David Whitaker's disappearance. That figured. A high-profile former school board member who suddenly vanished was bound to move to the top of the list. Meanwhile, Erlene Spencer could just take a number and stand in line. Or, rant and rave in his office for all it was worth.

As much as I loved our bistro food, sometimes there was nothing quite as good as an authentic Italian sub with all the fixings. I made a quick stop at Morgans' Market, a small neighborhood place that had been in the village of Penn Yan for decades, and ordered the giant size to go. That way, dinner would be covered as well. When I got home, there were two phone messages for me—Madeline Martinez and Stephanie Ipswich.

As I tore into my sub and guzzled a Coke, I hoped they weren't calling to fill me in on the latest winery disaster. At least it wasn't Catherine. The only thing I feared from her was a pre-arranged date with her son.

Chapter 24

Madeline's voice sounded chipper when I returned her call. "Thanks, Norrie, for getting back to me so soon. I'm phoning everyone in WOW about our next meeting. I hope you don't mind, but I really need to postpone it until after the Federweisser. We're absolutely swamped over here, not that it's going to get any easier in October, but by then, my in-laws will be on their way to Pompano Beach for the winter and I'll be able to pitch in."

"Sure. That's fine."

"I'm so glad you understand. Besides, I already spoke to Rosalee and she said she wouldn't be able to make it to the meeting anyway. Something about an appointment with her lawyer. She's really quite distraught over that arrest. It's not easy to find a capable and honest handyman."

"I think there's more to it than that." *Geez! Why oh why did I open my big mouth?*

"What do you mean?"

"The sheriff's office might have reason to believe Rosalee put him up to it in order to prevent her winery from closing. With Roy Wilkes out of the picture, the land situation could've been revisited."

"Poppycock. I don't care how devoted an employee may be, they're not going to commit murder to save their employer's rear end. Now, saving their own hide is quite a different story. If you ask me, Roy Wilkes' killer had to be someone who was looking after himself. Could be there was something going on between Kelsey Payne and Roy Wilkes. Guess all of that will come up in the trial. It's been all over the local news. You'd think they'd have something else to report on in the Finger Lakes."

"I'm not convinced it was Kelsey Payne."

"The article in yesterday's newspaper said they found his fingerprint on the victim's clothing. That would pretty much squash that evidence you mailed us a photo of—the little jacket tab. Stephanie says she's got a regular crew all lined up to look for the jacket during the Federweisser. I told her I thought that was unnecessary at this point, but she was going to chat with you."

Oh no! She's going to call it off. No bowlers. No quilters. No chance to scrutinize the guests. "Um, it was a blue Eddie Bauer windbreaker, and it might belong to the real killer."

"I hope for Rosalee's sake you're right. I'll tell my staff to keep their eyes open, but if I were you, I wouldn't be too optimistic."

By the time the call ended, not only wasn't I optimistic, I was ready to throw myself off the Main Street Bridge over the Keuka Lake Outlet in the center of Penn Yan. It was awful. Someone tried to kill me. The sheriff's deputy didn't believe me about the murder. And now, the only plan I really had to catch the killer was about to implode, thanks to Madeline Martinez's words of wisdom.

The Italian sub that I inhaled was now pressing on my chest and no amount of Tums was going to make it get any better. I picked up the phone and returned Stephanie's call.

"Norrie! Good. You got my message."

"Um, I got a message that you called, but not a message, message."

"It's the twins. I swear they're making me so scatterbrained lately. I called you about the Federweisser and the folks I had lined up to, uh, well, you know. Anyway, there's been a change. That's why I called."

I knew it. Why did Madeline have to open her mouth? One lousy fingerprint does not constitute a conviction. "Stephanie, just because Kelsey Payne got arrested doesn't make him the killer. That's why it's so important we follow through with this plan. I admit, I wasn't all gung ho at first, but now I really am. If we don't, he'll be railroaded and Rosalee might be the next one in line."

"Norrie, what are you talking about? Of course we're going through with the plan. That's why I called. Rosalee's an absolute basket case, even if she covers it up pretty well. I called to tell you the stupendous news."

"I could use stupendous news. What is it?"

"Okay, my husband's bowling team only has four members. But, get this! He talked to the league and got a few more of them to sign up."

"Like how many more?"

"Twelve. I think it's twelve, and that's not all. The quilters from my church belong to a quilting guild that takes in Seneca, Wayne and Schuyler counties, in addition to Yates and Ontario. Some of them offered to help out as well. Isn't that fantastic?"

Oh dear God! It'll be like the cast from Star Wars—*Stormtroopers and all.* "I'm almost afraid to ask, but do you have any idea how many?"

Stephanie paused for a moment and mumbled to herself before throwing out a number. "Twenty-three. I think it's twenty-three. Plus the twelve bowlers. That's thirty-five in all."

"Wow. Thirty-five."

"I know. I know. I don't think they have that much surveillance at the state fair."

Or that many free lunches we'll all be comping.

I envisioned a smaller group of people that would virtually go unnoticed, but thirty-five was substantial. Especially if they weren't exactly sure what their role would be, other than looking for a blue windbreaker and getting free food. I had planned on meeting with the original crew forty minutes before the Federweisser opened to the public so I could spell things out, but now it was even more paramount that I hold some sort of training or orientation or whatever-the-heck someone called what I was planning.

"Stephanie, we really have to have all those volunteers meet in my tasting room an hour before the Federweisser opens so I can explain what they should do. Or shouldn't, for that matter. Can you help?"

"Absolutely. Count me in. I'll e-mail you their names with either a B or a Q next to them so you'll know if they're a bowler or a quilter. I'll also e-mail all of them with explicit directions to be at your winery at least an hour before the event starts. So it would be nine, right?"

"Right. Nine o'clock. Tell them we'll have coffee for them."

"Sounds good."

Suddenly the Main Street Bridge over the Keuka Lake Outlet was no longer front and center in my mind. Instead, I wondered how on earth I was going to manage such a huge group of self-appointed spies. Even Agatha Christie had her limits.

I looked at the time and it was already past three. The day was practically wasted as far as my writing was concerned. Instead of firing up my laptop, I jogged down to our tasting room to see if I'd missed anything from the rumor mill.

Glenda spotted me the minute I walked through the door and gestured frantically for me to get over to her table. She was in the midst of a tasting with three middle-aged women and all of them were laughing and giggling.

Like Glenda's table, Cammy's was also occupied, as was Sam's. Roger had the day off, but everyone seemed to be doing okay with the crowd. It was a weekday afternoon, in between two major events, so it wasn't that hairy.

I approached Glenda's table cautiously, on the off chance she'd want to rid me of foul spirits or something equally bizarre in her realm of thinking. She was a sweet soul but, honestly, I wasn't prepared for the "Potteresque" experiences she seemed to thrive on.

"Must be the phase of the moon we're in because your love life is picking up," she said when I stationed myself next to her customers.

Picking up? From where? "Huh? What do you mean?"

"Don't be coy. First the flowers from that developer friend of yours two months ago and now a box of Aunt Lena's fudge. It's in the kitchen. Funny, but usually that stuff ships Fed Ex. One of those local delivery couriers brought it. The guy was only here two seconds and left. So, care to tell us who the new man in your life is? And to think, only last month I considered making a love potion for you. Kind of like pheromones but with better results."

The women at the tasting table looked at me as if I had three heads.

"I don't have a secret admirer, or an overt one for that matter, either. Fudge, huh? I'd better check it out."

I walked into the kitchen and, sure enough, there was a bright blue box on the counter that said "Aunt Lena's Fudge, a Martha's Vineyard Favorite." It was tied up with a white ribbon and a small card was attached with my name on it. I opened the card and read the typed message. All it said was, "Enjoy this with my compliments." Hardly a love note. And whose compliments? Who the heck sent it?

My first, and only, thought was Bradley Jamison. But why didn't he own up to it? Then I thought of Rosalee. Was this her way of thanking me? Nah. She'd given me those wonderful cinnamon rolls, but I seriously doubted she had time to place an Internet fudge order for herself or anyone else. That left, well, absolutely no one. Still, it didn't stop me from untying the ribbon and walking the box out to the tasting room. Maybe I did have a secret admirer. *Oh dear God. Please don't let it be Sam or Roger. Especially Roger.*

There was a slight lull in the room as the customers had all completed their tastings and were perusing the wine racks and gift items.

"Hey, guys," I said. "Someone sent me fudge. We might as well enjoy it. I'll grab a knife from the kitchen. I should've snagged one while I was in there. Give me a second."

I handed the box to Cammy, who put it on her table, while the others quickly gathered around. "Go ahead, open it up. I'll be right back."

When I walked back into the tasting room, everyone looked at me as if it were a funeral.

"What?" I asked. "Was this a joke? Was there a dead mouse in there or something?"

"No," Cammy said, "but something's not right. My aunt Luisa orders fudge from Aunt Lena's all the time. Pumpkin, Cappuccino, Bittersweet Chocolate…you name it, she orders it. She spent a vacation on Martha's Vineyard a few years ago and got hooked on the stuff."

I looked at the classy blue package and shrugged. "So, what's wrong with this box?"

"The box is genuine, all right," Cammy said, "but I'm not so sure about the contents. Aunt Lena's fudge doesn't come packaged in those thin roundish slabs like you see in your box. They come in one huge chunk and it's wrapped in wax paper with the store's logo on it. Your fudge is wrapped in plain wax paper."

"Are you saying what I think you're saying?"

"I don't know what I'm saying, but I wouldn't eat it if I were you."

I pushed the lid down hard on the box and grabbed it. "Did anyone get a good look at the delivery guy?"

A chorus of "sorry" and "no" followed.

Lizzie seemed particularly rattled. "I should've been more observant. Nancy Drew would've been observant. I'll do better next time, Norrie. Honestly."

"Might as well throw that sucker in the trash and call it a day," Sam said, "unless you want to bring it to the sheriff's office to have them check for food poisoning."

"I've got a better idea," I said. "Meanwhile, beware of Greeks bearing gifts."

"Good thing Roger has the day off," Glenda said, "or he'd be telling us that awful story about those blankets tainted with smallpox that some British commander gave to the Indians. I mean, Native Americans. I don't know why I can't say 'Indians.' It was the French and Indian War, not the French and Native American War. Good grief, after working with Roger, I feel as if I could write a book."

"We could write a thesis," Sam said. "And it was William Trent, a militia captain. I had to listen to Roger for two whole hours the day before yesterday."

The three or four minute lull ended abruptly when customers approached the tables.

"Next time I'll bring in a box of donuts," I said. "Have a good afternoon, everyone."

As I headed out the door with the fudge tucked under my arm, Cammy tapped me on the shoulder. "Seriously, girl, you should have that checked out. Maybe someone's trying to give you a not-so-subtle message to leave things alone as far as the Roy Wilkes' murder is concerned."

"Yeah, well, we both know that's not going to happen." I held the box of fudge in the air. "I've got this covered. Don't worry."

Okay, so maybe I lied. I didn't have anything covered, but I did have a thought. The minute I got back to the house, I picked up the phone and called Godfrey Klein at the entomology department.

"Norrie! Are you calling about the image I sent you of the Aedes bahamensis? I got it off to you in a rush, but I can send you better images."

"Oh no. Please don't. I mean, the image was fine. Just fine."

"Oh good. Are you calling about Jason and your sister? Nothing much to report really. We're getting their transmissions and everything seems to be going smoothly."

Yep, as long as they've got enough DEET for an army. "Actually, the real reason I called was to ask for your help. I know you're in the entomology department, but I was hoping you might know someone in the chemistry department who could help me out with something extremely confidential."

Without going overboard, I gave Godfrey the gist of what had happened regarding my brakes and now the possibility that someone might've sent me a poisoned box of fudge.

"Shouldn't you be going to the police?"

"It's a long story, but they don't believe me. So, can you help?"

"I think so. A colleague of mine works for the department of food science. Let me give him a call and I'll get right back to you. Are you going to be at this number?"

"Um, yeah. I'm home. But you have my cell number, too, right?"

"Indeed I do. It's with Jason's file."

"Thanks, Godfrey. You have no idea how much I appreciate this."

It must've been a really slow day at the Experiment Station because Godfrey called me back less than twenty minutes later.

"Can you get over here with that box of fudge in the next thirty minutes? Michael Liu, that's my colleague, said he'd stop by on his way home."

"I'm on my way!"

"Wait! Hold on a second. You'll need to bring your identification with you when you enter the building. Some people leave their driver's licenses in their cars and have to walk all the way back to get them. Didn't want that to happen to you. The security in this building is very tight."

For bugs? They're worried about someone stealing bugs? "Uh, thanks for the heads-up. I'll be right over."

The mere thought of going into the entomology building made my skin crawl. I envisioned tons of corkboard and Styrofoam boxes with all sorts of dead insects set out for display—wings spread wide open and tiny pins holding them in place.

I was being silly, but I wiped some of Francine's Burt's Bees Insect Repellent on my arms before I left the house.

Chapter 25

Godfrey Klein lived up to the mental image I had of him from when we first talked. He was shorter than me by a few inches, was slightly overweight, had a round face and had a receding hairline with wispy light brown hair that looked as if he'd been through a wind tunnel. Round, dark brown glasses completed the look. He was Jason's age and, judging by the two framed posters of assorted beetles that hung on the wall behind his desk, shared the same enthusiasm my brother-in-law did for his profession.

"It's so nice to meet you in person, Norrie. Would you like a tour of the facility? We have the most amazing specimens you'll find anywhere."

"Oh, gee, as much as I'd love to, I really need to get back to the winery. It's our busy season, you know."

I handed him the box of fudge and thanked him again.

"I'm glad I could help you out. Poisoned, huh? How unnerving, to say the least. Michael should be here any time now if you want to wait."

"Again, thanks, but I really need to get going. Do you have any idea when he'll be done with the analysis?"

"He's going to get started on it tonight. He's going home for dinner and then he'll be back in his lab. Forensic toxicology isn't his field but he's got the equipment and the expertise to conduct a preliminary scan for major toxins."

"That's fantastic."

"Norrie, just because he's getting started on it tonight, don't expect a fast turnaround time. These things can take days...weeks."

"I don't have weeks. Can you tell him that?"

"Sure. Look, this isn't any of my business, but if I were you, I'd make sure I knew where my food was coming from. And I'd only eat candies that were properly sealed."

"You sound like my mother when we went out trick or treating for Halloween."

Godfrey's face flushed slightly. "Yeesh, I'm beginning to sound like *my* mother."

I had to admit, I liked the guy. Not in a Bradley Jamison sweep-me-off-my-feet kind of way, but there was definitely something endearing about Godfrey Klein. Even if he worked with bugs.

Since the Experiment Station was only a few blocks from Wegmans, I phoned Theo and Don to ask if they'd like to drive up the hill to my place for an impromptu dinner. Impromptu meaning an assortment of culinary dishes that the Wegmans chefs prepared for takeout.

"Wegmans takeout?" Theo asked and, in the background, I heard Don shouting, "Tell her yes."

From chicken French to Cavatappi pasta with vodka blush sauce, I brought home an assortment that would make anyone's mouth water. I even paid close attention to selecting vegetables that were eye-catching as well as tasty.

"You remembered my favorite," Theo said as we sat around the kitchen table. "Butternut squash with baby spinach and Craisins."

"It's the least I can do. You and Don feed me all the time."

I also indulged Charlie with pieces of boneless turkey breast I put into his kibble. It was the only way to stop him from begging at the table.

When we had finished our second, and in the case of Don, third, helpings, I put my fork down and groaned.

"Eat too much?" Theo asked.

"Yeah, but that's not why I'm groaning. There's something I need to tell you. I think someone's trying to kill me."

"What???" Theo and Don's voices exploded across the room.

"I was going to tell you about the first incident when I found out about it this morning, but then the second thing happened."

"What thing? What incident?" Theo asked.

"The first attempt on my life happened yesterday, but I didn't know it was sabotage. Vehicular sabotage, to be precise." I then expounded on the incident worse than when Roger went on one of his rants about the French and Indian War. Before Theo or Don could say anything, I told them about the fudge and how Godfrey Klein's chemistry colleague was going to give it the once-over for poisoning.

Don pushed his plate toward the center of the table and straightened his arms. "Unbelievable. This is absolutely unbelievable. What gets me is the fact that Deputy Hickman dismissed the whole car thing as if you reported someone smoking in the boys' room."

"If you must know the truth," I said, "I'm getting kind of freaked out about this. The worst part is, he wouldn't believe me at all about the evidence Theo and I found. Or Bethany's statement."

"We still have a last-ditch attempt," Theo said. "The whole blooming county and then some shows up for the Federweisser. In fact, last year we had winemakers and vineyard managers from all over the lake, not to mention the locals and the tourists. Don't worry. We'll find out who really murdered Roy Wilkes."

"I hope so. Because the wrong guy is headed for prison. And worse yet, his brother may be the one who's trying to get me out of the way. You don't suppose Cal's the real killer, do you? Remember that fight he had with Roy Wilkes? And the timing of the murder? He could've done the deed once he got done locking lips with Bethany."

"Cal doesn't strike me as a murderer," Theo said. "True, I don't really know him but I do know about his reputation. He's been Rosalee's vineyard manager forever."

"It doesn't mean he's innocent," I said. "He was there at the courthouse around the time my car was tampered with."

"You think he'd really let his brother take the blame for something he did?" Theo asked.

I let out a slow breath, plopped my elbows onto the table, made two fists, and rested my head on top of them. "I honestly don't know. And if it was him, who was the other person?"

Theo and Don looked at each other and shook their heads.

"Guess only time will tell," Don said. "So, about the Federweisser, Theo and I talked about it and decided that he's going to be there all day in case the murderer shows up."

"Don, you don't have to—"

"Oh yes, we do. We've got the Grey Egret covered and besides, the giant crowd is going to be at your place all day. Think about it. What if one of those bowlers or quilters spies someone in that blue windbreaker? Then what? At least you and Theo will be able to detain them or whatever you had planned."

"Um, that's the trouble. I haven't planned anything. Not really."

"Good. It'll give you and Theo something to think about all week. You've only got about a week and a half."

"Aargh. Don't remind me."

"By the way, what were you able to find out about the dates of employment for Roy Wilkes and David Whitaker?" he asked.

"Oh no! Not again! Not a second time. I am such a dunderhead! When Hank Walden called about my car this morning, everything else in my brain shut down. I swear that won't happen again."

I stood up and grabbed a piece of scrap paper from the counter. In bold print I wrote "Beecher Rand" and used one of Francine's magnets to stick it to the refrigerator. "There," I said, "unless all hell breaks loose, their human resources department will hear from me in the morning."

"I wish our newspaper searches yielded something more than what we already knew," Theo said. "The only thing I managed to pull up was an old police report that referenced a minor disturbance in one of the break rooms at the Athens, Pennsylvania, facility and guess what? Roy Wilkes was cited for grabbing a photo from a woman, which apparently caused her distress so she phoned the police. They showed up, talked to both parties, and dropped the whole thing as being inconsequential, but it still made the news. Talk about making a mountain out of a mole hill. Small town news and all that."

"First I've heard of it," Don said.

Theo gave him a pat on the hand. "Uh, sorry. I must've forgotten. I'm getting as bad as Norrie."

"Hello. I'm right here, you two."

We topped off the night with a mini dessert tray that featured tiny Wegmans cheesecakes and assorted mousses. If nothing else, I knew how to shop.

"Do you think I'm putting all my eggs in one basket?" I asked when the guys got up to leave. "I mean, pinning my hopes that the killer will be wearing that windbreaker?"

"It's the only thing we've got, Norrie," Theo said. "That hang-tab had fallen to the ground recently. It was spotless. Let's trust our instincts on this one."

It was past eleven when I finally got to bed and turned off the lights. Charlie took his usual spot on my feet and was oblivious to the numerous attempts I made to get him to move to the other side of the bed. At the very moment when I finally got the leg room I needed in order to sleep, the phone rang. *Now what?* I didn't hear any fire alarms or any alarms, for that matter, but a phone call after eleven was never good.

"Norrie! It's me. Cammy."

"My God! What's happened?"

"Nothing. Nothing like that. And I'm sorry it's so darn late, but you won't mind once I tell you what I found out. I'm at Rosinetti's. Long story. One of my idiot cousins, Nico, dropped a bottle and cut his hand so they were short a bartender for the rest of the night. Family, you know. I couldn't say no."

"Is he—"

"He'll be fine. Forget about Nico. I called you because I found out what Roy Wilkes and David Whitaker were fighting about that night and you won't believe it."

I was now sitting bolt upright on the edge of my bed and taking in her every word.

"Two women, on and off again regulars, were talking about it tonight. They were reminiscing about bar fights they'd seen. Anyway, they were more than happy to include me in their conversation. Are you ready for this? Roy Wilkes was already at the bar when David Whitaker came in. The women were a few seats away. David took the seat next to Roy and said something like, 'I've been asking around and I knew I'd find you here.'"

"Oh my gosh. Go on. Go on."

"So then Roy said something like, 'So, what's the big deal?' Then the bartender took David's order and walked away. David then gave Roy a poke in the arm and said, 'What's the big deal? What's going on with you and my wife?'"

"Whoa."

"I know. I know. So then Roy said, 'Ask your wife if you want to know.'"

"Then what? Then what did they say?"

"They stopped talking and got physical. So, was it worth me calling you so late?"

"Oh hell yes! We can put the puzzle together. Roy Wilkes was having an affair with David Whitaker's wife, and that's what got him killed. I still don't understand who the second person was. Kelsey Payne said there were two of them."

"The wife? Maybe Roy and the wife were getting it on behind the pump house and got caught in the act by the husband."

"At dawn? It's downright chilly in the mornings. Doesn't sound like a place for a rendezvous."

"No, it sure doesn't."

"Maybe David Whitaker and some strong-armed buddy of his knew about the pump house and threatened to do some serious damage to it if Roy Wilkes didn't show up. It's a possibility, isn't it?"

"Heck, anything's a possibility, but now we have something ironclad—a motive. David Whitaker had a damn good motive for murdering Roy Wilkes. Cammy, I could give you a hug right over this phone line!"

"Thought you'd appreciate the call. Get some sleep."

Was she nuts? After a call like that, Cal Payne slid into second place. My mind bounced around with more scenarios for love triangle murders than Danielle Steel and Jackie Collins combined. I finally managed to slip into a light sleep around three, only to be awakened at five by the sound of the harvester, fast at work. Another glorious day in the wineries.

Chapter 26

As much as I wanted to call Deputy Hickman and tell him I found the real motive for murder and that it had nothing to do with Rosalee's winery, I knew I'd be wasting my time. Instead, I focused on my writing, with occasional trips to the tasting room each day in order to give the crew some breaks.

Theo and Don both agreed with Cammy that David Whitaker was the likely killer. Instead of penning a country western song about his cheating spouse, he could've gotten straight to the point and eliminated the competition. That being said, why was someone going through a heck of a lot of trouble to mess with me? It couldn't be David, since he'd been AWOL for over a week. As far as I was concerned, Cal Payne wasn't out of the picture.

I poured myself a Coke and watched the bubbles rise to the surface. One popped. Another one appeared. Then it hit me—Kelsey said there were two people behind the pump house. Sure, one of them disappeared, but the other one, the *partner in crime*, might very well have been Cal. And he had his own reasons to loathe Roy Wilkes.

It was a longshot, but if Cal Payne were to show up at the Federweisser wearing the blue windbreaker, it would be "game over." Too bad Rosalee never mentioned him owning one when I sent that e-mail around about the hang-tab. Then again, I didn't pay attention to what our vineyard crew wore.

The grim mood I was in lifted slightly. At least there were no more attempts on my life. I credited that to the fact I rarely left the house. It was Thursday afternoon and I seriously considered updating my Facebook profile to read "Homebody." Thankfully the phone rang before I went any further with my idea.

"Norrie? It's me. Godfrey Klein. Listen, I don't want to alarm you, but you were right. That fudge was tampered with. Sorry it took so long for the analysis, but, like I told you, those processes take a great deal of time. Michael e-mailed me the report and I can forward it to you. I know Jason left your e-mail address with his contact information."

"What was it? Arsenic? They always use arsenic. Rat poisoning? Cyanide? What?"

"Ex-lax. Well, not exactly Ex-lax, Dulcolax. I don't think Ex-lax is still on the market."

"A laxative? That's what was in there? That sounds like a middle school prank. Who would pull such a sophomoric stunt?"

"Um, it wasn't a stunt. Not according to Michael. There was enough bisacodyl in there to cause some serious damage, anything ranging from dehydration to—"

"Just spit it out and say it! Death! It could cause death!"

"Um, that isn't exactly where I was going with this, still…it's a concern."

I tightened my grip on the receiver and didn't say a word.

"Norrie? Are you still there? Are you all right?"

"What? Yeah, sure. It's sinking in, that's all."

"What's sinking in?"

"Remember that murder at Terrace Wineries a couple of weeks ago? Well, I might have stumbled upon the real killer, even though they've arrested someone else. What's worse is that the lead deputy on the case refuses to look farther than his nose."

"Is there anything I can do to help?"

"You've already helped, and I really appreciate it. In fact, why don't you come to the Federweisser this Saturday? Bring some of your colleagues. Lunch will be on me."

"This Saturday, huh? I've got to release some ladybird beetles into the community gardens that day, but I should have enough time."

"Great. Catch you then. And thank your friend Michael for me, will you?"

"Sure thing. Oh, and by the way, he's secured the evidence if you decide to call the sheriff's department."

"Okay. Thanks." *Sheriff's department, my you-know-what.*

Sticky stuff on my brakes and now Dulcolax. Whoever tried to harm, or worse yet, *kill* me, had to be an absolute amateur or a blithering idiot. Still, it didn't make them any less dangerous. I'd ruled out David Whitaker because it was tough to pull a vanishing act and attempt to kill someone at the same time. Even Penn and Teller would be hard-pressed. I tried to tell myself that whoever did those dastardly things to me was only trying to scare me. Got news for you. It worked. I *was* scared. And not just for me, for the entire winery. I tried not to dwell on it, turning my thoughts instead to Kelsey Payne. Well, not exactly Kelsey Payne. His legal counsel—Bradley Jamison.

Bradley had no idea about the brakes or the fudge. Maybe it was time he did. If nothing else, it would substantiate the fact that that there was someone "out there" who wanted to prevent me from snooping around. And that someone couldn't possibly be Kelsey.

It was four fifty-six when I made the call, informing the secretary who I was and that the matter was extremely important.

"Hold on for just a moment, would you?" she asked. "I thought Mr. Jamison was on his way out. Our office closes at five."

Terrific. Banker's hours. I tapped on the floor and took a breath while I waited for him to pick up.

"Hi, Norrie! The secretary said it was urgent. Is everything all right?"

"For now, anyway. Hey, I'm sorry I caught you on your way out, but I'm more convinced than ever that Kelsey Payne isn't our guy."

Before Bradley could say a word, I told him about the gooey stuff on my brakes and the Dulcolax poisoning.

"Really? The stuff is that lethal? I'm sorry, you just caught me off guard. I don't suppose you're willing to notify the sheriff's department. One incident could be a prank, but two…they have to listen to you."

Again with the sheriff's department. "Um, yeah. I suppose you're right. But I don't think it'll do anything to further our cause as far as Kelsey's innocence is concerned."

"It's a starting point. I'll be sure to convey it to his criminal attorney once he or she is officially hired."

"Okay, then. Um, have a nice evening."

"Norrie, wait a sec. What time did you tell me that big event of yours starts? I know it's the day after tomorrow."

"The Federweisser? At ten in the morning. Goes on all day, with food and entertainment. Not to mention wine tours. Are you, um, planning on coming?"

"As a matter of fact, I am. I thought I'd bring my—"

And like that, he stopped mid-sentence. "Uh, sorry. Marvin needs to catch me for a minute. See you on Saturday."

Bring your what? Girlfriend? Fiancée? Who? Like I don't already know. I saw her cute smiley face on your cell phone. Pam. That's who.

Pam. With the tussled blond hair. At least she gave me something to think about other than another possible attempt on my life. I knew Godfrey and Bradley were right about calling the sheriff's department, but I really wasn't ready for another lecture from my favorite deputy. Besides, he'd have to pick up the evidence and the Experiment Station would be closed until morning. I figured it could wait.

I took a sip of my Coke and went back to my laptop when I realized something—Bradley Jamison didn't sound the least bit concerned about Kelsey's predicament. Almost as if he resigned himself to the fact that nothing, short of a miracle, was going to get that guy out of a full-blown trial. I didn't want to admit it, but I was beginning to feel the same way.

The term "snowball's chance in hell" bounced around my head every time I thought about the one paltry little clue we had. *If* it was a clue at all. I prayed to the gods the Federweisser wouldn't turn out to be a colossal bust as far as catching the killer was concerned. If it did, I could always ask Glenda to contact Roy Wilkes' deceased spirit.

I went to bed that night with a slight pounding in my head, but it was real pounding that woke me up at a little past five. A rhythmic thud that wouldn't stop. I knew it wasn't the sound of our harvester or any other machinery for that matter. Those sounds I had gotten used to. Even the dog looked up from the foot of the bed every few minutes. The sound woke him, too, but obviously didn't concern him.

Pulling the curtains back, I squinted at the hazy dawn and scanned the vineyards. A huge blue and white striped tent had appeared out of nowhere, connecting the tasting room building to the winery. *Oh my God! The Federweisser tent!* John told me he'd made arrangements with Carter's Canopies to put up the tent Friday morning, but somehow it slipped my mind.

"Carter's crew should have the tent and the stage areas ready to go by midday," he had said. "Then our vineyard guys will bring in the folding tables and chairs from the back of the barn, as well as the large propane grill. We should be all set way before closing time."

I must've glossed over that conversation, but I did remember Cammy telling me something about tablecloths and centerpieces. Was I supposed to do something? It was early enough in the day, an obscene time, really, that I didn't have to worry about it. I fed the dog, ate an early breakfast and took a long shower before venturing down to the tasting room.

With the fall rush, Cammy had arrived an hour earlier to restock and setup. She was already at work when I walked into the tasting room.

"Did you catch the forecast for tomorrow?" she asked as soon as I waved.

"Oh no. Please don't tell me it's going to pour. That's the last thing we need."

"Partially sunny and breezy. Highs in the low seventies, with winds picking up, and a forty percent chance of rain in the late afternoon."

"Late? How late? How do they define late?"

"I'm hoping their definition of late is any time after we close. Hey, don't get all worked up. It's the Finger Lakes. Those forecasts change every hour. Besides, we've got the tent, and the grill's located under the overhang by the winery building. We'll be fine."

"Except for the turnout. Any mention of rain and people stay home. You'd think they were afraid of melting."

"Relax, Norrie. It'll be okay."

"If you say so. Um, was I supposed to help out with centerpieces or anything like that because I can't remember."

"Nope. We're all set. Fred and Emma have got the food under control and their assistants are topnotch, according to Fred."

"That's a relief."

"Oh, before I forget, the reporter from the *Finger Lakes Times* called to let us know they'll be sending a photographer over sometime tomorrow. They couldn't be more specific than that."

"Great. The reporter can take a picture of Bradley Jamison and his girlfriend enjoying our wine."

"Huh?" Cammy raised her eyebrows. "He has a girlfriend? Did he tell you that?"

"He started to but got interrupted. I called to tell him about my brakes and the fudge being poisoned when—"

"WHAT? You didn't say anything about the fudge being poisoned. So I was right after all. Was it arsenic? That seems to be a popular poison. Agatha Christie and all that. And how'd you find out, anyway?"

"From one of Jason's scientist friends at the Experiment Station. And no, it wasn't arsenic. It was Dulcolax. And before you start laughing, it was serious. Apparently too much of that stuff can do serious damage."

"Ugh. Remind me to stick to prunes if I have to. Did you let the sheriff's office know?"

Great! The third person insisting I call the sheriff. "Um, not yet. I'm not exactly Deputy Hickman's person of the year. And it's not as if he can do anything about these threats. He'll only tell me to be careful. Duh. What I really need to do…what we *all* really need to do…is to be on the lookout for anyone wearing that Eddie Bauer jacket without its hang-tab. I doubt David Whitaker will be waltzing through the door, but Cal Payne might, and if it's not him, then maybe we'll get lucky and find out who it really is. One way or the other, it's got to be the accomplice or the killer."

"And to think of it, up until a few weeks ago, the highpoint of the occasion would've been the wine," she said.

"Very funny."

"So you're all set with your never-ending cadre of spies?"

I steepled my fingers and gave her a smile. "If you're referring to the bowlers and the quilters, the answer is yes. I spoke with Stephanie last night, and our volunteers agreed to be in the tasting room at eight thirty for the briefing."

"The briefing? As in Pentagon and White House briefings?"

"It sounded better than breakfast meeting. Especially since we're not giving them breakfast, only coffee and donuts. And Fred's got that covered."

Cammy shook her head and smiled. "I'll give you this much, you certainly know how to persevere."

Yeah. Too bad I don't know how to catch a killer.

Chapter 27

The first clue that the covert operation I had loosely planned for the Federweisser might not go down as I expected came when two elderly women pulled me aside the moment I stepped into the tasting room at precisely eight fifteen the following morning—Federweisser morning.

"You must be Norrie," the first woman said. "You look exactly the way that lady over there described you."

She pointed to Cammy, who was refilling some of the T-shirt bins.

I gave a quick nod.

"I'm Eunice and this is Cecile. We're from the Schoolhouse Quilters in Seneca Falls. We brought our binoculars with us and told the other three ladies from our guild to do the same. Did you want us to station ourselves in a particular place and scan the area? We got here especially early to be sure. Of course, we'll need a description of the suspect. We *are* on the lookout for a murderer, aren't we?"

Then she poked Cecile in the arm. "Isn't this the most exciting thing we've ever done? And aren't you glad I told you to bring your seam ripper with you in case you got attacked?"

If my jaw had dropped any lower, it would've hit my chest. I didn't want to sound ungrateful, but Eunice's enthusiasm really scared me. "Well, thanks. And welcome. Coffee and donuts will be served right over there in the bistro." I pointed across the room to where Fred and Emma were setting up. "You won't need binoculars and certainly not seam rippers. All you'll be doing is mingling around and keeping an eye open for anyone wearing a blue windbreaker that's missing its front pocket hang-tab. I'll explain more when everyone gets here."

In the next fifteen minutes, bowlers and quilters streamed into the tasting room. I welcomed them and ushered them over to the food.

One hefty guy, who looked as if he bench pressed on a daily basis, grabbed me by the wrist. "I've got a concealed weapon permit and my Glock is locked up in my car, but I can get it if you'd like."

I assured him it wasn't necessary. Then it got worse. Another man told me he had a black belt in Tae Kwon Do and was itching to put it to good use. Three women informed me they were knitters and had stashed their knitting needles in their handbags "just in case."

By eight thirty I was convinced Stephanie Ipswich had inadvertently gathered an assortment of rogues and self-styled crime hunters. It was frightening.

"Good morning, everyone!" I called out as the unofficial crew helped themselves to an assortment of donuts and coffee. "I really appreciate you giving up your Saturday to help us out."

I then went on to explain what a covert operation was and more specifically, what it wasn't. "So you see, all you need to do is keep an eye out for someone, male or female, wearing the aforementioned windbreaker. If you spot them, don't approach them. Let Cammy or me know. Cammy's the brunette in the tasting room. The one with her hair pulled into a bun. She's wearing an orange T-shirt that matches the ribbon on her bun. If you can't locate either of us, tell whoever's working on the cash register and they'll know what to do."

For the most part, it would be Lizzie at the cash register, but, in case she was on a break, it could be any of our tasting room employees. All of them were told to remain calm and find me.

"Are we being assigned to a particular position?" someone asked.

"No, not at all. Please wander around the place as if you were one of the partygoers. Feel free to take a wine tour, enjoy the polka music, everything we have to offer. It's best that all of you are scattered throughout the event. I've got lunch tickets for everyone, as well as drink tickets. Also, coupons for fifteen percent off our wines. It's the least we can do. Keep in mind, you're observers, not a militia. Everyone understand?"

A cacophony of uh-huhs, yeahs and okays followed, but I had a dreadful feeling this crew was going to be as unpredictable as they come.

"Enjoy your coffee," I said. "The event starts at ten and the entertainment tent is through those back doors. I'll be right here handing out your tickets. Again, thanks."

The group was orderly as they waited in a makeshift line to pick up their meal tickets. Unfortunately, a few side comments really rattled me.

Things like, "Mary Sue carries a can of mace with her if she needs to spray it," and "No one can wield a two by four like Timmy."

By the time I got done handing out the tickets, I was downright jittery. So jittery, in fact, that I nearly jumped out of my skin when Theo approached me from behind.

"Whoa! Didn't mean to scare you. That polka band sounds really good, by the way. I heard them practicing as I was coming up here. It's gorgeous outside, so I walked. I don't suppose you could hear them from inside the building. Trust me, they're great."

"That's a relief. At least one thing's going right."

"What do you mean?"

"I don't know. I'm kind of worried about our volunteer spies. Some of them think this is *Mission Impossible*."

"Relax. Once everything gets underway, they'll be fine. All they have to do is look-see."

"Tell them that."

"Come on, you can fill me in over coffee. I spied that collection of donuts and one of them's got my name on it."

Theo was in absolute stitches when I got done recounting my introduction to Stephanie's operatives, for lack of a better word. "Hey, if nothing else, there'll be lots of eyes on the visitors. And as soon as I'm done with my donut, I'll be playing *I Spy*, too. Stop worrying, Norrie!"

If nothing else, the weather forecast was right. It was cool with partial sunshine and a breeze. Perfect weather for wearing a windbreaker. I left the tasting room and bistro in order to check out the tent and the festivities, but instead of cutting through the building, I walked outside to get a look at the parking lot.

It was filling up fast, and we didn't open for another twenty minutes. Thankfully John had roped off a portion of our unused land, adjacent to the barn, for extra parking. I glanced at Alvin. He was busily munching on some fresh hay. His enclosure looked better than ever since John and his crew rebuilt much of it following that disaster two months ago when I was attacked and Alvin broke through his pen.

I prayed we wouldn't have anything quite as dramatic with this event. And for the first two or three hours, my prayers were answered. The Polka Meisters from Buffalo were really as good as Theo said. They played all sorts of old favorites, which prompted the audience to get on the large platform and dance. Not only that, but they had singers, too, and even a few comedians.

The tantalizing aroma from the sausages cooking on the grill permeated the tent. So far so good. Inside the tasting room, the canapes were quickly getting gobbled up and our tasting room tables were filled to capacity. I was on "standby" duty if needed, but Cammy reassured me they had plenty of part-time college students working. That left me plenty of time to scout out the area for Roy Wilkes' elusive killer.

In theory, that was exactly what I should've been doing, but the reality was, I got sidetracked by all of the winery friends and acquaintances who came by so that the event would be a success. Madeline Martinez had two handfuls of sausage cheese balls when I spotted her outside the far end of the tent in front of the Chardonnay barrel that held our precious Federweisser.

Herbert and Alan were assigned to the task of pouring out the Federweisser and serving it. Since it wasn't bottled, and the barrel was adjacent to the winery, it made sense for the winemakers to handle that task.

"Norrie!" Madeline shouted when she spied me. "The Federweisser is outstanding! Bubbly and bright! If it wasn't so deceptive, I'd be drinking it by the gallon."

"I know. People forget there's an alcohol content to it."

"Have you seen Catherine or Stephanie? I know they're both here because I ran into them a few minutes ago in the tasting room. Still no news on catching that killer, huh?"

"Not as far as I know."

"Well, if it's any consolation, we're all on the lookout. By the way, I think that goat of yours has gotten bigger. My husband mentioned something about us purchasing some llamas for the winery, and I told him if he did, he could count on sleeping outside with them. It's enough work growing grapes and turning them into wine."

No truer words said.

Just then, I heard someone calling my name and when I spun my head around to see where the voice was coming from, I saw Mallory and Bethany from the blue ranch house waving to me.

"Excuse me, Madeline," I said. "I need to get over there. Enjoy the Federweisser and thanks so much for coming."

"My pleasure!"

I walked to the opening in the tent where Mallory and Bethany were standing. "Hi there! So glad you could make it."

"Did the e-mail I sent you work?" Bethany asked. "I mean, did the sheriff's department release the wrongly accused guy?"

I shook my head. "Not yet. But it'll help the guy's defense lawyer, that's for sure. Listen, we owe you some complimentary wine. Ask for Cammy in the tasting room before you leave. She'll take care of it."

"Sure thing. Say, this party's a blast. I never thought I'd be into polka music, but it's like you can't stop dancing once you start. Oh my gosh! Do you hear that? They're playing the 'Macarena'. I don't want to miss it." Then she grabbed Mallory by the arm and gave her friend a tug. "Hurry up, Mallory. Get a move on!"

Looking around, it was obvious people were having fun. Kelsey Payne was all but rotting in a jail cell, but as far as the attendees at our Federweisser were concerned, all was right with the world. I stepped inside the tent and stood for a minute watching the "Macarena." Or, to be more precise, watching to see if any of the Macarena dancers had on a blue windbreaker. No luck. I moved to the tasting room.

No sooner did I get one foot in the door than Catherine Trobert caught me by the arm and wouldn't let go. "I knew I'd find you sooner or later. Too bad Steven isn't here to enjoy this with you. But never fear, he'll definitely be home for the holidays in December."

Dear God. Where can I escape to in December? Aruba, Jamaica? My God, I'm reciting that Beach Boys song. And yes, Kokomo. I'll go there. I'll go anywhere. "Um, sure…December."

"Did you get to see Stephanie? She was here earlier but had to leave. Her babysitter called. Threatened to quit. Stephanie said she'll try to get back later today. But you know who else is here? Rosalee's sister, Marilyn. With some friend of hers. A big woman who reminds me of a woodcutter. What was her name? Oh yes, Erlene. Erlene Spencer."

Terrific. No sign of Bradley Jamison, but Erlene Spencer's here. Must be my lucky day. "Did Marilyn or Erlene mention if Rosalee plans to stop by?"

"They didn't say. Anyway, I can't wait to taste the Federweisser."

"It's on the other side of the tent. Walk straight through and you can't miss it."

"Wonderful. And remember, December's less than four months away."

Terrific. I'll buy a giant wall calendar.

The aroma from those sausages had really gotten to me, and I charged over to the bistro as fast as I could. Not that it mattered. I waited in line like everyone else for a sausage on a bun. That was when I overheard someone talking about "the windstorm that was supposed to hit Seneca Lake sometime late in the day."

I immediately clicked the weather app on my phone but couldn't seem to pull up an hourly forecast the way I could on my laptop. Instead, I got the temperature and some idiotic graphic of light rain. I tried to tell myself that "late in the day" could be anything, but all I envisioned was that humongous tent coming loose from its tethers and landing on everyone.

I'd seen videos of bouncy houses lifting off the ground with toddlers still inside, but I tried not to think about it.

"Hi, Norrie!" Fred said when I finally reached the front of the line. "It's going great, isn't it?"

He handed me a sausage sandwich. The giant link was barbequed exactly the way I liked it, brownish on the skin and a few splits. I couldn't wait to sit down so I took a bite. The warm juices started to run down my chin and I wiped them with the back of my hand. Francine would have rolled her eyes.

"You haven't heard anything about a rain or windstorm, have you?" I asked.

"Sorry, no. I've been too busy running back and forth to the grill. Don't worry. Those reports are always exaggerated. Besides, last night's news said late in the day. I take that to mean after dark."

"Geez, I hope you're right."

"Any luck with your other endeavor? You know, the blue windbreaker."

"Nope. Nothing yet, but we still have three hours left."

I didn't want to hold up the line, so I told him I'd catch up later and stepped aside so the next in line could get a sausage. I thought I caught a glimpse of Marilyn Ansley and Erlene Spencer near the T-shirt bins, but when I got closer, they were gone. Instead, I found myself face-to-face with none other than Bradley Jamison and the adorable blonde. I wanted to puke.

"Norrie! I was looking all over for you," he said. "We've been here for over an hour. What a terrific event. This is Pam, she's—"

I cut in before he finished the words. I really didn't want to hear them.

"It's nice to meet you, Pam. I hope you're enjoying your visit to our winery."

"I am. Thanks. This is the first chance I've had to see Brad in ages. When he called to suggest it, I couldn't wait to drive down here. I'm only in Cazenovia but it feels like a zillion miles away."

I'll bet it does.

Bradley gave her a quick glance. At least he wasn't holding her hand or nuzzling her. "Pam teaches fifth grade and when she's not in the classroom, she's working on lessons. Even our parents don't get to see her as much anymore."

What? What did I miss? "Your parents?"

"Good grief. I never made a full introduction. Pam's my older sister, by a year."

"Your sister. How wonderful. How absolutely wonderful. That she could be here, I mean."

Pam reached out and shook my hand. "Brad's told me all about you and how you've been working day and night to catch a killer. I've got to admit, I'm impressed."

And at this very moment, I'm relieved. "Don't be. I haven't gotten anywhere."

Suddenly, a grey-haired lady from one of the quilting guilds rushed over to me. I recognized her from earlier in the day because she was wearing a chartreuse top with a screaming loud purple jacket.

"The killer! The killer! I saw him. Doris and Deborah have got him trapped in the restroom. Doris is barricading the door so he can't get out and Deborah is right behind her. Hurry. He could be armed and dangerous. This is the most exciting thing that's ever happened to the Merry Stitchers."

Apparently Doris and Deborah forgot about my directive to observe and report. They were working off their own playbook—corner and trap.

I bolted out of the tasting room and ran straight for the corridor where the restrooms were located. I wasn't sure if Bradley and his sister were following me, and there was no time to look. Behind me, I could hear a jumble of voices screaming, "Killer? There's a killer in here?" And that's when I knew we were in major trouble.

Chapter 28

Sure enough, two ladies stood in front of the door to the men's room, their arms crossed in front. If I didn't know any better, I would've sworn they were blockers for a national roller derby team.

Behind me, the voices were getting louder, but thankfully there was one I recognized—Theo's. "I heard the commotion and got right over here. What's happening?"

"Doris and Deborah over there think the killer's in the men's room. Now what?"

"Oh brother. If we don't do something right away, this is going to get out of hand. You go over there and talk to them while I deal with the crowd."

He turned away and I could hear him shout, "Just a plumbing problem in the men's room. There are lots of portable toilets outside until we get it fixed."

Meanwhile, I sprinted over to the ladies and whispered, "What's going on?"

"We saw it!" one of them said. "The blue windbreaker. That *was* a windbreaker, wasn't it, Doris?"

"I thought it was a poncho, but you said it was a windbreaker."

I bit my lip and forced myself to stay calm. "Okay. We can take it from here. Why don't you wait over by the cashier, and I'll let you know what we find out."

"Are you sure you're going to be safe?" Doris asked.

"I'm sure."

At that instant, Theo, Bradley and Pam rushed over.

"I overheard the conversation," Theo said. Then he turned to Bradley. "What do you say we walk in there and see who may or may not be our murderer."

With that, Theo opened the door and he and Bradley walked in.

"Honestly, Norrie," Pam said. "Here you are tracking down killers and do you know what the high point in my life is?"

I shook my head.

"On Wednesday, the school cafeteria serves fried chicken."

Both of us laughed as the men exited the restroom.

"We almost had to hire Bradley ourselves," Theo said. "Thank goodness the guy in the men's room isn't going to press any charges. Said two ladies chased him in there shouting, 'Murderer, Murderer!'"

My cheeks felt warm, and I swore there was a giant lump in my throat. "I'm almost afraid to ask. What was he wearing?"

Theo and Bradley burst out laughing and answered simultaneously—"a blue hoodie."

"Remind me to never listen to Stephanie Ipswich again," I said.

Bradley and Pam went off to listen to the Polka Meisters after Bradley pulled me aside for a split second to tell me he'd give me a call tomorrow. I wanted to ask him if it was business or pleasure, but I wound up saying, "Okay."

It was midafternoon and no sign of our suspect. However, there were signs of a possible rainstorm, and that wasn't good. The sky, which had been partially sunny, was now overcast, but that didn't seem to matter to any of our guests. The tent was packed and the lines for food were long. I moseyed back to where Herbert and Alan were serving the Federweisser to see how it was going.

"If this keeps up," Alan said, "we won't have any feeling left in our hands from all that pouring. Franz is going to work for the next two hours while Herbert and I take breaks in between winery tours. Franz says if he has to answer one more question about how wine is made, he's going to make a video and tell everyone to find him on YouTube."

I was about to go back to the tasting room when I realized something. I had locked Charlie in the house because I didn't want him to position himself in front of the outdoor grill begging customers for a handout. Francine had mentioned the dog had a propensity for doing things like that. That, along with other reasons, was why he wasn't allowed in the tasting room.

It was a quick jaunt back to the house. I let him outside for a few minutes, fed him some kibble, and freshened up. I figured what was fifteen or twenty minutes more. No one would miss me. As I was about to leave the house, I noticed the flashing red light on the answering machine.

The message was from Gladys Pipp at the public safety building. "Managed to locate your home number. Didn't want to leave a message at the winery. You didn't hear this from me. David Whitaker's son, Richard, was in to see Deputy Hickman first thing this morning. And it wasn't about his missing father. It was about Kelsey Payne. Couldn't hear the whole conversation, but I did hear the kid say, 'Don't ask me how I know, but you made a mistake. Kelsey's not your killer.'"

I replayed the phone message three times, waiting for it to sink in. Darn it! It was after three and Gladys would be gone for the day. I opened the cupboard where Francine kept her stack of yellow phone books and flipped frantically to find Gladys' number. *If* she even had a landline. My eyes bounced all over the last names beginning with P. Finally, a number. I dialed it as fast as I could only to get her answering machine.

My message was short and to the point. "Gladys, it's Norrie. I need to know more. Call me on my cell."

I recited my number and took a breath. Not that this news was a particular game changer, but it was important. It meant that someone, other than me, knew Kelsey Payne was innocent. And that someone was David Whitaker's son, of all people. I remembered reading that David Whitaker had two grown sons, but couldn't remember if they lived at home or not.

Again, I tore through the pages of the Penn Yan phone book but came up empty.

What did I expect? It's the twenty-first century. Everyone has a cell phone.

With less than two hours left of the Federweisser, I figured I'd better get back there. At least I could find Theo and tell him about the call. I gave Charlie a few biscuit treats and locked the door behind me.

Once I was back in the tasting room, I looked all over for Theo. I couldn't believe it was possible, but the crowd seemed to have swelled. Cammy, Glenda, Roger, and Sam were all swamped, not to mention the part-time college students, who were also assisting with the tastings.

Lizzie and her helper were also mired under with customers. That, at least, was the good news for the day. No blue windbreaker sightings, but a red banner day as far as sales were concerned.

I blew past the tasting room tables on my way to the tent when, all of sudden, Godfrey Klein raced toward me. He was carrying a small cooler meant for a six-pack.

"Norrie! I've been looking all around for you! Can I please put this cooler in your kitchen or another safe place?"

"Uh, sure. Don't tell me you brought your own drinks?"

"Drinks? No. These are the ladybird beetles I need to release in the evening. They have to remain dormant, so they're in this cooler with the appropriate cooling element. I didn't want to trouble you by asking if I could put them in your refrigerator."

Oh thank God! "Come on. You can put them in my office. They'll be safe there. They won't escape, will they?"

"Not unless someone opens the chest. Still, it would take a few minutes for them to adjust to the temperature and become active."

When Godfrey set the small chest under my desk, I noticed the warning label affixed to the top. It read, "Caution—Live Insects, property of Cornell Entomology Department."

Thank goodness he told me it was ladybird beetles. The cutesy factor outweighed everything gross I'd come to expect of insects.

"Have you eaten yet?" I asked. "Or tasted the wines?"

He shook his head.

"Come on. You'd better taste the sausage and try the Federweisser before we run out. The crowd's much bigger than we expected. Oh, I should've asked. Are you with other people from your department? Or friends?"

"No. I spent most of the day working and when I stood up to stretch, I noticed the time and figured I'd better get over here before the event closes."

"You've still got plenty of time."

"Er, uh, look, I don't mean to pry, but I sure hope you informed the authorities about that fudge."

I nodded and mumbled, hoping he'd let it go. Then I tapped him on the elbow and motioned for him to follow me. "Come on, it's shorter to get to the barrel tasting and sausages if we go outside and walk past the parking lot."

Godfrey surveyed the area as we walked downhill. "Impressive. Absolutely impressive. I'd love to see your winery's plan for dealing with agricultural pests."

"Pests? Huh?"

"Sure. You've got your chewing insects like the cutworm or the berry moth. Oh, and let's not forget the root borer."

Naturally. Better not forget that one.

"And then there's the sucking insects like mites and leafhoppers."

"Yeah, leafhoppers. I'm sure our vineyard manager has a plan." *Spray it, fumigate it, burn it, whatever.* "I'll, uh, look into it and get back to you. Well, here we are! Federweisser today and then after more fermentation, Chardonnay."

"I imagine you know quite a bit about winemaking, considering you grew up here."

I grimaced. "I should, shouldn't I? But I don't. I mean, I *do* have a general background but truthfully, I was never into winemaking or growing grapes. Not like Francine. I was always too busy holed up somewhere reading."

Godfrey laughed. "Now I don't feel so bad. I come from a long line of dentists. That's right. Prosthodontists, endodontists, you name it. And the family members who aren't dentists are oral hygienists. Growing up, I had more toys that consisted of those silly false teeth than anyone I knew. And every Halloween I got a new toothbrush kit. Can you imagine? My parents still haven't gotten over the disappointment that I chose entomology as my career and passion. But honestly, think about it—would you want to stick your hands into someone's mouth? It gives me the creeps."

"And the bugs don't?"

"Well, I wouldn't enjoy getting bitten, but I've always been fascinated by them. And please don't get me wrong. I certainly don't want them infiltrating my house, but studying them is a different story entirely."

I didn't know what it was about Godfrey Klein, but for some inexplicable reason, it was really easy talking with him. He was close to my age and not full of himself, like so many of the guys I'd dated. Then again, he was into bugs.

"I left your name with our bistro and tasting room crews. All meals and drinks are on us. I really should get back to work. The grill is straight ahead, and you can't miss the polka tent."

"Thanks, Norrie. I'll pick up my cooler when the event closes. Plenty of time for me to get to the community gardens by dusk."

"Great! Lizzie or Cammy will let you into the office. They have the key. Have fun!"

I had to find Theo and let him know about Gladys Pipp's phone message. And why David Whitaker's son? Shouldn't he be more concerned about his missing father? And speaking of missing people, Erlene Spencer practically had a meltdown at the sheriff's office from what I heard, but then again, she didn't seem all that broken up when she was flitting around with Rosalee's sister, Marilyn. Maybe her anguish comes and goes in spurts.

Then I had the strangest thought. Something that should have occurred to me days ago. Something only Gladys Pipp could answer.

I took the short walk back to the tasting room via the parking lot. Alvin was in his glory, getting petted by two little boys, and I was glad John had made a large sign that read, "Please do not feed the goat. We are not responsible if he throws up on your clothes." Nothing like getting right to the point.

The tasting room was buzzing with customers, and the energy was palpable. I wove in and out of the crowd, focused on finding Theo. The noise level took some getting used to, but no one seemed to mind. In fact, they all seemed to be chatting at once. That was why I didn't hear my cell phone right away. Or at all, for that matter.

A man standing next to me gave me a quick pat on the arm. "I think your phone's ringing."

Oh my gosh. It has to be Gladys Pipp. "Hello! Hello! Hold on a second! Give me a second to get out of this crowd!" I elbowed my way through the customers until I was outside the building. It had gotten cloudier but no wind or rain. I looked at the screen on my phone and shouted, "Hi, Gladys! Thanks for calling me back."

"Of course. So, what do you think? David Whitaker's son. Why would he be concerned about Kelsey Payne?"

"That's why I wanted you to call me back. Did you hear anything else? Did Deputy Hickman say anything after Richard left?"

"Not to me, he didn't. But I did hear him telling one of the deputies that he thought the kid, meaning Richard, knew where his father was."

"Knew where he was or is actually hiding him? The possibility exists that David Whitaker killed Roy Wilkes."

"What are you saying?"

"This is kind of third-hand knowledge, but Roy Wilkes might've been sleeping with David Whitaker's wife. Richard's mother. There's a motive for you—jealously. Or revenge. Take your pick."

"Or lunacy. Roy Wilkes doing the nasty with the wife? Have you ever met her?"

"No. Why?"

"Honey, I don't like to speak ill of people, but any one of those mules my uncle Ralston has on his farm in Dundee would've been a better choice. And much more personable. The only interest Deputy Hickman has regarding the Whitaker family is a missing person, not a possible jealous husband and murderer."

Strange thought, hell. I think I've pieced something together.

"Gladys, is David Whitaker's disappearance the only one that's been reported?"

"Yes, why?"

"Oh my gosh. Is his wife Erlene Spencer?"

"In the flesh. Erlene Spencer Whitaker, but she kept her maiden name."

"That explains it. That's why I thought, well, quite frankly, everyone thought there were two missing people."

"Only one."

"Thanks, Gladys, for cluing me in. I really appreciate it."

"No problem. Sorry I couldn't make your event today, but by the time I got out of work, my feet were killing me, and all I wanted to do was throw myself on the couch. Hope you understand."

"Absolutely. Have a good weekend."

Deputy Hickman might get more than he bargained for if he was tracking down a missing person who turned out to be Yates County's only killer in what? The past God-knows-how-many years. Well, aside from the other murder on my property this summer. Where would the kid hide his dad? Especially if they all lived under the same roof with Erlene breathing down their necks.

A few yards away from where I was standing, the crowd sang along with the band. It was a mishmash of words but I did hear "roll, barrel and fun." I pictured Franz pouring wine from our barrel, but I doubted he was having fun. We had a little more than an hour left, and I was resigned to the fact that my plan was a total bust

Miserable, I walked directly to the entertainment tent, hoping the music would cheer me up. When I stepped inside the tent, the "Beer Barrel Polka" had ended and one of the MCs announced a new line dance for the occasion—the "Picnic Polka." As soon as I heard the first few notes, I recognized the song from my nephew Shane's wedding. (At least we referred to him as our nephew even though he was Jason's relation.) Right toe, left toe, shuffle, shuffle, whatever.

I took a seat at one of the tables, propped my elbows up, and watched. At first only a few brave souls took to the platform stage, but within minutes, that number had doubled. For the most part, people danced along to the music with light, lively steps. Except for two women who all but stepped on everyone's toes. And that was no easy feat, considering it was a line dance. I leaned forward to get a better look at them when I realized it was none other than Marilyn Ansley and Erlene Spencer.

Granted, Erlene's husband was AWOL and not dead, but should she really be having that much fun? Most people I knew went nuts if their cat went missing, and here's this woman acting like what? The Merry Widow one day and Ophelia the next? She ran hot and cold like a faucet.

I was about to leave the tent when, all of a sudden, a man I thought I recognized strode across the platform and yanked Erlene off to the side. If his voice was any louder, it would've loosened the tent fasteners.

"You, you Jezebel! You made Dad take the fall for you!"

Dad! So this kid is Erlene's son.

Suddenly, everyone stopped dancing and turned their attention to Erlene Spencer, who told the guy to "hush up."

The Polka Meisters, not sure of where this was going, decided to switch tunes and began to play the "Chicken Dance." And not only play it, but play it in such a way as to drown out Erlene and her son. Unfortunately, it had the opposite effect. The two of them got louder and the dancers more energized. It was like watching some bizarre competition, but what? It was anyone's guess.

Chapter 29

"He had to get the hell out of town, thanks to you," the son said. "Were you going to sit back and wait while they arrested him?"

Erlene, who was still on the platform, only off to the side, threw her hands in the air. "If you haven't noticed, your father wasn't arrested, that handyman of Rosalee's was."

Meanwhile, the "Chicken Dance" got louder and louder. People were clucking, snapping fingers, and shaking their collective booties. It seemed, with each verbal assault coming from Erlene or her son, the clicks, snaps and shakes intensified.

"We both know *he* didn't kill Roy Wilkes," the kid shouted.

More clucking music. Amplified this time.

The music made my head spin as I tried to process what was being said. I felt as if I had walked into a feature film an hour late.

Erlene pointed her forefinger and poked it into her son's chest. "How did you know I'd be here?"

Now clicking music. I thought my eardrums would explode with each click, click, click.

"I didn't! The only thing I knew was that you'd be within a four-foot radius of wherever your friend Marilyn was. And since I knew her sister was Rosalee Marbleton from Terrace Wineries, I called and asked *her*. That's when I found out how close Norrie Ellington was to catching the real killer. That's right, Norrie Ellington, the owner of this winery. That's her, right over there. She looks exactly like the description Rosalee gave me." He pointed to me, and I thought I'd retch.

And then, in a flash, the shake, shake, shake of chicken "booties" from the dancers as Erlene Spencer shoved her son away with the push of a hand and charged toward me.

"You tell me what you know right now, missy, or someone's going to be sorry."

Again, my mind was total sludge. I had no idea why Erlene Spencer was going after me.

"I don't know what you're talking about," I said.

By now, she and her son were only a few feet from me and I got a good look at the guy. For a split second, I thought I was seeing things. It was the same guy whose photo I took at Rosinetti's bar that night. The night Cammy called me insisting I rush over there because she was sure she had seen David Whitaker. At the time, Cammy and I thought the skinny kid might've been Kelsey Payne because he resembled Cal, but a few nights later, one of the bartenders overheard him talking to a girl and she called him Richie. My brain was now on fast-forward and, oddly enough, things were beginning to make sense.

"Oh my God!" I shrieked. "You're Richie—Richard Whitaker. David Whitaker's son. You're the one who went to the sheriff's office!"

And then, a thunderous crescendo as the "Chicken Dance" reached its frenetic conclusion. The band immediately began playing a more traditional polka song, but no one was dancing. Instead, they were all gathered around a more interesting spectacle—the Two Witches Winery version of the *Family Feud.*

Richard ignored my outburst and took a step forward, effectively blocking his mother from lunging at me. I leaned to the side so I could see the expression on Erlene's face as her son continued with his diatribe. "You were having an affair with Roy Wilkes and Dad found out. How could you?"

"Is that what you think? An affair?"

"I don't think it, I damn well know it. Why else would you sneak off to meet him?"

We were suddenly interrupted by the MC's voice. "Grab your polka partners, everyone, for the 'Polka Twirl Around.' And if you don't have a partner, grab the nearest person."

The music started up but, instead of partners pairing up, the crowd was vying for a decent spot near us. I bit my lower lip, moved forward and bumped Richard so I was face-to-face with Erlene. "Not here! Not in the middle of the entertainment. You need to take this family squabble outside."

Preferably in the next county.

Marilyn, who had been pretty quiet up until that point, tapped Erlene on her shoulder and said, "Maybe it's best if we go outside. You don't need to make a spectacle over some rumor your son heard."

"Rumor my butt!" Richard yelled. Then he turned to me. "According to Rosalee Marbleton, you've got the whole thing figured out. Well, I've got news for you. My dad's not about to take the blame for something he didn't do."

I opened my mouth to speak, but it was too late.

Erlene slapped Richard across the side of his face with such a wallop I swore I could feel the sting. "You blithering moron. We've got a patsy sitting in the jail. Why couldn't you leave well enough alone? And where's your father, by the way? Hiding out until the coast is clear? Like he did when he delivered that classified information to one of Beecher Rand's competitors? I was the one who had to clean up that mess for him."

Holy cannoli, the patent infringement or whatever it was called. Yikes—our beloved school board member was a real bottom feeder.

Erlene's voice had reached a fever pitch. "You tell me right now where that lowlife scoundrel is hiding. Do you hear me? The whole county's out looking for him. Tell me now!"

"Like hell I will."

With those words, Richard bolted out of the tent, followed by Erlene, Marilyn, and a few onlookers.

Meanwhile, I fumbled for my cell phone and pushed speed dial for Theo. "Up the hill. They're heading up the hill. Hurry. Get to the front of the tasting room building."

"Norrie? Who's running? Who are you talking about? What's going on? The blue windbreaker?"

"Erlene, that's who. And Marilyn. Only I think she's innocent. And Richard."

"Who?"

"Long story. Possible killers. Hurry. I'm moving as fast as I can."

Up ahead, Richard had the crowd beat by at least seven or eight yards. If this was a horse race, my money would've been on him. Erlene and Marilyn were slowing down but not stopping. It was only a matter of seconds and I'd be neck and neck with them. Then, out of nowhere, the sound of a motorcycle starting up. By the time I realized it was Richard Whitaker under the red helmet, he had given all of us the finger as he headed down the driveway.

Erlene must've caught me out of the corner of her eye because she spun around like that kid from *The Exorcist.* "Say a word about this and it'll be the last thing that comes out of your mouth."

We were now a few yards from the tasting room parking lot on a grassy area between the driveway and the pavement. And we had a new audience watching the show—attendees who were getting into their cars. Some of them were craning their necks to get a better look at us. I hadn't realized how loud and downright masculine Erlene's voice was.

"Say a word about what?" I asked. "Your husband's industrial espionage or whatever it's called? Your affair with Roy Wilkes? And believe me, I really don't care about that. But I do care that you're letting an innocent man take the blame for something you did."

"You better not be accusing me of murder."

"Um, if you want to be specific, I think it was your son who made that accusation. Well, more like an insinuation, but—"

"Norrie!" Bethany's voice rang out from the first row of cars. "I thought that was you. Hang on. I want to say good-bye."

Before I could shout to her to stay put, she rushed over with Mallory a few feet behind her.

Meanwhile, Erlene had grabbed me by the wrist and tightened her grip. "I mean it. Keep your mouth shut."

She let go just as the girls from the blue ranch arrived.

"My mouth shouldn't concern you," I stated calmly, "but if I were you, I'd be more worried about your son."

"That blithering moron! He's an absolute idiot!"

Suddenly Bethany and I locked gazes. We heard it—"id-jut." A loud, raspy voice.

"Is it—?" I mouthed to her and she, in turn, mouthed back, "OMG."

Bethany eyeballed Erlene and, after a few more OMGs, finally spoke. "I heard your voice. It was dawnish." She turned to me. "That's a word, isn't it? Dawnish. Around dawn."

I nodded back because, for some reason, I couldn't form words.

Bethany, however, seemed to have a never-ending supply. She crinkled her brow at Erlene. "Your voice is unmistakable, and I heard it. It was the morning that guy got killed down the lake. You were getting into a car in front of the creepy house on Route 14."

"That doesn't prove anything," Erlene said.

Finally, my vocal chords started working. "Not by itself, but it puts you in the vicinity of a murder with an eyewitness."

"Who? Those stinking little punks with the fishing rods? They took off before anything happened."

Oh my God! How could I have missed it! Eli Speltmore wasn't referring to Rosalee, he had an encounter with Erlene before Roy got murdered.

The witness *I* had in mind was Kelsey. So what if he was the one being accused of the crime. As far as Erlene was concerned, there might be another player out there. I had to keep her on edge while I figured out what to do next.

"Not your 'stinking little punks,'" I said, "although they'll corroborate what my witness saw. I'll let the sheriff's department piece this together."

"Don't you dare reach for your cell phone or I'll be forced to use what's in my handbag."

Part of me wanted to get really snippy and retort with something like, "What? Your mirror?" But I wasn't dealing with someone who was entirely rational. My eyes darted back and forth, hoping I'd spot Theo but instead, Godfrey Klein meandered over, his right hand clutching the small cooler with the ladybird beetles.

"I had a blast, Norrie! Thanks for inviting me. I need to get going. It looks like it's going to rain pretty soon."

"Um, sure. Anytime."

"I'll keep in touch." He seemed oblivious to what was happening in the small circle that surrounded me.

He turned away and walked slowly to his car. And that was when two things happened at once. I grabbed the cell phone from my pocket and Erlene pulled out a syringe from her handbag. She was inches from me and ready to take a jab at me. It was probably a small needle, but, to me, if looked as if it could tranquilize a large mammal.

"I meant what I said, Norrie."

Bethany let out a scream and so did Mallory.

Suddenly, Godfrey spun around and yelled, "I wouldn't do that if I were you. Inside this nifty little cooler are Brazilian Killer Bees. They're the most lethal of their species. One move with that syringe and you'll wish you were never born."

Erlene held the syringe in her hand and didn't move. Meanwhile, everyone else took off, including Marilyn, who shouted, "You're on your own, Erlene." She set the world's record for the fifteen-yard dash.

"If they're so lethal, you'll be bitten, too." Erlene didn't take her eyes off of Godfrey or the cooler.

Godfrey appeared unfazed. "Norrie Ellington's brother-in-law and I happen to be Cornell Entomologists, and, along with our family members, we've been immunized. The bees won't have an effect on us, but you'll be struggling to breathe if you make one move. Now drop the damn syringe."

With the needle tip only an inch or so from my neck, I was afraid any sudden move on my part would spook her and she'd stab me with God knows what. Some powerful horse tranquilizer? Some stolen narcotic?

And then, out of nowhere, a car raced up the driveway and all but skidded into us. Whoever was behind the wheel slammed on the brakes with such force that the noise startled Erlene and she dropped the syringe. Godfrey immediately kicked it aside as the car door slammed.

"Can't you ever leave well enough alone, Miss Ellington?" Deputy Hickman shouted as he exited the car. "Against my better judgment, I listened to your friend Theo Buchman and didn't blast the siren or use the flashers."

"Theo? Theo called you?" My voice took on a weird whiney tone.

"Yep, something about you chasing after a killer. And, given that little scenario I caught on my way up the hill, I believe you, Ms. Spencer, have some explaining to do."

Erlene stamped her foot on the ground and pointed her finger at Godfrey. "Me? You need to arrest him! He was about to unleash a swarm of killer bees on all of us! He's got them contained in that cooler of his. I demand you arrest him this instant."

Godfrey could barely keep himself from laughing. "Um, upon closer inspection, I must've grabbed the wrong cooler because according to the labeling, these are ladybird beetles that need to be released into the community gardens. In fact, I should be heading over there right now. Looks like we're in for some rain, and that's perfect for them."

I took a step toward Godfrey and, for some inexplicable reason, most likely nerves, I threw my arms around him and gave him a hug.

Godfrey kept his voice low and whispered in my ear, "I think we may be looking at Betty Crocker herself. Have the deputy ask her for her fudge recipe."

I don't know what got into me, but I didn't wait for the sheriff. Mainly because he had no idea about my near miss with the Dulcolax. Instead, I lit into Erlene like a madwoman.

"It was you! The fudge! My car brakes! It's all making sense. Back when you and Marilyn were at Rosalee's, I mentioned finding a witness who could corroborate Kelsey Payne's story. That must've scared the daylights out of you, considering it was you all the time! So, what did you stick on my car brakes when you sent Marilyn back into the house to look for some sunscreen/bug spray of yours that was never there to begin with? Sound familiar? Tell me, what did you use? And by the way, you're paying for the labor charge!"

Deputy Hickman gave Erlene a cold stare. "Now isn't the time to start lying."

"Hairspray. I used hairspray. Extra hold."

Terrific. Wait 'til I tell Hank Walden at the garage.

"That's attempted murder!" I shouted. "And if you press her, I'll bet she'll admit to putting a laxative in a gift box of fudge for me."

"Really, Ms. Spencer? A laxative?"

"Sounds like attempted murder to me," Godfrey said.

Erlene clenched her fists and gritted her teeth. "You have to believe me, I wasn't trying to kill Norrie. I only wanted to slow her down."

"Slow me down!" I yelled. "I could've wound up in a ditch! And what about that syringe? What was in that? Ketamine?"

"If you must know, it was insulin for Sir Puss-in-Boots, my cat. He's diabetic."

I thought I remembered her saying something about having a diabetic cat when she was at Rosalee's with Marilyn, but I never made the connection when she pulled the needle out of her bag.

Deputy Hickman took out his little pad and looked directly at Erlene. "I'm one step away from placing you under arrest, so you'd better think out your answer carefully. What did you mean about 'slowing her down'?"

"I know my rights. I want a lawyer. Right here. Right now."

I wouldn't have believed it in a million years, but the minute Erlene demanded an attorney, who rushed over to us but Bradley Jamison, looking even more adorable than he did earlier in the day.

"Whoa! Hope I'm not interrupting anything, but your friend Theo sent me out here to find you. Some woman came running into the tasting room screaming her head off about killer bees in the parking lot. She got everyone in the tasting room into a near hysteria. Theo's trying to calm down the crowd because they're afraid of leaving the building."

"Where's your sister?"

"Helping Theo."

Deputy Hickman looked directly at me. "Do you think you can handle this, Miss Ellington? Or should I send for backup?"

I could envision the headline in the Finger Lakes Times—*Federweisser Flops Over Bee Hysteria.*

"It'll be fine. Honest. I'll get on the sound system in the office and thank everyone for coming. I'll reassure them that there's nothing but cars in the parking lot."

"What about my lawyer?" Erlene demanded. "What about my—" Then, it was as if she had an epiphany. She extended an arm and pointed to Bradley. "Aren't you Marvin Souza's helper, or whatever you call it? Get him on the phone right now and tell him he's hired."

Bradley shook his head and spoke softly. "I'm afraid that's not possible. It would be a conflict of interest. I heard everything that was said, even though I was a few yards away. Voices carry, you know. Our firm is representing Kelsey Payne. And, for your information, I'm a partner, not a helper."

As much as I wanted to remain standing to see what Erlene would do next, I had to get into the tasting room and convince the public it was safe to leave.

"I've got to get to the tasting room," I said to Deputy Hickman. "But I can tell you this—Erlene's son is Richard Whitaker, and he lives in Geneva, near Rosinetti's bar. He knows all about the affair his mother was having with Roy Wilkes and how she manipulated everything to cover up murdering him. I'll bet anything you'll find David Whitaker safe and sound in his son's apartment. Heck, he's probably scared out of his mind she'll murder him next."

It was funny how some people got fixated on one or two words. Because, for Erlene, it was the word "affair." Apparently, that was all she heard before she went totally ballistic.

"You stupid little fool!" she screamed at me. "An affair? With Roy Wilkes? I wouldn't let that man so much as touch my little pinky finger! I wasn't having an affair with him, I was blackmailing him!"

The instant she said it, she gasped. The words must have flown out of her mouth before her brain had a chance to censor them.

Something my mother warned me about when I was in my teens. "Don't ever open your mouth in anger, Norrie," she told me, "because once those words leave, you'll never get them back."

"Ms. Spencer," Deputy Hickman said, "I need to bring you in for questioning. If you resist, I will be forced to place you under arrest. Do you understand?"

The last words I heard as I raced to the tasting room came from Erlene's mouth. They were aimed at me and they certainly weren't censored.

Chapter 30

Theo was standing a few feet from the front door as I stormed in. "You won't believe what happened out there. It was Erlene Spencer. Erlene Spencer Whitaker, to be precise, and if it wasn't for you and Godfrey Klein, she would've killed me, too. With a syringe!"

"Norrie, I—"

"I know, I know. Scared the hell out of me, too."

"Not that—the crowd. Look around. No one wants to leave. They're all clumping up in groups, talking about killer bees. You've got Marilyn Ansley to thank for that. And the only people who aren't talking about bees are the quilters and bowlers. They're waiting for you in the kitchen and banquet room. A big guy with a scary tattoo said you'd be conducting a debriefing. What the heck! You've got to do something. Maybe start with the bees. Does your sound system have a microphone?"

One second I was thinking about crazy Erlene and the next about quilters, bowlers and our sound system. "Okay, okay. I'll see if I can make an announcement. I used to mess around with that old sound system when I was in high school. Pretending to be a DJ and all that."

"Well, pretend again and hurry!"

"Fine! Can you please go to the kitchen and tell everyone I'll be there soon?"

Theo let out a moan and took off while I raced to the office. I switched off the mellow mood music that was piped in over our sound system and picked up the small microphone that my father installed sometime during Calvin Coolidge's administration. It was an antiquated setup but it worked. No reason for Jason or Francine to go all high-tech when they didn't have to.

"Thank you, everyone, for attending this year's Federweisser at Two Witches Winery. We hope you had a wonderful time and will be back to taste the Chardonnay. It's perfectly safe to exit out front to the parking lot. Someone thought they saw some bees but most likely they were ladybird beetles. Cornell University releases them this time of year. Very helpful for pest control. Again, thank you all for coming."

Then, like a madwoman, I made a beeline for the kitchen and the small banquet room connected to it. At first glance, the crowd reminded me of a middle school dance—the men on one side and the women on the other. The instant I arrived, I was besieged with questions.

"Did anyone find the blue windbreaker?"

"Did you catch the killer?"

"Did anyone get arrested?"

"Should we wait for reporters?"

I clapped my hands a few times and shouted for everyone to be quiet. The irony wasn't lost on me. "No one saw the blue windbreaker, but there was a break in the case and one of the sheriff's deputies is questioning someone in the driveway. That's all I can tell—"

"In the driveway?" someone shrieked. "I say we head out there right now and see what's going on!"

"I don't think that's such a great idea since—"

I never got to finish my sentence because I was too busy trying not to get trampled as the quilters and bowlers vied for the nearest exit to the parking lot. Unfortunately, it was our main entrance and they wound up pushing and shoving the other guests, who were headed out the door. All sorts of horrible thoughts ran through my mind, including bodies underfoot, loss of our liquor license, and a melee that would make front page news. It was past five thirty, and we should've closed ten minutes ago. I prayed for a major storm, but the only thing Mother Nature delivered was a light sprinkle of rain.

"Slow down! Slow down!" I yelled but nobody listened. The only good news was that none of our patrons fell, no one was face down on the ground and Deputy Hickman's car was nowhere in sight.

"It's all right." Bradley tapped me on the shoulder. "The crowd will disperse. Theo's playing traffic cop. He told me to tell you he got out of the kitchen before 'all hell broke loose.'"

"My God, this is a nightmare."

"If it's any consolation, I think Deputy Hickman's in for a worse one. He's got to listen to Erlene Spencer all the way back to the public safety building. I can't believe you got her so worked up she admitted to blackmail."

With that, the two of us burst out laughing.

"Too bad I couldn't get an out-and-out murder confession from her."

"I'm sure Deputy Hickman will persist," Bradley said. "Come on, I think it's safe for you to go in the tasting room. I'll go out the side door and give Theo a hand. See you in a few minutes."

Pam was at the front entrance when I walked back into the tasting room. "Have you seen my brother?" she asked. "I barely managed to escape from some lunatic woman screaming about Brazilian Killer Bees. I think she's gone now. In fact, other than the staff, I think everyone's gone now."

I stood for a few minutes and surveyed the room. The crowd might've been unwieldy, but there was no sign of damage, unless, of course, I considered our staff—Cammy, Glenda, Lizzie, Roger, Sam, Fred, Emma, and the part-timers. All of them looked as if they had barely survived a tornado.

"Holy Crap Fest!" Sam blurted out from behind his tasting room table. "I've never seen anything like that in my life!"

"Lots of unsettled auras in that crowd," Glenda said. "Norrie, you really need to consider a smudging of sage and lavender."

"I, um, er…"

Cammy gave her a look. "Not on my watch." Then she turned to me. "We've been so busy working, none of us knows what's going on. Did anyone find the blue windbreaker? The killer?"

"I was just about to ask the same thing," Theo said.

He and Bradley returned from their impromptu role as traffic cops and walked toward us. By now the staff had gathered next to Cammy's table and they were all looking at me.

"Everyone might as well hear this at once." I wanted to be clear and succinct. Poised and direct. Instead, I rambled on like one of those recipients of an Academy Award who didn't know when to stop talking.

"It was Erlene Spencer. Not an affair with Roy Wilkes. Blackmailing him. Don't know why. Tried to kill me, too. It was her fudge. And her hairspray on my brakes. Oh, and she thought Bradley was Marvin Souza's errand boy. And her cat is diabetic. She tried to jab me with his needle. The killer bees held her off. But they were ladybugs. Did I mention the fudge was laced with a laxative?"

Theo tapped me on the shoulder and motioned for me to calm down. "Maybe we should go over the events sequentially."

We didn't. But somehow, I was able to explain how Erlene's own son outed her during the "Chicken Dance."

"Whoa. Never saw that coming," Cammy said.

"Me either. I wonder if she'll give a full confession or try to squirm out of it. Either way, I'm hoping it'll be enough to get Kelsey Payne released."

Bradley gave a nod. "We'll be working on it."

"Oh my gosh," I said. "I still have to tell the winemakers and the vineyard guys. They're probably down by the tent cleaning up."

Fred nodded. "Yeah, about that, we'll still be another hour or so. We've got the grill to scrub as well as the tables in the tent area. According to John, the rental company will be back on Monday to take down the tent and pack up their furniture. We'll put our own tables back in the barn. We had terrific sales, but I don't want to see another sausage for a long, long time. Lucky for us, we won't have to. Next year, the Federweisser will be someone else's turn from that WOW group."

I swear the color drained from Theo's face. "I hope the Grey Egret's last on the list. It'll take me years to get over this one. Hey, everyone, it was great working with you today, but I'd better get back to my own winery before Don puts out an all-points bulletin."

"Gotta run, too," I announced. "I can't believe I forgot about Franz and his crew, not to mention the vineyard guys." I turned to Theo. "You're the best. Call you later."

I scurried out of there and was halfway across the parking lot when I heard Bradley's voice. "Norrie! Hold up a second, will you?"

"What? What is it?" I turned and stood still as he approached.

"Hey, I know this has been, well, a frenetic day, to say the least, and I know I'll be up to my neck with phone calls and paperwork tomorrow. Even if it *is* Sunday. But I was wondering, maybe you'd like to go out to dinner or something next weekend. We may have cause to celebrate if all goes well with Kelsey. *May*, not will."

Kelsey. That was right. I should've been concerned about wrongful imprisonment and all that, but the only words that really sunk in were "dinner or something."

"Uh, sure."

"I'll call you to let you know what happens regarding Erlene being charged for murder. Remember, she didn't admit to it."

"Aargh." I brushed the loose strands of hair from my face. "Look, if Deputy Hickman can round up her missing husband, there'll be a confession all right. Of course, that means getting the Geneva Police involved since Richard lives there."

"That part of it shouldn't be a problem. The tricky part is the motive. Why would she kill someone she was blackmailing? The old payola would come to an abrupt halt. And I don't know about you, but I'm curious as all get-up-and-go to find out what that shrew had over Roy Wilkes."

"Yeah, that makes two of us. I'll bet you anything it had to do with those dealings at Beecher Rand."

Bradley headed back to the tasting room, where Pam was waiting, and I rushed downhill to the Chardonnay barrel and our winery crew. The vineyard guys were a few feet away, cleaning off the tables in the tent.

"John left about an hour ago," one of them said. "I'm surprised he stayed as long as he did. He hates these things."

Small wonder.

I took a step closer to where they were working. "We may have caught the real killer."

"Already?" they said in unison. "Herbert just found that blue windbreaker a few minutes ago. He's over there with Alan by the Chardonnay barrel."

"The what? He did? The windbreaker?"

I all but tripped over myself as I darted the few yards to the barrel that was adjacent to the back of the winery building.

"We were about to call the tasting room," Alan said the second he saw me. "Herbert and I found this all crumpled up and stuffed in the bushes behind the barrel. Is this the evidence that goes with that hang-tab? I still have that photo you e-mailed us."

It was evidence, all right, at least in my book. But it was also contaminated with everyone's fingerprints from here to the Pennsylvania border. I figured what difference would a few more fingerprints make? Herbert handed me the jacket, and I immediately shook it out and held it upright to see the front pocket.

"It's the very one we've been looking for," I said. "See for yourselves, there's a slight tear where the hang-tab was attached. Do you have any idea who was wearing it or how long it has been hidden?"

"It wasn't there this morning," Alan said. "I can tell you that much. I would've noticed it when I was setting up the napkins and glasses. And Franz most certainly would've said something before he left for the day."

Herbert nodded in agreement. "Someone probably stashed it while we were inundated with tasters. By the way, what was that ruckus in the driveway? Was that a sheriff's car?"

"Yes. Without the flashers or siren."

I proceeded to tell Alan, Herbert, and the vineyard workers about the entire debacle with Erlene.

"Yahoo!" was the response I got, followed by someone saying how glad they were that Kelsey Payne wouldn't have to take the heat for something he didn't do.

"It's not over yet," I said. "Erlene Spencer hasn't confessed."

A series of groans followed as I shoved the jacket under my arm but, instead of traipsing back to the tasting room, I ran down the driveway straight to the Grey Egret.

"We've got it! We've got it!" I yelled as I ran toward Don and Theo. They were locking up their building and hadn't made it past their front steps.

"Here! See for yourself!" I thrust the wadded-up jacket at Theo and let out a long sigh. "I know, I know. It's laden with fingerprints. Too bad it doesn't have someone's name on it, like those little iron-on tags for campers."

"Did you check any of the pockets?" Don asked.

I felt my face get warm. "Um, no."

Theo was already ransacking the windbreaker, while Don and I held our breath.

"I believe we've just hit pay dirt and, if I'm not mistaken, we've cracked the case."

"What? What did you find?" I was practically shrieking.

Theo unfolded a small piece of paper from the Eastside Veterinary Animal Clinic.

"It's a receipt for Sir Puss-in-Boots Spencer's special diet food. Wow! Fifty-eight dollars for ten cans. Looks like that cat's out of the bag, huh?"

At that moment, I grabbed him by the arm and shouted, "What are you waiting for? Call the sheriff's office!"

Chapter 31

I waited with Theo and Don at their place while Deputy Hickman sent over two young deputies to "secure the possible evidence in the Roy Wilkes case." To be on the safe side, and because I was more than a little dubious of the outcome, I had Theo take a photo of the windbreaker, along with the cat food receipt.

"You know this would never hold up in court," he said.

"I know, but it's still a paper trail, more or less."

* * * *

While I was anxious for some news about Erlene the following day, nothing came. No phone calls. No texts. No e-mails. Nothing. I tried calling Deputy Hickman's extension, but all I got was his answering machine and a recorded message that said if I was calling about an emergency to "hang up and dial nine-one-one."

If I thought our tasting room staff looked wiped out at the end of the day yesterday, they looked like the living dead today. Glenda told me she needed to take an herbal shower infusion, whatever the heck that was, in order to strengthen her inner soul for the day. Cammy and Sam were both commiserating about how many shots of espresso they'd need to stay awake, while Roger was so tired he didn't even try to mention the French and Indian War. Not even once.

Lizzie had the day off but left a note for me the night before. It read, "You may need to re-read Chapter One in the *Nancy Drew Handbook*, especially the part about 'staying poised in dire situations.'"

You stay poised with a lunatic woman at your heels, Nancy. And no amount of tap dancing Morse Code is going to help.

Everyone kept asking me if I'd heard anything from the sheriff's department and after the fifth or sixth time of saying, "No, not yet," I trudged back up the hill and spent the rest of the day drafting a new script. I had made all of the "thoughtful changes" my script analyst suggested for the prior one.

Charlie was like a wild dog that day, having been cooped up during the Federweisser. He took off as soon as it was dawn and literally ran circles around the house before coming back inside to gobble down his food.

I promised Cammy that if I heard anything about Erlene, I'd let her know. I called the tasting room at five ten to tell her, "No news is good news."

Theo and Don checked in with me as well and informed me that there was "radio silence" as far as they knew.

It wasn't until the next day that I learned the fate of Kelsey Payne and Erlene Spencer. And I learned it not from Deputy Hickman or any one of our news or radio stations, but from the voice of none other than Gladys Pipp. It was Monday morning and I was sitting at the kitchen table working on some dialogue for my new screenplay when the phone rang.

"Norrie! It's me. Gladys. I have to speak fast. I'm on break and I have to be back at my desk by ten forty-five sharp. You didn't hear this from me, but Kelsey Payne's going to be released. A cadre of Geneva lawyers has been down here and at the courthouse all morning. Along with Rosalee Marbleton and her sister, Marilyn, although they left a little while ago. Lots of hubbub yesterday, and I missed it."

"What did you miss? What happened?"

"First of all, the Geneva Police located the husband, David Whitaker, and brought him in for questioning. He was staying at his son's apartment in Geneva. Can you imagine?"

"Yes, yes. Go on."

"Well, when he found out that his wife accused him of stabbing Roy Wilkes to death, he went berserk. Took three deputies to hold him down."

"So she really did it, huh? She was the one who killed Roy Wilkes."

"No, she wasn't. She didn't. Not exactly, anyway."

"What? What are you saying?"

"It's kind of complicated. You see, oh phooey. I've got to hang up. Deputy Hickman's headed this way." Then she said, "That's right, you can request a wellness check for your elderly aunt at any time. Please call the office number and not nine-one-one."

I held the phone in my hand for a moment before putting it back in the receiver. This was worse than one of those cliff hanger dramas that end with "To Be Continued."

Gladys had mentioned a cadre of lawyers, and I knew Bradley Jamison had to be one of them. I wasted no time calling his office.

"I'm sorry," the secretary said. "He and Mr. Souza are out of the office right now. I don't expect them back until after lunch. May I take a message?"

Suddenly, I realized something. I might not be able to get the details from Bradley, but Rosalee had been there, too. She *had* to know something. I tore off the grubby clothes I was wearing, washed up and put on something that didn't make me look as if I was a street urchin from a Dickens novel. Then I drove straight to Rosalee's house.

I recognized Marilyn's car in the driveway and pulled up next to it. I got out and walked up the porch steps to the front door. The little flowerpot stakes were still lined up in their pots against the wall. One quick knock and the door opened.

"Come in, come in," Rosalee said. "I take it you've heard the news. My sister is consoling herself with sugar cookies and a can of frosting."

Marilyn gave me a wave as I stepped into the kitchen. "I had no idea. Honestly. No idea. To think I could've been an accomplice to murder."

"Well, you weren't," Rosalee said. "So, let it go."

Then Rosalee turned to me. "I suppose you've gotten all the details by now."

"Um, actually, no. Not really. I know they arrested Erlene, but did she or didn't she kill Roy Wilkes? Or was it her husband? Their son thought she did it but was going to save herself by accusing the husband. And what were she and her husband doing there in the first place?"

Marilyn popped a handful of small sugar cookies in her mouth and reached for a cup of coffee to wash them down.

Rosalee poured a cup for me and motioned for me to sit down. "This may take some time. Do you want to explain, Marilyn, or should I?"

Marilyn tore into another handful of cookies. I wondered how many Rosalee baked. "I'm too upset. You tell her."

Rosalee groaned and leaned back. "Take notes. You might be able to use this for one of your screenplays. Roy Wilkes, David Whitaker, and Erlene Spencer all worked for Beecher Rand. Erlene was in personnel, so that should tell you something right there and then. She found out that Roy Wilkes lied on his résumé but did she report it? Of course not. She saved that tidbit of information to blackmail him when it came time for him to retire. He'd lose all of his pension and the company profit sharing, which was a substantial amount. Wasn't that so, Marilyn?"

Marilyn looked up from her cookies and gave a nod.

"Anyway," Rosalee went on, "she had to do a little woggie-doogling of her own when it came to the shady stuff her husband was involved in. But getting back to Roy Wilkes, it seems Erlene had a set time to meet with the guy behind the pump house to get payment for keeping her mouth shut. To compensate for the hush money he paid her, he raised our land use rent. That dirty rat!"

"You got that right," Marilyn said.

"Shh. Let me finish. As I was saying, Erlene and Roy met at dawn so she could sneak out of her house unseen and unheard. I'd venture as far as to say separate bedrooms, but I'd be gossip mongering at that point."

"Whoa. This is beginning to make sense," I said. "What happened on the morning Roy was killed?"

"Apparently Erlene didn't tiptoe out of her house and her husband pursued her in his car. He was convinced she was seeing someone. Which, of course, she was, but not for the reason he had in mind. Erlene parked by that vacant lake house on Route 14, so as not to be noticed, and her husband did the same when he followed her."

Marilyn began to sniffle and Rosalee told her to "pull it together."

"When Erlene met with Roy Wilkes, he refused to pay the money and they started arguing. That's when the husband showed up. He thought it was a lovers' spat and got into a physical altercation with Roy. Erlene was worried David would get hurt but had no way to stop the brawl. She said she tried to throw some rocks but that didn't work. Then she remembered those re-purposed metal flowerpot stakes I had on my porch. Erlene and Marilyn had helped me replant some geraniums a while back and knew the stakes were like Roman weaponry. She ran back to my porch, grabbed one, and charged Roy Wilkes, intending to scare him off. Unfortunately, it didn't work out that way."

"So she stabbed him to death?"

"Not quite like that. She took jabs at him and succeeded in tearing his jacket, but it was her husband who finally wrestled the flowerpot stake away from her and, in a fit of anger, went straight for Roy Wilkes."

"So he was the one who stabbed Roy to death."

"More or less."

"Huh?"

"He had the flowerpot stake in his hand and was aiming it at Roy when Erlene gave him a hard push from behind and he reacted without thinking. So hard, in fact, he hurt his arm. In a way, they both stabbed Roy to death."

The hurt arm. The person who couldn't open the car door. It's all making sense.

"Yeesh. I should be taking screenplay notes."

"Erlene and her husband panicked when they realized what they had done. David wasn't sure what to do about the murder weapon. He still had it in his hand as they made their way back to their cars. Erlene pointed out our winery building's porch and he stashed it there, on a window ledge. He managed to wipe off the prints."

"But what about the blue windbreaker? It was hers, after all."

"Yes indeed. Finding her windbreaker helped to get my handyman off the hook. Erlene figured it got torn a bit in the scuffle, but the hang-tab didn't fall off until she was on her way back to the car. She hadn't worn it again until the day of the Federweisser, and she took it off when she went to taste the Chardonnay. She said she put it over some bushes and forgot about it. Too bad she left an old cat food receipt in one of the pockets, huh?"

"I'm glad Roy's killers were caught," I said, "but one thing's still plaguing me—the intruder on your porch that night. Was it—"

"The old bat herself," Rosalee said. "Once Erlene started confessing, it was like a leak in a dam. She'd torn off a piece of Roy's jacket during the altercation and was going to stash it in one of my potted plants, but my scream scared her off. Can you believe it? She tried to plant false evidence."

Then Rosalee spoke directly to her sister. "Next time you get chummy with one of those ladies from the Yates County Senior Center, run a background check!"

Marilyn kept muttering how sorry she was, all the while ingesting more cookies. I was tempted to try one but thought she might slap my hand.

Rosalee thanked me profusely and walked me to the door. "Good work, Norrie. I'm glad you're back at Two Witches."

Only temporarily! And if my sister and brother-in-law don't find that damned bug, I'll go down there myself and hunt for it!

By the latter part of the day, I had heard all about Erlene's confession, this time from Bradley Jamison, who called to let me know that all charges against Kelsey Payne were dropped. We also set a time and place for dinner on Friday—Port of Call on the lake.

I wasted no time sharing the information with the guys from the Grey Egret and our staff. As far as everyone else was concerned, every news channel in the Finger Lakes had it covered by five o'clock.

At six thirty-nine, the phone rang again. This time it was Godfrey Klein. "I turned on the news a few minutes ago. Too bad that sheriff's deputy got all the credit for solving the murder. You were the real sleuth, you know. I wanted to call to let you know that."

"Not without your help. You literally saved me."

It was funny, but I wanted to reach over the phone lines and hug him again. What on earth was going on with me? I had a date coming up with one of the hottest guys I'd ever come across and yet, there was something so compelling about this down-to-earth entomologist that made me wonder if I needed one of Glenda's aura cleansings to figure out where I really stood.

At least I knew one thing—I was never, ever, going to go out on a limb to solve another murder. That was my plan on paper, anyway. I wanted to enjoy the rest of the fall season. The Federweisser would now continue to ferment and become Chardonnay. Its bubbly froth would mellow and, with it, the promise of a buttery wine that I hoped would never be laid to rest.

Meet the Author

J.C. Eaton, the wife and husband team of Ann I. Goldfarb and James E. Clapp, is the bestselling author of Booked 4 Murder, Ditched 4 Murder, and the Sophie Kimball mystery series. Ann has published eight YA time travel mysteries.

Visit their website at www.jceatonauthor.com.

Staged 4 Murder

While waiting for Norrie Ellington's next adventure in the third book of
THE WINE TRAIL MYSTERIES
(March 2019)

Don't miss J.C. Eaton's bestselling
The Sophie Kimble Mysteries!

STAGED 4 MURDER

Available now at your favorite bookseller or e-retailer

Turn the page for a quick peek!

Chapter 1

Sun City West, Arizona

The wet sponge that hung over the Valley of the Sun, sapping my energy and making my life a misery for the past three months, wrung itself dry and left by the end of September. Unfortunately, it was immediately replaced by something far more aggravating than monsoon weather—my mother's book club announcement. It came on a Saturday morning when I'd reluctantly agreed to have breakfast with the ladies from the Booked 4 Murder book club at their favorite meeting spot, Bagels 'N More, across the road from Sun City West. I arrived a few minutes late, only to find the regular crew talking over each other, in between bites of bagels and sips of coffee.

"Who took the blueberry shmear? It was right in front of me."

"It still is. Move the juice glasses."

"I hate orange juice with the pulp still in it."

"If it didn't have pulp, it'd be Tang."

Cecilia Flanagan was dressed in her usual white blouse, black sweater, black skirt, and black shoes. Don't tell me she wasn't a nun in a former life. Shirley Johnson looked as impeccable as always, this time with a fancy teal top and matching earrings, not to mention teal nail polish that set off her ebony skin.

Judging from Lucinda Espinoza's outfit, I wasn't sure she realized they made wrinkle-free clothing. As for Myrna Mittleson and Louise Munson, they were both wearing floral tops and looked as if they had spent the last hour at the beauty parlor, unlike poor Lucinda, whose hair reminded me of an osprey's nest. Then there was my mother. The reddish blond and fuchsia streaks in her hair had been replaced with . . . well . . . I didn't even know how to describe it. The base color had been changed to a honey blond and the streaks were now brunette. Or a variation of brunette.

The only one missing was my Aunt Ina, and that was because she and her husband of four months were in Malta, presumably so my aunt could recuperate from the stress of moving into a new house.

"You look wonderful, Phee," Myrna announced as I took a seat. "I didn't think you'd ever agree to blond highlights."

My mother nodded in approval as she handed me a coffee cup. "None of us did. Then all of a sudden, Phee changed her mind."

It was true. It was a knee-jerk reaction to the fact my boss, Nate Williams, was adding a new investigator to his firm. An investigator that I'd had a secret crush on for years when I was working for the Mankato Minnesota Police Department in accounting.

"Um . . . gee, thanks. So, what's the big news? My mom said the club was making an announcement."

Cecilia leaned across the table, nearly knocking over the salt and pepper shakers.

"It's more than exciting. It's a dream come true for all of us."

Other than finding a discount bookstore, I couldn't imagine what she was talking about.

My mother jumped in. "What Cecilia is trying to say is we have a firsthand opportunity to participate in a murder, not just read about it."

"What? Participate? What are you saying? And keep your voices low."

"Not a real murder, Phee," Louise said. "A stage play. And not any stage play. It's Agatha Christie's The Mousetrap, and we've all decided to try out for the play or work backstage. Except for Shirley. She wants to be on the costume and makeup crews."

"Where? When?"

Louise let out a deep sigh. "The Sun City West Footlighters will be holding open auditions for the play this coming Monday and Tuesday. Since they've refurbished the Stardust Theater, they'll be able to use that stage instead of the old beat-up one in the Men's Club building. All of us are ecstatic. Especially since we're familiar with the play, being a murder and all, and we thought in lieu of reading a book for the month of October, we'd do the play."

I thought Louise was never going to come up for air, and I had to jump in quickly. "So . . . uh, just like that, you all decided to join the theater club?"

"Not the club, just the play," my mother explained. "The play is open to all of the residents in the Sun Cities. Imagine, Phee, in ten more years you could move to one of the Sun Cities, too. You'll be fifty-five."

I'd rather poke my eyes out with a fork.

"She could move sooner," Myrna said, "if she was to marry someone who is fifty-five or older."

"That's true," Lucinda chirped in. "There are lots of eligible men in our community."

I was certain Lucinda's definition meant the men were able to stand vertically and take food on their own. I tried not to shudder. Instead, I became defensive, and that was worse.

"Living in Vistancia is fine with me. It's a lovely multigenerational neighborhood. Lots of activities . . . friends . . . and it's close to my work."

Louise reached over and patted my hand. "Don't worry, dear. I'm sure the right man will come along. Don't make the mistake of getting a cat instead. First it's one cat, and then next thing you know, you've got eleven or more of them and no man wants to deal with that."

"Um . . . uh . . . I have no intention of getting a cat. Or anything with four legs. I don't even want a houseplant. I went through all of that when my daughter was growing up. Now she can have pets and plants in St. Cloud where she's teaching."

The women were still staring at me with their woeful faces. I had to change the subject and do it fast.

I jumped right back into the play. "So, do all of you seriously think you'll wind up getting cast for this production?"

My mother nodded first and waited while the rest of the ladies followed suit. "No one knows or understands murder the way we do. We've been reading murder mysteries and plays for ages. I'm sure the Footlighters will be thrilled to have us try out and join their crews."

Yeah, if they don't try to murder one of you first.

"Well, um . . . good luck, everyone. Too bad Aunt Ina won't be able to try out. Sounds like it's something right up her alley."

My mother all but dropped her bagel. "Hold your tongue. If we're lucky, she and your Uncle Louis will stay in Malta until the play is over. It's bad enough having her in the book club. Can you imagine what she'd be like on stage? Or worse yet, behind it? No, all of us are better off with my sister somewhere in the Mediterranean. That's where Malta is, isn't it? I always get it confused with the other one. Yalta. Anyway, leave well enough alone. Now then, where is that waitress? You need to order something, Phee."

The next forty-five minutes were spent discussing the play, the auditions, and the competition. It was ugly. Like all of the book club get-togethers, everyone spoke at once, with or without food in their mouth. I stopped trying to figure out who was saying what, and instead concentrated on my meal while they yammered away.

"Don't tell me that dreadful Miranda Lee from Bingo is going to insist on a lead role."

"Not if Eunice Berlmosler has any say about it."

"She's the publicity chair, not the director."

"Miranda?"

"No, she's the lady who brings in all those plastic trolls to Bingo."

"With the orange hair?"

"Miranda?"

"No, those trolls. Miranda's hair is more like a honey brunette. Perfectly styled. Like the shimmery dresses she wears. No Alfred Dunner for her. That's for sure."

"Hey, I wear Alfred Dunner."

"You're not Miranda."

"Oh."

"What about Eunice?"

"I don't know. What about her?"

"Do we know any of the men who will be trying out?"

"I'll bet anything Herb's going to show up with that pinochle crew of his. They seem to be in everything."

I leaned back, continuing to let the discussion waft over me until I got pulled in like some poor fly into a vacuum.

"You should attend the auditions, Phee. Go and keep your mother company." It was Cecilia. Out of nowhere. Insisting I show up for the Footlighters' tryouts.

"You can scope out the men, Phee. What a great opportunity."

Yep, it'll be right up there with cattle judging at the state fair.

In one motion, I slid the table an inch or so in front of me, stood up, and gave my best audition for the role of "getting the hell out of here." "Oh my gosh! Is it eleven-thirty already? I can't believe the time flew by so quickly. I've got to go. It was great seeing all of you. Good luck with the play. I'll be sure to buy a ticket. Call you later, Mom!"

As I raced to my car, I looked at the clear blue sky and wondered how long I'd have to wait until the next monsoon sponge made its return visit to the valley. Weather I could deal with. Book club ladies were another matter, and when they said they were going to participate in a murder, I didn't expect it to be a real one.

Printed in the United States
by Baker & Taylor Publisher Services